DCPL0000312648

D0518808

Withdrawn From Stock
Dublin City Public Libraries

Degrees of Guilt

By the same author

Scapegoat

Degrees of Guilt

Patrick Marrinan

ROBERT HALE · LONDON

© Patrick Marrinan 2010
First published in Great Britain 2010

ISBN 978-0-7090-9074-8

Robert Hale Limited
Clerkenwell House
Clerkenwell Green
London EC1R 0HT

www.halebooks.com

The right of Patrick Marrinan to be identified as author
of this work has been asserted by him in accordance with the
Copyright, Designs and Patents Act 1988

2 4 6 8 10 9 7 5 3 1

Typeset in 10/12pt Sabon
Printed in Great Britain by the
MPG Books Group, Bodmin and King's Lynn

one

Dawn was lazily breaking over Sandymount village in Dublin. It was the second Sunday in November, and cold and grey. At the southern end of the village a row of red-bricked terraced houses bordered a diamond-shaped park. The uninviting black front door of Number 14 opened into a small communal hall. A staircase rose steeply to the upstairs flat. Through a red door, a narrow corridor was dimly lit. To the left was a double bedroom, with a bed placed against the far wall. Heavy green-velvet curtains were closed and the room was in almost total darkness. A small figure was lying neatly in the bed. There was no sound.

Across the hallway a bay-windowed sitting room overlooked the park. The curtains were partly drawn and the remnants of a fire were visible in the tiled fireplace. Four elaborate antique silver-framed photographs were displayed on a console table. One in black and white was particularly striking. Professionally taken, it looked like a family portrait. Two handsome dark-haired men were standing behind two striking blonde Eastern-European-looking women who were seated on a settee. The men looked like brothers and the women sisters. Seated at the women's feet were three young children. A pretty young girl, of about six years old, sat in the middle, and was flanked by two older boys. They, too, looked like brothers, possibly twins. Beside the photograph was a leather pouch for a hunting knife with the letters YK engraved in gold. The knife was missing. Further down the hallway was a small kitchen. It was neat and clean and in a far corner a Formica table was set for breakfast with two bowls, spoons, cups and saucers.

Directly opposite the kitchen an open door led to a small bedroom. Inside, a narrow shaft of morning light shone through a slightly open curtain, throwing a column of light across the single bed. On the floor beside the bed an alarm clock lay on its side, its hands frozen at 11.30. A glass ashtray was overturned and the remnants of two joints and a packet of Rizla papers were scattered across the carpet. An empty bottle of Jack Daniel's and a glass were perched precariously on a wooden

Leabharlanna Poiblí Chathair Bhaile Átha Cliath
Dublin City Public Libraries

bedside locker. The naked body of a young man lay face down on the bed with his arms outstretched.

The short, shrill sound of the front doorbell abruptly broke the silence. The young man didn't stir. After a short while the doorbell rang again. The sound echoed around the flat, but the young man remained motionless. A few moments later the bell rang again. But there was no response from within the flat. Suddenly there was a loud thud, followed by the sound of splintering wood as the front door crashed inwards. The thunderous sound of heavy soled boots was deafening as a rush of blue-uniformed bodies flooded the hall and panned out frantically into each of the rooms. Two gardai rushed into the back bedroom. Seeing the young man lying on the bed one of the officers prodded him in the back with his baton. He didn't respond and appeared lifeless. The officer prodded him again, aggressively. There was still no movement. Kneeling beside the young man the garda cautiously felt the side of his neck for a pulse. He then slapped the back of the young man's head, but he didn't respond.

'This will wake him,' one of the officers said, as he threw a mug of cold water over the young man's head.

There was only a slight reaction, and the gardai looked at each other in bewilderment.

'What's wrong with him?' They rolled him onto his back. He was certainly alive and appeared uninjured. They slapped him around the face, with little effect. Eventually the young man groggily came to. He looked up at the officers through bloodshot eyes, tensing as they came into focus. He went to sit up, but the officers pinned him down by his arms.

'Gardai,' they roared. 'Don't move.'

As he looked from one officer to the other, the fear that gripped him was all too obvious to them. After a short time he appeared to relax, and they released his hands. He was shivering and pulled the quilt to his chest. Then, without warning, he cried out in Russian.

Detective Sergeant Barry Murphy was in the front bedroom looking for a light switch that worked. He called on another officer to draw back the curtains and a stream of morning light flooded the room. An elderly woman lay on her back on the bed. Her face, despite her age, was angelic in the brightness. A large area of blood was visible on the white sheet and quilt below her breasts. The outer areas of blood were brown and appeared dried. Just above and to the left of her breastbone were several stab wounds, some of which were gaping. The detective gently took her frail hand in his and felt her tiny wrist for a pulse. Her hand was cold and stiff; rigor mortis had already set in. The detective sighed heavily as he gazed down at the brutality he witnessed with growing regularity. He then walked down to the bedroom where the young man had calmed down and was seated on the side of his bed with his head bowed. The detective ushered the uniformed officers from the room and closed the door after them. He stood, with his hands buried deep in his trouser pockets, looking down at the young man who momentarily glanced up at him and then hastily looked away.

'What's your name?' The detective asked.

The young man shrugged his shoulders. 'Who is the woman in the front bedroom?' There was still no response, just more shrugging of shoulders. The detective became firmer as his impatience grew.

'Who is she?' he demanded.

The young man didn't reply and appeared unaware of the fact that a woman was lying stabbed to death only yards from where he sat.

'Do you speak English?' the detective enquired.

The young man looked up and shook his head. The detective sighed heavily, then pointed to some clothing draped across a chair in the corner of the room and gestured him to dress. The young man stood up and pulled back one of the curtains on his way to the chair. The room was now more brightly lit and, on the floor beside the bed, the detective saw a knife. He observed fresh blood on the blade and the handle; the carpet beneath was also bloodstained. He was distracted by the sound of his detective inspector being directed down to the bedroom by one of the uniformed officers. Detective Inspector Harrington, a tall erect man, pushed open the door and entered the room.

'What's the story here, Barry?' the inspector enquired.

'It looks like some sort of domestic argument, Inspector. The old one in the front room was stabbed to death, and she's been dead for some time.'

The inspector glanced down at the bloodstained knife.

'This chap doesn't speak English and is obviously spaced out on something,' the detective observed.

The inspector noted the empty bottle of Jack Daniel's and the remnants of the two joints lying on the carpet. Looking at his suspect, he eyed him up coldly.

'He looks sober enough to me, make sure you get a blood test done back at the station, and the sooner the better,' he said firmly. 'Have you arrested him yet?' the inspector continued.

'No, not yet.'

'Well, get on with it, and bring him in immediately – and get this scene preserved for Christ's sake, it looks as though a herd of elephants has been through here.'

As the inspector was leaving the room he noticed a framed photograph on a chest of drawers. In the photograph was a handsome elderly woman being hugged affectionately by a young man. He picked it up, examined it closely, and then showed it to the detective.

'That's our corpse,' said the detective.

'And that's clearly our suspect,' replied the inspector, as he left the room.

The detective placed his right hand on the shoulder of his suspect and formally arrested him. He then led him by the arm down the hallway towards the hall door. As they reached the front bedroom, the door was slightly ajar. A white sheet had been respectfully pulled over the woman's corpse. The young man looked into the bedroom then suddenly lunged towards the open door, roaring in a loud indecipherable voice that echoed throughout the flat. The uniformed guard went to the detective's assistance by blocking the doorway. Both guards struggled with the suspect, who was screaming and appeared to have lost all control. It was impossible to understand what he was saying, but a few of his words were universally understood:

'Mama, mama!'

He was subdued and forced chest down onto the floor, where his hands were brought swiftly behind his back and cuffed. He was crying uncontrollably as the detective led him down the stairs and out the front door. Detective Sergeant Murphy sat beside his prisoner in the rear of the garda car as it sped along the coast road towards Pearse Street Garda Station. He closely studied his suspect's face. He was in his mid-twenties, of average height and slightly chubby. Though his head was shaved, his large blue eyes gave him an almost childlike appearance. The young man looked back at the detective. Tears welled in his eyes and he appeared distraught. He spoke softly in a language the detective didn't understand, but thought might be Russian.

two

Pearse Street was a busy city centre garda station. In the stark hallway a smartly uniformed station sergeant stood imperiously behind his desk. A formidable-looking man in his fifties with a large handlebar moustache, he peered down at the distraught young man standing before him.

'What's your name, bucko?' the sergeant demanded with authority, his strong Donegal accent booming around the small hall. The young man took a step back and looked at the sergeant respectfully, but didn't reply.

'Where are you from?' the sergeant demanded more firmly. The young man looked bemused at first, then pointed awkwardly to his back pocket with his hands, which were still handcuffed behind his back. Detective Sergeant Murphy, who was standing behind him, removed a small leather wallet from the pocket and handed it to the sergeant who opened it and emptied its contents onto the desk. Amongst a few notes and coins were some loose travel documents, one of which had a photograph of the suspect. The sergeant read aloud from the document.

'It says here, that you are Yuri Komarov, from Rostov-on-Don in Russia. Is that correct?'

Yuri looked at him and nodded. The sergeant let out a heavy sigh.

'Not another Rooski,' he declared.

A photograph had fallen from the wallet onto the desk. It was a smaller copy of the one Detective Sergeant Murphy had seen in the bedroom. He picked it up and inspected it.

'I'll take that if you don't mind, Sergeant,' he said, putting it in the inside pocket of his tweed sports jacket.

The sergeant glanced around at Garda Patrick O'Shea, a fresh faced young garda, who had joined him at the desk.

'Take him down to the cells, Pat, search him, and I suppose you better get him a cup of tea.'

Yuri was led down a dark corridor to a small, damp cell. The handcuffs were removed and he was searched. Pat asked him to remove his shoes, but he didn't seem to understand, so Pat removed them for him.

The garda returned to the sergeant who was at his desk making a careful note with a fountain pen in the large station diary.

'Pat, the lad doesn't seem to speak a word of English. I have made an entry in the station diary that the prisoner hasn't been advised of his rights and that this has been postponed till the arrival of an interpreter.'

'Yes, Sarge.'

'And get onto one of those translation agencies and get someone down here as soon as possible.'

'Actually they've already been on, and an interpreter is on her way.'

'That was quick.'

The sergeant looked suspiciously at Pat who shrugged his shoulders.

'It's a competitive business.'

'I wonder who she was,' the sergeant pondered aloud.

'Who?'

'His victim of course.'

'I have no idea, Sarge, but he seems quite relaxed about it all, doesn't he?'

'What do you mean?'

'He doesn't look like a fella who just got caught for murder.'

'And pray tell me, Pat, how does such a person usually look?' the sergeant asked sarcastically.

'Well, I would have thought he would look nervous, but, of course, you would be a lot more experienced than me about such matters, Sarge.'

The sergeant nodded approvingly at the young guard's observation.

'You're right, he should be nervous, but you know these Eastern Europeans, they have absolutely no emotions.'

'I suppose not, Sarge.'

'Look at Putin, cold as ice!'

three

A tall, blonde and extremely beautiful young woman wearing a scruffy black leather bomber jacket and black Armani jeans loped into the station and presented herself to the sergeant at the front desk. He looked her up and down admiringly.

'Hello! My name is Marina Petrovskaya, I'm from the agency.'

She took out an identity card from Tenko Translations and handed it to the sergeant.

'Hello, Marina,' the sergeant said beaming at her. 'I remember you well; you were here translating for us in that big cocaine case last June. Lithuanians, weren't they?'

'Yes, that's right; I was here for four days.'

'You got here real quick this morning,' he said, as he glanced at Pat, who was lurking in the background smiling at Marina.

'I have to pay the rent somehow,' she replied, as she glanced over the sergeant's shoulder at Pat and smiled at him.

'Do you want to get acquainted with the prisoner first?'

'Where's he from?'

'Rostov.'

'Yes, I only need about ten minutes with him.'

'Pat, show Marina down to the interview room and supervise the visit – and don't forget this guy's in for murder, so take good care of her.'

Pat brought Marina down a narrow hallway and into a good-sized room with a glass door but no window. There was a sturdy table in the middle of the room with three chairs on one side and one on the other. The walls were bare and painted a lifeless grey. A solitary bulb, with no shade, hung from the ceiling. She removed her jacket, hung it on the back of the chair in the middle and sat down. Wearing a white long-sleeved jersey polo-neck jumper, she was conscious of Pat's eyes settling on her small breasts. She took out her notebook and the *Pocket Oxford English Dictionary*, and placed them on the table.

Yuri was brought in by a garda and Marina remained seated. He went to sit beside her, but she gestured to him to sit in front of her on the far side of the table, which he did. Pat sat on a chair in the far corner with one eye on the prisoner and one on Marina. Yuri appeared pleased to see her and spoke anxiously, words flooding forth. She opened her small black leather backpack, took out a packet of Marlborough and offered him a cigarette, which he accepted. His hand shook as she leant across the table and lit it for him. She also lit one for herself.

Yuri was animated, waving his arms up and down in an aggressive but non-violent way and Marina appeared to be trying to calm him. At one stage, as the protests became vociferous, Pat glanced up anxiously from his paper and offered to intervene, but she glanced around and shook her head. After another cigarette and considerable dialogue she got up and walked over to Pat.

'Right, we can get started whenever you're ready.'

Pat picked up a phone on the wall and shortly afterwards the sergeant came into the room. He read aloud from a document entitled 'Notice of Rights for Persons in Custody' and explained the powers available to the gardai. Marina, who was fully familiar with all these regulations from past experience, translated his words with ease for the benefit of the prisoner. Yuri then spoke in Russian, and she translated his words. He didn't want anyone notified of his detention, he said. He didn't require the services of a solicitor, as he had done nothing wrong.

Yuri looked closely at the sergeant as Marina translated his words, as if to check his reaction, but there was none.

'He also suggested that you do … I don't know how to translate it,' she said in a frustrated tone.

'Is it some sort of examination?' the sergeant enquired.

'Yes, a test to see if he is telling lies.'

'You mean a polygraph.'

'Yes, that's the word I was looking for.'

The sergeant laughed. 'We don't carry on with that sort of rubbish in this country.'

'I know, and I already explained that this is Ireland, not America. I think he understood all right.'

'Good girl, Marina. Detective branch want to interview him after the doctor has examined him. Explain to him that the interviews will be video-taped, to protect his interests.'

After this was done Pat led Yuri into a small room where Dr Zuharry took four samples of his blood and also requested him to provide a sample of urine. Two samples of blood and the urine sample were to be tested for evidence of any intoxicants. The remaining blood samples were for DNA-profiling purposes. All the samples were placed in glass vials and carefully labeled. The doctor then conducted a cursory medical examination, looking for any signs of injury to Yuri's body. There was none. Yuri was returned to the interview room looking dejected and slumped into the chair opposite Marina.

four

The door opened and Detective Sergeant Barry Murphy and Detective Garda Ruth McNamara, a dark-haired woman in her early thirties, casually dressed in a pair of pale-blue denim jeans and a black sweatshirt, entered the interview room. Pat, who was sitting inside the door, left immediately. The female detective looked Marina up and down and then gestured to her to move from where she was and to sit at the end of the table.

Marina had met Detective Sergeant Murphy before; he had been in charge of the drugs case during the summer. He was a portly man in his fifties who had lost most of his hair, but had a cheerful rotund face, indicating that he had not yet lost his sense of humour. Marina had been impressed by his sense of fairness and he seemed to avoid some of the sharper tactics employed by many of his colleagues. He commenced asking questions, his tone was soft, almost friendly. Marina translated his questions.

'Yuri, we now know the woman in the bed was your mother. You know she is dead, don't you?'

Yuri buried his head in his hands.

'Sir, I can't believe my mother is dead.'

Yuri looked at Marina and became emotional as she translated his answers. After a short time he composed himself, wiping the tears from his cheeks he looked at Detective Sergeant Murphy.

'How was she killed, sir?'

Detective Sergeant Murphy raised an eyebrow and there was a long pause.

'You tell us,' he replied eventually.

Yuri appeared surprised when the question was translated and shrugged his shoulders.

'I have no idea how she was killed,' he said, through Marina.

'Come on Yuri, you know that she was stabbed to death.'

A look of astonishment crossed Yuri's face. 'My mother, stabbed?'

'Yes, four times, as you well know.'

Yuri stared down at the table, looking confused and deep in thought.

'You know who did this, don't you?' the detective pressed.

Yuri raised his head and looked at the detective sergeant.

'Sir, I can't think of anyone who would want to do such a thing to my mother. She only had a few friends, but she had no enemies.'

Detective McNamara intervened.

'We believe you killed your mother in cold blood,' she declared.

Yuri appeared taken aback by her accusation and laughed nervously. Marina glared at him disapprovingly and he immediately adopted a more sombre pose.

'We believe you stabbed your mother,' she continued. 'And then got drunk and fell asleep.'

Yuri placed his hands on the table and, raising himself slightly from his seat, glared at the woman detective.

'You're crazy, I loved my mother and she loved me. We lived for each other.'

The detective sergeant intervened.

'Please calm down,' he said firmly.

Yuri slumped back into his chair. The detective sergeant placed his elbows on the table and leant towards his suspect, looking him directly in the eye.

'Yuri, I want you to listen very carefully. Your mother was stabbed four times in the chest whilst she lay in bed. Do you understand?'

'Yes, sir.'

'No one broke into your flat.'

'You checked the door lock, sir?'

'Yes, and all the windows too; they were all shut when we arrived. There was no way anyone entered the flat without a key.'

'Has anyone else a key to the flat?' Detective McNamara asked.

Yuri became agitated and spoke to Marina.

'No, just me and my mother; no one else except the landlord.' He looked at Marina as he spoke and avoided eye contact with his inter-rogators.

'Please, there must be some mistake, are you sure she is dead, sir?'

Detective McNamara intervened. 'Yes – and you know it, because you killed her,' she said flatly.

'It's not true … it's not true … it can't be true,' Yuri protested.

'We know you killed your mother, so stop wasting our time and let's get on with this,' she responded aggressively.

Yuri pulled back slightly, and then slumped forward with his head in his hands. It was clear that he was availing of the change in tone to gather his thoughts. He rubbed his eyes, as if hoping that when his vision refocused he would see the walls of his bedroom, but when he lifted his head all he saw were the grey walls of the interview room and the stern faces of his interrogators.

Detective Sergeant Murphy stood up and left the room for a moment. He returned with a paper cup of water and put it in front of Yuri. He sat down, took a packet of Marlborough from his pocket and offered one to Yuri, who took it without hesitation.

'Look, Yuri,' Detective Sergeant Murphy said, as he lit Yuri's cigarette, 'the knife I found beside your bed is yours, isn't it?'

'Yes sir.'

'Why do you have a knife?'

Yuri hesitated.

'For fishing and stuff.'

Even Marina appeared unconvinced by his reply as she translated his answers.

'My mother gave me the knife for my birthday.'

'Come on, stop this nonsense,' Detective McNamara intervened. 'Tell us the truth and stop wasting our time.'

'I didn't kill my mother! I never hurt a soul in my life.'

As minutes passed in silence, Detective McNamara glared at Yuri and tapped her long red fingernails on the table. Again Detective Sergeant Murphy intervened.

'Yuri, your knife caused the wounds to your mother.'

'If you say so, sir.'

'And it was found beside your bed.'

'I know, I saw it myself.'

'And it was covered in blood.'

'Yes, sir, I saw that too.'

'And we believe that the blood will turn out to be your mother's blood.'

Yuri looked at Marina and then turned back to Detective Sergeant Murphy.

'Sir, are you sure of all this?'

'Yes, and what's more the early indications are that fresh blood was found smeared on the wall of the hall leading to your bedroom. It's all pointing to you, Yuri. So, tell us the truth about last night; you will feel much better if you get it off your chest.'

Yuri shook his head and remained silent.

'Was there some sort of an argument between the two of you?' Detective Garda McNamara asked.

'No.' he replied with conviction.

'How can you be so sure? You had a lot to drink and smoked some grass.'

'I would remember an argument with my mother,' he replied firmly.

'I loved her and would do nothing to hurt her. Why won't you believe me?'

There was another pause. Detective Sergeant Murphy scribbled some notes on the sheet in front of him and then sighed heavily. He took the photograph that had fallen from Yuri's wallet and placed it on the table in front of him.

'OK, Yuri, start at the beginning and tell us in your own words what happened last night.'

Yuri didn't answer.

'Where were you last night?'

He looked up at his interrogators with despair etched on his face. He turned to Marina and shook his head.

'Come on,' the detective sergeant pressed.

Yuri didn't respond and sat in silence staring at the photograph. The detectives glanced at each other. Their suspect was now totally unresponsive and had regressed into a world of his own.

'OK, do you want some breakfast? We could all do with something to eat. We will talk to you later.'

On the way out of the room, Detective McNamara gestured to Marina to leave. Yuri was to be denied any companionship and all three left together.

Marina sat at a small table in the Strada restaurant sipping a cup of black coffee. She had a few boyfriends here and there, but had never met anyone special. She found it difficult to hold down any sort of relationship with Irish guys, and felt she had little in common with them. She had even fewer female friends. She rarely went to pubs and didn't much like discos either. It wasn't that she was more the outdoor type – a drive in the countryside was her worst nightmare. She had simple needs – work and food on the table. Intellectually she felt she had potential, but so far had realized none of it. It dawned on her that she spent too much time with Russian immigrants and met most of them in garda stations. They were usually on their way to prison, or about to be deported, neither of which was a good starting point for a long-term relationship. She spent most of her time in the company of losers, illegal immigrants who were going nowhere, who thought Chekhov was a brand of vodka, and Tolstoy a computer game. She smiled inwardly. Perhaps Yuri needed a solicitor. Sometimes she recommended solicitors to prisoners, though she wasn't supposed to, and in return got backhanders from them for the referral. She worked now and then with Dermot Molloy who did a lot of legal aid work. Perhaps she would give him a call; there again perhaps not. She checked her watch and hurried back to the garda station.

five

Detective Sergeant Murphy had used the break to keep himself abreast of developments as news filtered in from the crime scene. An incident room had been set up at the station, with his detective inspector in charge. All initial reports went through the incident room and were collated there.

Dr Carmel Hudson, the State Pathologist, had provided a handwritten report on her initial findings. Of relevance was the approximate time and cause of death. Apparently Mrs Komarova had died of shock, due to loss of blood through four incised wounds to her chest. The wounds were all in a horizontal line, spaced approximately a quarter of an inch apart. The entry wounds were jagged on one side and smooth on the other, suggesting a single-edged blade. The depth of the wounds indicated a blade of little more than three inches in length. There was some slight bruising around the area of entry; the blade had probably been thrust in to the hilt, causing bruising to the underlying tissue. She had examined the knife found in the suspect's room. It was a single-edged blade with a small handle. The blade and handle were heavily bloodstained. There was dried blood and tissue in the gap between the blade and the hilt. The blade, three and a half inches in length, was sharp, as was its tip. In her view, the knife found in the suspect's bedroom was similar to the weapon used to kill the deceased. DNA profiling would be carried out in the laboratory to confirm or disprove this hypothesis. It was also her opinion that a minimal degree of force was required to inflict the injuries sustained, because of the sharpness of the knife. She had also observed several lacerations on the outer palm of the deceased's left hand. These injuries were more than likely defensive, the hand raised in a feeble effort to ward off the blows catching the outer surface of the blade. There was also some bruising and abrasions on her right wrist, which could be due to the attacker holding the woman down from above. This made sense. The injuries to her free left hand were consistent with her trying to ward off the knife thrusts and the lack of similar injuries to her right hand suggested that it had been immobilized. Examination of the nails on her right hand indicated the presence of dried blood and tissue. This suggested a scratching or clawing action against her assailant, perhaps in a last and desperate effort at defence. Adhering to the dried blood found beneath one of the fingernails was what appeared to be a human hair, approximately three inches in length? This would be sent to the laboratory for analysis. There was also some reddening and bruising, together with loss of hair, at the back of the victim's scalp; probably due to having her head held violently by the hair. The close pattern of the injuries to the chest strongly suggested accuracy and purpose in the attack. These injuries were not random in nature and this was not a frenzied attack but, in her view, bore all the hallmarks of deliberate injuries inflicted to an area of the body traditionally known to be vulnerable. The injuries were clearly intended to cause maximum injury and probably death.

The temperature of the body and the room had been measured and the body had cooled considerably. She estimated the time of death as between 11 p.m. and 1 a.m.

Detective Sergeant Murphy scratched the back of his head. The scenes-of-crime examiners were still at the scene and a preliminary report radioed in from them indicated that the sheet and quilt in the woman's bed were both heavily bloodstained. The blood on the outer perimeters had dried. This tied in with the pathologist's opinion on the time of death. There were some small splashes of blood on the wall behind the bed. Opposite Yuri's wall in the hallway were two droplets of blood on the skirting board and some small smears of blood were also observed on the wall nearest his bedroom. These were located at waist level.

There was a small area of dried blood on the carpet beside Yuri's bed. The bedclothes and pillow from Yuri's bed had been sent to the laboratory for detailed examination, but the preliminary view was that there was an absence of blood on all these items.

The bottle of Jack Daniel's and the glass were not contaminated with blood, nor were the two remnants of the joints found in the ashtray. A tiny area of dried blood had also been found on the right-hand side of the staircase leading down to the front door. It was not known if this was recent in origin. Samples had been taken of all the blood at the scene and would be subjected to DNA profiling.

Dr Zuharry had found no injuries on Yuri's body. There was also no blood on his clothing, though this still had to be confirmed by microscopic examination in the laboratory.

Barry called in to the detective inspector's office.

'It looks pretty straightforward, Barry,' the detective inspector said cheerfully.

'Yes, I suppose so.'

'Who tipped you off this morning?'

'I don't know, Inspector.'

'Was it an anonymous caller?'

'Yes, someone called 999 and said there was an intruder in the flat.'

'Has he confessed yet?'

'No, he claims to be suffering from amnesia.'

'Any theories on this one, Barry?'

Barry shrugged his shoulders.

'What about motive?' asked Detective Inspector Harrington.

'None; quite the opposite, he appears to have been devoted to his mother.'

six

Detective Sergeant Murphy and Detective McNamara returned to the interview room where Marina was chatting to Yuri.

'OK, Yuri, you have had enough time to gather your thoughts. Are you going to save us all a lot of trouble and tell us what happened?' Barry asked.

There was a long silence. Yuri eventually looked up at Detective Sergeant Murphy and spoke slowly.

'Sir, I do not want to cause you any trouble. If I had done this, I would tell you. Everybody seems to believe I killed my mother – nobody else in the flat, just me and Mama, and then the Jack Daniel's and the grass. My knife on the floor beside my bed covered in Mama's blood. What horrible thing have I done? Mama, forgive me, please forgive me.' He buried his head in his hands and he began to shake.

Marina lit a cigarette and smoked nervously as Yuri started to sob uncontrollably.

'Come on, Yuri, get it off your chest,' Detective Sergeant Murphy implored him.

But there was no response.

'You don't expect us to believe you don't remember killing her, do you?' Detective McNamara said aggressively.

Yuri glared at her.

'I don't care what you think; you think I care what you or anybody else thinks?'

'Yuri, stop this,' Detective Sergeant Murphy pleaded with him.

'Is she alone? Is she alone right now? Don't leave her alone. Please take me to her. She never liked being alone. She won't know where I am. I must light a fire for her. She doesn't like the cold.'

Yuri rambled on and Marina was struggling with the translation. Suddenly he stopped and looked vacantly into space. His bloodshot eyes set against his pale face seemed to be peering into his future. There was another long silence.

'When can I go home? I don't like it here.'

Suddenly, and without warning, he slammed the desk with his clenched fist. He began to sob uncontrollably. Detective McNamara looked at Detective Sergeant Murphy and arched an eyebrow.

After what seemed like an eternity, Yuri appeared to compose himself, looked down at the table and muttered, 'Did I kill Mama? Did I kill her?' He broke down again, but this time started wailing in Russian, and Marina stopped translating his words. His body shook as though with fever and he appeared oblivious to the others in the room. Detective Sergeant Murphy stood up and, though Yuri might well have been on the verge of confessing, he decided to leave him alone at this moment, a moment when it appeared that Yuri accepted that he killed his own mother. He touched Detective McNamara on the shoulder. She looked up at him, but was slow to leave. He gestured Marina from the room. Outside, she looked back through the glass door. There was no sound in the interview room, just Yuri rocking back and forth in his chair, with his head buried in his hands.

seven

Marina sat in a small room awaiting further instructions. The detectives' office was two doors down and she could hear raised voices emanating from there. She moved closer to the door so she could eavesdrop.

'Barry, he was on the verge of confessing and you let him off the hook.'

'That's not the way it works, Ruth, and anyway you know my style.'

'We know he killed his mother, now let's get a confession out of him and stop this molly-coddling.'

'We have our case, Ruth, why do we need a confession? The forensics will tie all this up.'

'Why leave any room for doubt, Barry?'

'There's no doubt, you said so yourself.'

'Are you not even vaguely interested in why he did it?'

There was a long pause as she looked at her colleague, who was sitting in front of her rubbing his eyes. He looked exhausted.

'Ruth, I honestly don't think the guy knows himself.'

'And you're not even going to test him.'

Barry looked at her with angry eyes.

'Look, are you blind or what, he's under a lot of pressure?'

Ruth shook her head and sighed heavily.

'Do you really believe all that shit about Mama and not remembering what happened last night?'

'Maybe I do, maybe I don't.'

'Barry, you're losing it.'

'We've got our man, the scene has been preserved and all the forensics are being done as we speak. It's all being done by the book. If he's got something to say, let him tell the jury. Maybe he's a psycho, or maybe his mother said something to provoke him, I don't know and to be honest, I don't give a toss.'

'But, Barry, he did it in cold blood.'

'Yeah, sure,' Barry replied, his tone heavy with sarcasm. 'And then went off to bed leaving the murder weapon conveniently by his bedside.'

There was a short silence.

'OK, you have a point, but there again, he was hardly expecting us.'

'Look, Ruth, what if he denies he killed her, what then?'

'I don't know.'

'Then we have to chase down every friend, enemy, relative, from Parnell Square all the way back to bloody Russia. Have you any idea of the donkey work involved in excluding the possibility that someone else did it?'

'But he now seems to accept he did it.'

'Yes, at the moment, but if we put more pressure on him, lean on him a little harder, what if he changes his tune and says he has been framed? Just think about that. Do you want to spend Christmas checking on every lying immigrant, every person his mother ever met who may have had a motive to do away with her? I can just hear it now, some bigwig for the defence: *And, Detective, when he told you he had been framed, did you check it out?*'

He gave Ruth a rueful smile; it was the smile of experience.

'OK, I see where you're coming from.'

'Ruth, his lawyers will plea-bargain with the prosecution and look for manslaughter; leave it to the wigs, let them sort it out.'

'Just give me one more go; one more crack at it. I can break him.'

'Sure you can, Ruth, but not on my turf.'

The detective sergeant wearily pulled himself from his chair.

'Go and get some lunch. I'll talk with the super and the inspector, OK?'

Barry sat in the detectives' office alone. He had been a detective for twenty-seven years and had never sought promotion, preferring the cut and thrust at the coalface. Paperwork had never been his forte, but he had the nose of a bloodhound and he was greatly respected in the force. And he always played it by the book, right down the middle. The punters respected him too. No planted verbals or concocted confessions. His approach made his life a lot easier. He believed suspects who respected their interrogators were more likely to confess to them. His own detection rate was legendary. The truth was, he knew about life more than most and had seen the extremes of human behaviour, both good and bad. Four years earlier he had returned home at five in the morning after a busy nightshift, to find his wife hanging by her neck in the hall of their small but comfortable home in Drimnagh. They had been married for twenty years and were close. She had never shown any sign of unhappiness, let alone depression. There was no apparent reason why she had decided to take her own life and she left no note. He had searched for a possible cause, but had never found one. His only child, Darragh, was fifteen when his mother died and shortly afterwards started to abuse heroin. Perhaps it had been the sight of his mother hanging by the neck that had prompted his withdrawal from reality. Barry spent all his free time with his son, down at the clinic, with drug counsellors. The care of his son consumed most of his free time and served as a distraction from his own sense of sadness and loss. He was tired now, very tired.

Marina strolled along the boardwalk that skirted the River Liffey, and found a bench. She took a tuna roll and a coffee she had bought in a nearby deli from her leather rucksack. The day had turned cold and grey, with a biting easterly wind whipping off Dublin Bay. Suddenly an overwhelming sense of loneliness and fear gripped her and sent a shudder down her spine. She took out a small make-up compact, opened it and took out a packet of Rizla papers and a small piece of cellophane with some good quality Moroccan in it. Looking furtively around the deserted boardwalk, she rolled a joint.

She sipped her coffee and her mind wandered. Had her work permit come in for New York? The translation work was part time and poorly paid, but she also worked as a model. However, that career was going nowhere in Dublin; she wasn't quite gangly enough for the catwalk and too shy up front for photo calls. Now twenty-four years old, she was quickly approaching her sell-by-date. However, an agency in New York had seen her portfolio and liked her look. Subject to her obtaining a visa, she had two months' guaranteed work, which would pay her rent for a year and buy some college books.

She finished her joint and was beginning to feel less stressed. Beyond the white granite columns of the Customs House, the river meandered gently and she gazed at the luxurious apartment complexes rising steeply in the docklands area beyond the Financial Services Centre, perhaps only a kilometre from where she sat, yet light years away from her own little universe. The heavy rumble of a freight train crossing Butt Bridge startled her. Looking at her watch, she saw it was two o'clock. She made her way along the embankment towards the garda station, giggling to herself as she tripped on some loose stones. That Moroccan stuff was stronger than she thought.

eight

Pat brought Yuri to the interview room where Marina, Detective Sergeant Murphy and Detective McNamara were already waiting for him. He looked tired and drawn and hadn't eaten. He mustered a smile for Marina, but she looked away, worried he might spot her dope-ridden eyes. Detective Sergeant Murphy commenced the interview.

'Yuri, are you feeling any better?'

He didn't answer.

'Are you going to tell us what happened last night?'

Yuri looked him squarely in the eye and took a deep breath.

'I watched Match of the Day. I was drinking Jack Daniel's. Chelsea beat Arsenal, two-one. I think I went to my room after and had a smoke. My mother was probably in bed reading, or else she was already asleep. I don't remember anything after that, except being woken in my room and water being thrown over my head. That is the whole truth, please believe me, sir.'

'And you had no argument with your mother last night?'

'No, I didn't.'

'Are you sure about that?'

'I told you we never argued; she only ever argued with— It doesn't matter?'

'With whom Yuri? Who did she argue with?' Detective McNamara intervened.

Marina didn't translate this, but instead looked at Detective Sergeant Murphy and said she had got the translation mixed up. He said they never argued and that was it. Barry nodded.

'Do you drink a lot?' Barry asked.

'Yes,' Yuri replied.

'Why?'

'Because I don't go out much and I get bored.'

'Would you normally drink as much as you did last night?'

'No.'

'Then why did you drink so much last night?'

'Because it's not every day Chelsea beat Arsenal.'

Detective Sergeant Murphy laughed, but Detective McNamara didn't, and looked at him disapprovingly.

'Had you or your mother any financial worries?' he continued.

'No, we were comfortable enough, and I worked in the park every morning.'

'Do you have a girlfriend, Yuri?'

'No, I don't.'

'Did your mother have a boyfriend?' Detective McNamara asked in a caustic tone.

Yuri glared at her, and didn't answer.

'Did your mother have any friends, male or female?' Detective Sergeant Murphy asked more diplomatically.

'Just the old people who lived in the flat below, but they were away visiting family in the country for the last week.'

'And money – had your mother any money?'

'She owned a bank.'

'What!' exclaimed Detective McNamara.

Marina looked surprised at her reaction.

'Ask him again,' she said angrily, glaring at Marina.

Marina was feeling a little groggy from the cannabis and feared it was beginning to show. She spoke to Yuri again.

'Just a little money in the bank,' came the reply.

The detectives visibly relaxed.

'Had she a life insurance policy?'

'Sorry, I don't understand,' Marina said to Detective Sergeant Murphy.

'A life policy.'

'What's that?' Marina enquired.

'An insurance policy, in case she died, Yuri would inherit money.'

Marina nodded, indicating she understood, and explained it to Yuri. At first he didn't appear to understand, but they spoke together for a little while.

'No, she didn't,' Marina translated eventually.

'Did she own anything of value?'

Again Marina spoke to Yuri and he replied at some length.

'No, she had nothing,' was the eventual translation of his reply.

'Where is your father?'

'He was killed in a fire at our home in Russia, along with my twin brother and cousin and her parents.'

'Have you any other brothers or sisters?'

'No, I'm the only member of the family left now; I'm alone.'

'Were you both naturalized here?'

Again, he looked bemused, and again Marina appeared to explain it to him.

'No,' came the eventual response.

'Were the immigration authorities putting pressure on you?'

Again, Marina entered into conversation with him. Detective McNamara become visibly annoyed at Marina's intrusion into the questioning.

'No, we were allowed remain here on compassionate grounds.'

'When were you going to return home?'

Marina again spoke at length with Yuri.

He shook his head and became agitated. Detective McNamara stood up and slowly walked around the room until she was behind Yuri.

'Look, Yuri, we know you killed your mother,' she said aggressively.

He remained silent. She moved to his side and stood, glaring down at him.

'Did she discover you were gay? Is that it?'

He didn't answer her and looked away.

'Did you let Mama down? No girlfriend, no education, no fucking English after all these years – and a stupid job in the park.'

Yuri lowered his head. She resumed her seat, but continued to glare at him.

'Do you get off on beating up women? Is that how you get your kicks?'

Yuri turned sideways in his chair facing away from her.

'You're a loser, little mama's boy! Maybe you sent her out on the street, and she didn't hand over the money to you – is that it?'

Yuri began to shake with rage and she leant forward and laughed into his face.

'You little pimp, Mama's little pimp.'

Marina stopped translating, but Detective McNamara didn't let up.

Suddenly Yuri lunged forward across the table at her. Grabbing his left hand she pulled him towards her, turning him over at the same time. He fell on his back on her side of the table. Detective McNamara leapt on him, pinning his right hand to the floor with her left hand, her right leg lodged firmly in his groin. She had a felt-tipped pen in her right hand and she stabbed down at him towards his heart. Yuri put up his free left hand to protect himself. She caught the outside of the palm of his hand several times as she stabbed down at his chest.

Marina looked away and started to scream. 'No, no!'

Detective Sergeant Murphy tried to pull her off him.

'Ruth, what the hell are you doing?' he exclaimed.

She released Yuri. He looked stunned as he lay on the floor. Detective Sergeant Murphy ushered Detective McNamara from the room. He returned, closing the door behind him, and helped Yuri to his feet. Marina was standing in the corner crying hysterically; he ordered her out and she left.

He put his arm around Yuri and helped him back to his chair. Kneeling down on his hunkers, he put his hands on Yuri's shoulders and looked into his eyes. He hadn't responded in any way to the dramatic reconstruction of his mother's death. Pat came into the room.

'Is everything OK here?' he asked.

'Yes, everything is fine.'

'Are you sure?'

'Just take him back to his cell.'

Barry remained alone in the interview room deep in thought. After ten minutes he got up and went into the detectives' office where Ruth was sitting at her desk, visibly upset. She looked up at him.

'Barry, I'm sorry, I lost it in there. I don't know what came over me.'

He placed his hand on her shoulder.

'It's OK; it can happen to the best of us.'

There was a long silence.

'It's just how the pathologist saw it and it meant absolutely nothing to him,' Ruth said.

'I know, it didn't register with him. Either he genuinely doesn't remember what happened, or else he deserves an Oscar.'

'What are we going to do? It's all on tape.'

'Ruth, just go home and get some rest.'

'But I'm finished, headquarters will boot me out.'

'Leave it to me, I'll see what I can do,' he said reassuringly.

Barry walked down to the dayroom, looking for Marina. The sergeant told him she was outside. He found her sitting on the stone steps, smoking. She was still shaking. He put his hands on her shoulders from behind, but she pulled away.

'Are you OK, Marina?'

'How could I be after that?'

'Come back inside and have a cup of coffee.'

He brought her into the detectives' office and called on Pat to get coffee for them both. He closed over the door and sat beside her.

'That should never have happened in there, Marina.'

She looked away from him.

'Forget it, everyone was a bit edgy.'

He cocked his head and smiled.

'I noticed you're not quite yourself since lunch.'

Marina felt he knew she was stoned and was making a point.

'Let's forget it, OK,' she said impatiently.

'It will look bad for Yuri,' he continued.

She flicked back her hair, which had fallen across her face and looked at him quizzically.

'How do you mean?' she asked.

'You saw it yourself; he lost control and went for Ruth.'

She appeared startled at this interpretation of what had happened.

'Come on. She provoked him; she wanted him to react that way and you know it.'

'But will a jury, Marina, will they understand?'

'Can you not just forget it? It's not fair on him; you know the atmosphere in that room.'

'Yes, and I don't want to see any injustice done to him, believe me.'

'Well then, forget it ever happened.'

'We can't, Marina, it's all on video tape.'

'Who is going to want to see those stupid tapes?'

'The defence lawyers for starters.'

A look of bemusement crossed her face.

'Why would they want to see them?'

'Because they check the translation; maybe some word out of place, I have seen it done loads of times. I have notes of most of what was said, and he has said nothing incriminating.'

'I know that.'

Barry lowered his voice to a near whisper.

'We could say the tape of the last interview was accidentally erased and we won't mention what just happened. That way, it will let Yuri and Ruth off the hook.'

She admired his belated candour.

'Will you speak to him, Marina, and explain the situation? It would get everyone out of this mess.'

'OK, what you say makes sense.'

Marina was shown to the cell and spoke to Yuri in private. Barry paced impatiently up and down the corridor outside for what seemed like an eternity. Eventually she knocked on the door and Barry let her out.

'Well?' he enquired anxiously.

'That's OK, he will agree to what you suggest, but only on one condition.'

'What's the condition?'

'He wants all the tapes destroyed, not just the tape of the last interview.'

Barry thought the request strange, but agreed.

nine

The Bridewell District Court was busy as usual, with all the usual suspects waiting nervously for their cases to be called. Criminal legal aid solicitors were selling their wares in the large grimy hallway adjacent to the courtroom. Most of them survived on a large turnover of uninteresting petty cases, committed by drunks, drug addicts, and the unemployed. Some of the more seasoned career criminals had their own brief.

Dermot Molloy had been plying his trade at this venue for over twenty years. Not much had changed in that time. District justices came and went, as did gardai. Criminal families, however, were a little more consistent. There existed a sort of old lags' network, identified not by the old school tie, but by the designer logos on their tracksuits. Dermot didn't much like his work, but made a handsome living out of it. He didn't much like his clients either.

Now and again Dermot got a dock brief, awarded by the presiding district judge to the least troublesome solicitor in court. Since most of his clients pleaded guilty, the judges liked Dermot. Everyone was saved a great deal of time and effort by this simple and noble gesture. Sometimes he picked up the odd indictable case, which was sent forward for trial to the higher courts before a judge and jury. Very occasionally he picked up the most serious case of all, a murder.

These more serious cases, though reasonably lucrative, were unwelcome, as they demanded some degree of preparation. Dermot was supposed to send a brief to counsel, whom he nominated to defend the case. Ideally, the brief contained the Book of Evidence, which was prepared by the prosecution and contained statements from all the witnesses that they intended to call at the trial, together with any forensic or pathology reports. The brief was also to contain his client's detailed written instructions, statements from defence witnesses, independent forensic reports and any medical or psychiatric reports the solicitor had commissioned.

Whilst all this sounded very interesting, Dermot didn't have the organizational structure to back him up. He had a photocopier in his dingy two-roomed office on Arran Quay, but little else. Of course there was Tracy, his leggy, flame-haired secretary-cum-accountant-cum-private-investigator. He usually dispatched Tracy to the circuit court wearing a short skirt and found that none of the male barristers ever complained of being inadequately briefed. Tracy returned from court to advise him of the verdict. She then filled in the all-important legal aid claim form and typed up the Notice of Appeal. Most of Dermot's clients were losers and he rarely disappointed them with an acquittal.

Dermot lived in a neo-Georgian house in Sandymount and was married, with three children. His wife seldom saw him, since he was always at the beck and call of criminals and spent a large portion of his day calling to garda stations to service their peculiar needs. His advice was always the same: 'Say nothing'. He had no ambition other than to own the latest Mercedes motor car and holiday twice a year in Marbella; an ambition shared by many of his clients. He showed no great interest in civil rights matters and didn't even subscribe to the *Criminal Law Review*. He never had a case that made new law and had long since ceased caring.

He had slipped Marina a few bob the first time she recommended him to a Russian immigrant who was caught reclaiming scrapped cars and selling them on as genuine. Since then, they had a mutual understanding, and she sent a bit of work his way. He liked Marina a lot and plagued her with dinner invitations. Dermot honestly believed he was still attractive to members of the opposite sex. His short stature, pot belly, bald head and bulbous nose he saw as no obstacle to his pursuit of young lovelies, a pursuit he engaged in enthusiastically, but with no success.

Marina had phoned him the night before with a murder; yet another mad Russian immigrant. And she had fought her corner bravely, negotiating a better than normal backhander. Having explained briefly what the case was about, she arranged to meet him the following morning at half past nine.

True to form, Marina arrived late, wearing a pair of well-worn black jeans and a scruffy black leather jacket that had seen better days.

'Hi, Marina, you're looking particularly well this morning,' Dermot lied with ease, but little charm.

She didn't respond. Instead she put out her hand and opened her palm and gave him a wink. Pretty mercenary, he thought, as he placed a white envelope with €200 in it onto her upturned hand. They then went down to the cells.

Yuri seemed glad to see Marina and they spoke together in Russian for a few minutes. She looked around and pointed to Dermot enthusiastically. Yuri nodded to him, apparently agreeing that Dermot should represent him. Marina informed Yuri that Dermot would come and see him in prison and discuss the case in detail.

Upstairs, Detective Sergeant Murphy was sitting in the courtroom waiting for the case to be called. Dermot went in and gestured Barry outside.

'Good morning, Barry, are you here for the Russian case?' Dermot asked.

'Yes, Dermot, are you in that?' Barry said, with surprise in his voice.

'Yes, I am. When will the Book of Evidence be ready?'

'Soon; it's a straightforward case.'

'Did you get a confession?'

'No.'

'That's not like you, Barry; you must have lost your powers of persuasion. Don't worry, he might confess after I talk to him,' Dermot said, only half joking.

Barry went to walk back into court, but stopped, looked around to see if anyone was in earshot, and then ushered Dermot into a corner.

'Get a good senior counsel into this case, Dermot.'

Dermot laughed. 'You know me, Barry, I always do.'

'No, I'm serious. There's something not right about this case; get the kid the best.'

Dermot was a little surprised at Barry's serious tone and his apparent concern.

'You're getting soft in your old age.'

'He's not the worst.'

'OK Barry, nothing but the best.'

After court, Dermot went to the Tilted Wig for a pint of Guinness and a bowl of Irish stew. As he entered the bar he saw two male colleagues sitting together in a corner having lunch. He waved over to them. They nodded at him acknowledging his presence, but made it clear he wasn't welcome to join them. He sat at the bar on his own.

'How in God's name did that cowboy get assigned to that murder case?' one of the solicitors asked.

'The bollocks probably paid off one of the coppers. You know his style, he has them in his pocket,' the other replied.

'The poor punter is a foreigner, so he has no idea what he has let himself in for. He would be better off defending himself.'

'God help him.'

ten

Marina checked her mobile for any missed calls. There was a text from the model agency asking her to call urgently. Whilst walking along the quays she opened the white envelope that Dermot had given her, a good morning's work, she thought.

She climbed the stairs to the office on Wicklow Street where Angela, a short, bubbly blonde in her early forties, was seated behind a large glass-topped desk. Angela leapt to her feet as soon as Marina entered the room, and gave her an enormous hug. Marina appeared uncomfortable with the show of affection and pulled away.

'What the hell is going on, Angela, did you win the lottery or something?'

'No honey, but you did!' Angela exclaimed enthusiastically.

'What are you talking about?'

Angela stood back and took a deep breath.

'New York, honey, you're going to New York.'

'What?' Marina asked incredulously.

'You heard, you're going to New York, the work permit arrived this morning.'

'Are you serious?' Marina asked in a daze.

'Yes, two months in the Big Apple! You'd better pack your cases – you're going next week,' Angela replied, bubbling with excitement.

'Great.' Marina responded coolly. She lowered her head.

'What's up? I thought you would be over the moon.' Angela observed.

'I can't go,' Marina replied flatly.

'What do you mean you can't go?'

'I just can't go.'

After a moment's awkward silence, Angela glanced down at Marina's tummy.

'Don't tell me you're pregnant.'

Marina gave a half laugh and shook her head.

'Then what's wrong with you?'

'I'm in a big case and I can't leave it right now.'

Angela breathed a sigh of relief.

'Don't be stupid, you're not the only interpreter in town. I'm sure they can get someone else to do the job. Doesn't Elena stand in for you sometimes?'

Elena was another Russian interpreter at the same translation agency and one of Marina's few female friends.

'I can't leave the case, Angela. I know you did all you could getting me the visa and I really appreciate it.'

This contract was worth a lot of money to the agency, and Angela's tone suddenly changed. 'Have you any idea of the trouble we went to getting you that work permit? You have to go, and that's it,' she said firmly.

Marina tensed visibly; her eyes became cold and steady and her lips tight, as though some passion had made her into stone. She glared at Angela. 'To hell with you and your stupid permit! Who do you think you are telling me what I can and cannot do? You stupid Irish bitch,' she roared.

Angela took a step back. 'You're off the books unless you go,' she said tersely.

'To hell with your stupid job,' Marina yelled as she stormed out of the office and down the stairs.

Back in her flat, Marina calmed down. The flat was a tiny room painted dusty pink. A single bed stood in a corner against the wall. Next to it was a small table with a chair on either side. On the far wall, a narrow bookcase held a stereo and a few DVDs. There was a much-thumbed book on tips for self-improvement and a book on practical philosophy given to her by Stephen, one of her few Irish friends. Beside the bookshelves was an open wardrobe, which held a few cheap tops and three pairs of jeans. On the floor of the wardrobe lay two pairs of designer runners and an old pair of black suede high-heeled boots. In the centre of the room was a much-used large television. There were no pictures or photographs and the only clue to the occupant's sex was the large make-up bag sitting in the corner.

She slipped out of her wet clothes and pulled on a pair of unflattering fleece pyjamas. She looked despairingly around her dingy room, turned off her mobile phone and slumped onto her bed. She was raging with herself. Yes, she had lost her temper on occasions before, but never with people who mattered. Why did nothing ever go right for her?

eleven

Dermot's office was above a property consultation service on Arran Quay. It comprised a reception area, where Tracy sat, with a splendid view across the Liffey, and two small rooms to the rear, one of which was Dermot's office.

A clerk from the Chief State Solicitors Office delivered the Book of Evidence and Tracy, wearing a denim mini-skirt and flat suede boots, brought it into Dermot's office. He was seated behind a desk in his shirt-sleeves and braces, smoking a cheap cigar; the desk and floor were littered with files. Tracy coughed disapprovingly and looked for some-where to place the file. She eventually gave up and handed it to Dermot.

'That's the Russian murder case, Mr Molloy.' She coughed again.

'Thanks, Tracy. By the way that's a nice outfit you have on today.'

She winked at him coquettishly. 'They had a shorter one.'

'Why didn't you buy it?'

'It was a designer label and I couldn't afford it on my salary.'

'We might have to review that then.'

She giggled, conscious of Dermot's eyes following her as she left the room.

Normally he just asked Tracy to photocopy the Book of Evidence and send it on to counsel. He seldom read the case himself. This time he did. Maybe it was the conversation with Barry that excited his interest.

The story he read in the statements intrigued him. This certainly was no ordinary case. Total amnesia, that was rare. After several more cigars, Tracy popped her head around the door.

'I am off then, Mr Molloy.'

He grunted by way of answer.

'Are you still reading that case?' she asked in amazement.

Dermot glanced up at her.

'Sorry, Tracy, what did you say?'

'It doesn't matter, see you in the morning.'

'Yes, thanks.'

He left the office at seven, and for once headed straight home, by-passing the Quill, a public house a few doors down from his office. Fidelma, his wife, was a petite, dark-haired, youthful-looking forty-something. She appeared surprised to see him home so early.

'Are you not feeling well, Dermot?' she asked, as he came into the kitchen, where she was baking a rhubarb pie.

'No, I have a bit of work to do, that's all, and decided to do it at home for a change.'

She glanced at the bundle of papers under his arm and raised a dubious eyebrow.

Dermot went into a small room he called a study, though it contained hardly any books. His law library consisted of a few textbooks that he had kept since his university days. He made himself comfortable in his leather armchair and began to read.

The report from toxicology showed there were 204 milligrams of alcohol per millilitre in the sample of blood taken from Yuri at eight o'clock on the morning following the murder. That's not so bad, he thought. But he read on. Leaving the body at the rate of eighteen per cent per hour, that gave an approximate reading of 350 milligrams at midnight. Traces of cannabis were also detected in his blood and urine samples.

He then read the forensic evidence. Splatters of blood here, there and everywhere. He could never read these damn reports. He concentrated harder. Blood on sheets and pillows in the old lady's room – hers. Blood on the wall behind her bed – hers. Blood on the knife –also hers; blood on the wall beside Yuri's bedroom – not hers. The partial DNA profile indicated that it belonged to a close relative – at least, the chances of it belonging to someone other than the accused or a close relative was about one in seven million. Pretty damning, he thought. Blood found in the hallway outside the flat, inadequate quantity for analysis.

He then turned to the medical report from Dr Zuharry; no injuries found on suspect when examined in the garda station. That's strange, he thought. He read on. No blood on the suspect's clothes, shoes or bedlinen. He turned to the interview notes. Yuri went to bed, it appeared, and had no recollection of anything until the gardai arrived. Next he read the statements from the gardai who found Yuri asleep in his bed. Initially they thought he was dead, because he was in such a deep sleep.

At around nine, Fidelma came into the room with supper looking pleased to have him home for a change. He glanced up at her as she came in with the tray, 'Oh! That's a nice surprise.'

'Well, it's not often you're home these days, Dermot.'

'Please don't start scolding,' he replied.

'I'm not,' she protested.

'I thought I detected a note of sarcasm in your voice.'

'No, I mean it Dermot; we're seldom together these days.'

Dermot detected unusual warmth in her voice. And she was right, of course. Dermot loved calling into the pub on his way home and invariably stayed there until closing time. It wasn't that there was a lot of excitement at the Quill, but at least there was hope of some new experience to brighten up the dullness of his life.

'Is it anything interesting?' she said, looking at the papers on his lap and on the floor.

'Yes, a murder,' he said proudly.

'A real-life who-dunnit?' she said.

'Well, not so much who, as why.'

'Who killed who?'

'A son killed his mother.'

Fidelma grimaced. 'That's awful.'

He was surprised at her interest. He smiled at her. 'I'll tell you all about it if you like when I've finished reading it.'

'That would be great, Dermot,' she said enthusiastically, 'Maybe we could talk about it over dinner tomorrow night.'

He looked at her and smiled. 'I would like that.'

There was a lightness to her step as she left the room. Poor Fidelma, he thought, he should talk to her more often. She was so pathetically pleased to be offered a chance to discuss something. How bad was it when there had to be a murder case before they had anything to say to one another? Life had just got so dull. He'd always thought it was her fault, the way she never took an interest in him or his life, but maybe he was partly to blame.

Dermot placed the case notes on his desk and sat back in his chair. There was something about Yuri, he thought; he was alone and looking to Dermot for help. In fact, he had no one else to turn to. Sure, his clients always looked to him for help and advice, but this was different. Yuri had absolutely no recollection of killing his mother. Even after being confronted with the overwhelming circumstantial evidence, it was obvious that Yuri still hoped the evidence would prove someone else had done it. He thought that at that very moment Yuri was lying in his dark, lonely cell with nothing but his thoughts, with no one to talk to. Dermot closed his eyes. If he genuinely had no recollection, how must Yuri feel? The isolation must be frightening. Dermot began to feel Yuri's pain. Yuri didn't know Dermot was a journeyman, who was ill-equipped to handle his plight. Dermot's feeling of uneasiness grew the more he thought about the case and a sense of panic swept over him. He had never felt like this before in all his years of practice. Yuri was his responsibility, and his future was in Dermot's hands. The thought didn't sit comfortably with him.

He rose from his chair, feeling clammy and unwell. He needed air. He went into the hallway and put on his raincoat. Fidelma came out from the kitchen where she was looking up recipes for dinner the following night. She looked disappointed when she saw him standing there ready to go out, no doubt to the pub, but said nothing.

'I don't feel too well, Fidelma, I'm just going out for a breath of fresh air. And, no, I'm not going to the pub.'

She smiled at him. He smiled back and left.

It was a still, foggy night as Dermot strolled across the park. The horror of Yuri's predicament had focused his mind on his own inadequacies as a lawyer. He wished now that he had kept himself abreast with developments in criminal law, forensic science and pathology. He stopped and sat down on a wooden bench. The fog had become dense and his mind, unhindered by visual distractions, became even more sharply focused. He took a deep breath and was suddenly inspired. He would withdraw from the case and ask the court to assign some other solicitor to handle the case. That was it. Claim there was an ethical problem with his client and he could graciously depart from the case. But would anyone believe that Dermot Molloy knew anything about ethics? Doubtful. So they would know he'd bottled out, that he wasn't up to it. What did that matter? Those bastards had no respect for him anyhow. That was it – an imagined ethical problem.

But what would he tell Fidelma? Perhaps he could tell her his client had sacked him; that he was discharged unceremoniously from the case. And good riddance to it, the trial would have tied up too much of his time anyway. All that work he would lose by being away from his busy practice in the district court. That was it. Perfect. All these feelings of inadequacy would go away with the case. He was already feeling better.

He decided to go to O'Reilly's Bar for a pint of Guinness. It was half past ten, and he hadn't noticed the evening flying by. As he was walking along Sandymount Road he passed the house where the murder had been committed. His steps grew shorter as he glanced across at the house, which was in darkness. His gaze was drawn to the upstairs windows. He looked to the right, at the bay window of the living room, and imagined how Yuri and his mother spent their evenings and thought perhaps she read aloud to him from her books. How isolated they were, living in middle-class Dublin suburbia. His gaze moved to the bedroom window. The curtains were drawn. He wondered what had really happened that night. For a moment he imagined the horror on the old dear's face as she looked into the eyes of her killer. What thoughts had gone through her head?

Maybe she went peacefully. No, the medical evidence suggested otherwise. She put up a dreadful struggle against her son and clawed at him in a desperate bid to survive. He turned away as his imagination galloped on. The scene he saw in his mind's eye was horrific. He had never seen himself inside any case before. Why this one? Why had Marina rung him in the first place? He was here because of his greed, and, of course, hers. But she didn't have the responsibility.

He moved on quickly, but felt the house moving with him in his corner vision. He stopped and looked back. They would still be there now, together, had Yuri not drunk so much that night. The lights would be on and maybe the sound of music would filter out onto the street, as they listened to some Russian ballad. But was drink really to blame? Could it turn a loving son into a monster? The more he thought of this the more he became convinced that drink was not the culprit. There must be some other reason why he killed her. He would have to get Yuri psychiatrically examined as soon as possible; he must be suffering from some form of psychiatric disorder. He should have done it long before then. He would get the best forensic psychiatrist in the Central Mental Hospital. That would be a good starting point. And he would prepare the best brief for the top silk in Ireland.

All thoughts of abandoning the case left him and he walked with purpose. What was the level of alcohol found in Yuri's blood again? He arrived outside O'Reilly's and continued walking. He had to get home and finish reading the case – for Yuri, and for himself.

twelve

When Dermot arrived home he went straight to his study. He picked up the Book of Evidence and studied the report on the alcohol level in Yuri's blood sample. It was as he remembered. He started to read the notes of the interview with Yuri in the garda station. He continued to read until exhausted, he fell asleep.

He was awakened by a dull thud coming from upstairs. At first he didn't remember where he was and was confused. He saw the papers at his feet and slowly came back to earth. There was another thud. He rose from his chair and nervously climbed the stairs, taking with him a baton he kept in a drawer in his desk. The landing light was off. As he got to the top of the stairs, he saw the outline of a figure in the darkness come from his right, from his daughter's room. The figure was walking slowly but purposefully. Dermot was terrified. His raised hand gripping the baton trembled as the figure emerged from the shadows. It was his daughter Andrea, dressed in her long nightgown. He breathed an enormous sigh of relief and lowered the baton. She didn't appear to notice him, even though he stood directly in her path.

'Are you OK, angel? You gave Daddy an awful fright.'

She didn't answer and, as she drew closer, he saw that she was staring vacantly ahead. She glided past him as though he wasn't there and continued into the bathroom where she climbed up onto the toilet seat.

'It's OK, it's only Daddy,' he said softly.

But she didn't respond. He stood at the door, not knowing what to do. The child climbed down from the toilet and went to the sink. She took the soap, washed her hands, and then dried them with a towel. Then she walked towards him like a zombie. Dermot was blocking her path to her bedroom, but she kept walking towards him, apparently oblivious to his presence. He stepped out of her way and she returned to her room, closing the door behind her.

'Good night, angel,' he said softly.

Dermot went back downstairs and into the living room, where he headed for the drinks cabinet and poured himself a large whiskey. Sitting down, he smiled to himself. He recalled when he was twelve years old he was found by his father walking down the road near their family home at four in the morning wearing his rugby gear, carrying a ball under his arm. God knows where he was going or why. His parents had taken him to the local doctor for advice. The doctor reassured them there was nothing mentally wrong with young Dermot, and that he was merely sleepwalking. Now here was Andrea following in her father's footsteps, only with the good sense, even in her sleep, to return to bed. He remembered the commonly held view that you should never wake a sleepwalker and this was why he hadn't attempted to wake Andrea. There was no obvious reason for this other than a fear of some violent reaction in the sleepwalker on being suddenly awakened from a deep sleep.

Then he recalled a documentary on television, about a man in Canada who got up in the middle of the night, drove fifteen miles in his car and murdered his mother-in-law, with whom, apparently, he got on famously. The scientists proved he was asleep at the time of the killing. Dermot had seen the documentary and was more than a little skeptical about the case. Perhaps he had been wrong.

Slowly it came to him: maybe Yuri had murdered his mother in his sleep. That was why he didn't remember anything. Well, it was a possibility at least. But it was a terrifying thought, and perhaps too bizarre to contemplate seriously.

thirteen

Yuri shared a cell with a drug addict called Darren who was awaiting trial on robbery charges. They were about the same age but had nothing in common. Darren was a thin young man whose gaunt, rodent-like face bore the scars of his conflict with anyone and anything that stood between him and his next fix. He was continually muttering to himself in a thick Dublin accent, and Yuri couldn't understand a word he said. The cell was small, with two concrete beds covered in wafer-thin mattresses. The walls were covered in calendar pictures of Baywatch babes interspersed with pictures of the Arsenal football team. Yuri knew the names of all the players and his only form of communication with his cellmate was to point to each team member and call out his name with a smile, hoping to provoke some sort of a response. Darren mistakenly believed that Yuri was also an Arsenal supporter, which was probably just as well.

Yuri had a photograph of himself and his mother taped to the wall beside his bed. Darren noticed that Yuri spent hours staring at it blankly with tears in his eyes and was convinced that he was half mad.

The inmates assembled in a large noisy communal dining hall for breakfast. Yuri sat alone at the end of a long wooden table looking curiously at the mayhem all about him. After breakfast the inmates were allowed time in the exercise yard and on this fine sunny morning they quickly grouped into two teams and started to play football. Yuri sat by himself on a wooden bench in the corner of the yard watching the game with interest. He would love to have joined in, but wasn't asked.

After a while a misdirected ball came hurtling towards him, and he instinctively leapt to his feet and caught it in both hands. A group of menacing-looking prisoners stood in front of him. He smiled at them and held out the ball. They glared at him with hard, twisted faces. Then they rushed him, viciously throwing kicks and punches, many of which met their target. He slumped to the ground and rolled himself instinctively into a protective ball, but still the kicks came flying in, mostly to his head, which was jolted from side to side with shuddering force. Shouts of 'mother killer' prompted more prisoners to join in, like sharks in a feeding frenzy.

Prison warders blowing whistles rushed to the scene and the prisoners quickly dispersed. Yuri lay on the ground motionless, blood streaming from his head and face. He was carried by the prison warders to the infirmary, battered and unconscious.

As he slowly came round he looked up and saw the angelic features of a young dark-haired nurse with porcelain skin who gently wiped the blood from his face. Her touch was light, but his wounds were sensitive even to her warm breath. He winced and reached out, taking hold of her delicate wrist. She pulled away, but he softened his grip and turned away in embarrassment, then began to cry. She looked down at him, patted his brow with a cold face cloth and tenderly wiped away his tears. He thanked her in Russian. She smiled at him and continued to clean his wounds.

After Yuri recovered, the governor moved him to a single cell in B wing, which was set-aside for high-security prisoners. Socializing amongst inmates was only permitted in a small exercise yard and was strictly monitored. His isolation was to become even more acute, through no fault of his own.

At first he hadn't been greatly concerned by his incarceration, but after the beating he was continuously on edge and unable to sleep. Most nights he lay awake in his cell thinking of his parents and Ivan, his twin brother, and their happy days together back in Russia. They were a closely knit family with strong orthodox beliefs and values. His father had been temporarily suspended from his post in the army pending a disciplinary hearing, something to do with selling arms to the Russian Mafia. However, Yuri was sure he would have been exonerated by the enquiry had he survived the fire.

Ivan had nearly finished his training in medical school at the time of the fire. He was engaged to Natasha, a beautiful blonde student nurse from Kiev, and had a good life to look forward to.

Yuri, on the other hand, was slow at school and left without any qualifications. He decided to join the army and follow in his father's footsteps. Despite his father's high rank and influence, he was turned down on what was tersely stated to be medical grounds. Since then he spent most of his time unemployed and idle. He knew a few girls from his school days but never had the courage to ask any of them out.

The difference between the twins couldn't have been more pronounced, yet their mother doled out love in equal measures. His father often took Yuri fishing, and they spent from dawn to dusk cloaked in intimate silence. He was convinced that his father had something profound to tell him, but had never managed to get around to it.

fourteen

Dermot sat behind the desk in his office and nervously dialled Blair Armstrong's number. He felt uneasy, as it had been ten years since they had last spoken and Blair had moved on to greener pastures. Dermot had briefed Blair in his early years when he was struggling to make ends meet at the Bar. Even then, starting out on his career, he was a cut above the rest, with a strong physical presence and a powerful voice. Despite his obvious brilliance, he was also modest, which was his most endearing quality and also his greatest weapon. Blair had progressed quickly through the ranks and his talents were well rewarded. Since he had become a senior counsel he was involved in most of the high profile criminal trials and was much sought after by solicitors and clients alike. How would he receive Dermot after all these years? Dermot thought. Would the success finally have gone to his head? The phone seemed to ring for an eternity.

'Yes.'

'Hello, Blair, Dermot here.'

Blair didn't respond immediately. Dermot knew it: he shouldn't have rung.

'Dermot Molloy,' he added.

'My dear friend, how nice to hear from you after all these years, how are you?'

'I'm fine, Blair, and yourself?'

'Great, Dermot, but it's been so long.'

'Yes, the years have flown by.'

'Is trade still thriving in the district court?'

'I am kept busy enough.'

'And Fidelma and the children, are they well?'

'Yes, great.'

There was a short pause.

'Well, what can I do for the man who gave me a leg up just when I needed it most?'

Dermot felt warm inside at the recognition. Blair was like that, always gracious.

'I have a difficult one, Blair.'

Blair laughed. 'A pickpocket in Henry Street, is it?' He was alluding to the first case that Dermot had sent him.

'No, Blair, it's a bit more interesting than that, it's a murder.'

Blair sighed. 'It's nice of you to think of me, but I must decline the case as I'm hanging up the old wig and taking early retirement. Money made and all that. I'm going out to pasture.'

'You're kidding me.'

'Nope, I'm deadly serious. Just finishing off a few bits and pieces and then I'm done.'

'But this one's a real challenge,' Dermot persisted.

'They all are,' Blair retorted.

'Is there any chance of meeting up with you to discuss it? I don't want to talk about it over the phone.'

Blair laughed at Dermot's paranoia. The years might have rolled on, but they hadn't changed him.

'Sure, Dermot, call around for a drink tomorrow evening, we can talk about old times, but you won't persuade me to change my mind.'

'We'll see about that. OK, tomorrow night it is.'

Marina sat in her bed-sit, her mood as dark as the threatening black clouds that loomed over the city. She took a tattered brown envelope from the bedside locker and fingered it hesitantly. Eventually she removed a black and white photo from the sleeve of the envelope and regarded it closely. Her father was a handsome man whom everyone respected and admired. Her mother, who was hugging him affectionately, was on the plain side and full figured. She remembered when she was eleven years old and the first time her father crept into her room at night smelling of drink. She began to tremble as she recalled the fear that gripped her when she felt his rough hands fondling her tiny breasts. She closed her eyes and tears flowed down her cheeks. The image of her mother's face peering in the door and closing it so Daddy could play his little game, ghosted into her mind.

After several weeks the touching gave way to violent penetration. But she learnt the rules and suffered in silence. Her mother continued to turn a blind eye for reasons Marina never understood. That abandonment was more painful than anything her father inflicted on her, and haunted her day and night. At school she felt different from the other girls. She was convinced they knew what was happening to her at home and thought her unclean. Her paranoia led to isolation, and then to prolonged silences. After school she spent hours walking the tree-lined streets near her home aimlessly, terrified to return. On one occasion she stood on the porch in her school uniform with her satchel over her shoulder and urinated in her pants as she heard her parents arguing inside; no doubt over her. Fear became so common that she began to think it natural. Her mother and she seldom talked, and Marina believed she resented her very existence. As the years rolled on she knew she needed help, but had no one to turn to. Isolated and alone she spent day after day lying on her bed sobbing into her pillow, clutching a photograph of her older brother who at the age of twelve, had drowned in a local river whilst fishing with some of his schoolfriends. Perhaps he would have protected her.

Then, one summer's day when she was sixteen, it stopped; abruptly and for no apparent reason. Her father never spoke to her again, and her parents stopped arguing. After the initial sense of relief subsided, she looked forward to recovery. But it never came. She remained depressed, alone and isolated. Sometimes she wondered whether it had all been one big nightmare and she would awake without the scars. But it wasn't, and for years she led a life detached from the real world, without family or friends.

Her parents looked happy in the photograph. Who would have guessed the brutality they dished out to their little princess? She placed the photograph back in the envelope, and rolled another joint to banish the everlasting images from her past. Eventually she fell asleep, fully clothed, on her bed.

fifteen

The following evening, Dermot parked his Mercedes on Fitzwilliam Square. Blair's apartment was situated in a fine Georgian house overlooking the wooded park. He walked up a flight of granite steps to a heavy panelled door and rang the bell. Blair answered and buzzed him in. He found himself in a large hall with a limestone floor and pale oak-panelled walls. As he entered a small lift, it automatically proceeded to the third floor. The lift doors opened directly into the apartment. Blair, wearing denim jeans, a navy-blue cashmere jumper and a broad smile, greeted him and shook his hand warmly. He had hardly changed in ten years, still the film-star looks, Dermot thought, as he handed Blair the bottle of Midleton rare single malt whiskey he had brought as a gift.

'That's very good of you,' Blair said, inspecting the bottle. 'We'll open it straight away.'

The apartment was exquisite, with a square hallway painted a creamy white. The limestone floor was also white and two gilt-edged Dutch paintings added muted colours to an otherwise clinical look. Dermot followed Blair through double doors framed by columns into a magnificent living room painted in burgundy and cream. The inlaid teak floor was covered in a variety of cream silk rugs. Three bow windows framed by heavy gold curtains looked out onto tennis courts in the centre of the park. There was a fine Georgian fireplace and a few modern *objets d'art* were well placed among comfortable antique furnishings. Quietly elegant, thought Dermot, as he settled into a large cream sofa, just like Blair.

Blair poured two whiskies into Waterford crystal tumblers and handed one to Dermot.

'Cheers, Dermot, to the good old days.'

'And to crime,' Dermot responded.

They both laughed.

'So, what has you so excited about this case, Dermot?'

Dermot burst into energy and enthusiastically described the crime scene and gave a sketchy account of the evidence. Blair listened intently, amazed that Dermot had had the patience and interest to read the Book of Evidence. When Dermot eventually finished, Blair looked at him quizzically.

'Dermot, what's the angle? It sounds pretty straightforward to me.'

'Automatism.'

'Automatism?' Blair said incredulously.

Dermot nodded.

'Epilepsy or hyperglycaemia?' Blair asked, testing Dermot's knowledge of a notoriously difficult area of the criminal law.

'No, Blair, somnambulism.'

Blair stood up, walked to the drinks cabinet and poured two more whiskies.

'Somnambulism?' he said, handing Dermot his drink.

'Yes, it's a term used for sleepwalking and I believe this is a classic case of it.'

Blair had never heard Dermot talking enthusiastically about anything except his motor car. Now he sounded as though he was on the scent of the Holy Grail. He looked at Dermot and smiled.

'I know what somnambulism is, Dermot, I'm a little surprised that you do.'

Dermot sat back, put his drink on a side table and folded his arms.

'Well, what do you think?'

'It sounds interesting. Have you strong medical evidence to back up your case?' Blair asked.

Dermot shifted nervously.

'No,' he replied sheepishly. 'Unfortunately the case isn't quite ready for trial.'

A look of bemusement crossed Blair's face.

'Then why in heaven's name do you say this is a sleepwalking case?'

'Well, to begin with, the guy had absolutely no reason to kill his mother.'

Blair laughed. 'It's not that simple, Dermot. You can't say he was asleep because he had no motive. Lots of crimes are motiveless. You should know that.'

'And what about his amnesia?' Dermot protested.

'If that's genuine – anyway the amount of drink your client consumed might well explain that.'

'So you're not interested in doing the case.' Dermot's disappointment was palpable.

'I'm sorry Dermot, but I can recommend some other good barristers if you like.'

Dermot knocked back his whiskey and was about to leave. Then he changed his mind and decided to give it one last shot.

'Blair, I have a gut feeling about this case and you would really have to meet the client to understand why. He has no fear whatsoever; it's as though his conscience is completely clear. Would you at least see him before you make up your mind?'

'Dermot, gut feelings don't win cases, hard evidence does. And, by the sound of things, you have none.'

'Come on, Blair, if you pulled this one off it would be a real feather in your cap.'

'And if I lost, I would be the laughing stock of the Law Library,' Blair retorted.

'The Blair Armstrong I remember never allowed fear of ridicule put him off accepting a case. If I remember correctly, you never turned down any cause unless you were too busy to take it on.'

A broad smile crossed Blair's face. 'Your memory serves you well, and I won't allow it affect me now. I told you, I've decided to retire and that's that. I have had enough of the law.'

'If you take it on you'll be working closely with a cute Russian interpreter; she's a real stunner.'

Blair let out a raucous laugh. 'That's the first time a solicitor has used that sort of bait to lure me into accepting a brief. You haven't changed one bit, Dermot, you're still a rogue.'

Dermot sensed that Blair was softening and leant forward clasping his hands together.

'Look, Blair, I know there are a lot of ifs and buts, and I haven't exactly done the groundwork yet, but I really need you in on this one. You know me and I won't be able to handle it without you. I beg you to take the brief.'

Blair paused and peered into his glass as though burrowing into his memories. Dermot sensed his growing vulnerability and fired an arrow.

'It's not just me who needs you; my client needs the best if he is to have any hope.'

Blair stood up and walked slowly to the fireplace. He poured more whiskey and sat down. 'OK, Dermot, with some reluctance, I'll agree to see your client.'

'That's great,' Dermot replied.

'And, by the way, it was the line about your client needing me that won your argument. I always had a soft spot for the underdog. The bit about the cute interpreter has nothing to do with my decision.'

The two men laughed and fell into conversation about old times and long-perished dreams.

sixteen

Marina stared blankly out of the window of the grubby taxi at the torrential rain that was beating relentlessly against the window. She was desperately trying to avoid conversation with Dermot, who was sitting next to her and irritatingly tapping his feet to the beat of the rain. He wore an old brown tweed suit that was two sizes too small for him, and his necktie strained to hold the grubby frayed collars of his shirt together. Marina was thinking about her studies. She had fallen years behind and was struggling with her degree. Truth be told, business studies didn't stir her interest greatly, but she struggled on, believing that a degree would give her respectability.

She glanced at Dermot, who grinned at her. She barely disguised her contempt for him as she glared at him. Too often she found herself in a taxi with a slimy defence lawyer going to see some low life in prison. And she seriously questioned the so-called Irish justice system: inebriated legal aid solicitors stopping off in court on their way to the next bar; the court appointment system, run by charitable district justices as some sort of benevolent scheme for down-at-heel solicitors.

She had lied about her qualifications when applying to the translation agency for a job; she simply had none. But she spoke good English, and believed she was reasonably good at her job, unlike many of the lawyers she had encountered.

'This lawyer we are meeting is the very best!' Dermot declared, interrupting her thoughts.

She glanced at him and warded him off with a half smile. Her past experiences with lawyers caused her to seriously doubt his assertion.

'We go back a long way – he taught me all I know,' Dermot continued.

Exactly, she thought, that's the problem.

Inside Cloverhill Prison, she felt the eyes of the wardens undress her; she was well accustomed to this and paid little heed. After the usual bureaucratic formalities were complied with, they were led into a large deserted waiting room.

'So, how's college?' Dermot enquired, trying to strike up a conversation.

'It's OK,' she replied.

She picked up a leaflet on the dangers of cannabis smoking and buried herself in it. Gateway drug. She had been smoking weed for years and it hadn't opened any doors for her! Her thoughts were interrupted by the faint sound of laughter, which seemed out of place within the austere walls. She looked up and saw a smiling prison guard, who minutes before, had been so abrupt with Dermot and herself, open the heavy steel door and usher a man into the room. Whatever quip the man had made had certainly brought the guard to life.

The man walked slowly towards them with a swagger. He was tall and athletic with broad shoulders. His greying hair was swept back off a strong face with hawkish brown eyes. Marina looked at him curiously and found it difficult to put a nationality on him. He wore an elegant dark-blue cashmere coat over a bespoke navy wool suit and a burgundy silk scarf. Marina thought him distinguished, almost aristocratic looking.

'Hello, Blair,' Dermot said warmly, and with a tone of respect that she hadn't heard from him previously.

'Good evening, Dermot.' The man's voice was powerful but melodic.

'We shouldn't be kept waiting too long,' Dermot said apologetically.

'There's no rush,' the man replied.

'Have you read the papers I sent you?' Dermot asked.

The man looked down at Marina, who was still seated.

'First things first, Dermot, where are your manners?'

'I'm so sorry, Blair,' – not Marina, she noticed – 'this is our interpreter, Ms Petrovskaya.'

Blair's warm brown eyes engaged hers. She stood up, flicked back a strand of hair that had fallen across her eyes and extended her hand. He shook it firmly and didn't avert his gaze. He smiled and his face lit up with expression and warmth.

'It's nice to meet you, Ms Petrovskaya. My name is Blair Armstrong,' he said, obliquely reprimanding Dermot for assuming Marina knew who he was and at the same time broadcasting a modesty that didn't presume she had been awaiting his arrival with interest.

'It's nice to meet you, too. Dermot has told me all about you,' Marina replied, enthusiastically.

They stood facing each other in silence, their eyes locked together for what seemed an eternity. Eventually Dermot coughed embarrassedly, and the trance was broken. Blair glanced down at her hand, which was still in his and she reluctantly let go.

'Dermot has told me you're the best lawyer in the country,' she continued.

'I think he might be exaggerating a little.' Blair looked out the window at the heavy rain. 'It's such a miserable evening,' he observed.

Marina cocked her head and looked quizzically at Blair. Could such a dynamic figure actually be shy? she thought. She felt an energy surge and a desire to engage him. At moments like this she wished she had something interesting to say, but she didn't.

Blair was impressed with her natural beauty and saw beyond her scruffiness. She was tall, with long colt-like slender limbs. Her pale-grey almond-shaped eyes, framed by perfect eyebrows, were delicately set in an exquisitely sculpted face. A small, slightly upturned nose perched between high cheekbones. Her shapely top lip curled gently upwards on either side and hovered seductively over a full lower lip. She had a flawless sallow complexion, untouched by make-up, and her blonde hair was casually drawn back in a bun. For once, Dermot had demonstrated remarkably good taste, he thought.

The silence was broken by the sound of the heavy steel door opening.

'We are ready for you now, Mr Armstrong. Sorry to keep you waiting, sir.'

Yuri was seated in the small visiting room. Pale and gaunt, his hair had grown since his arrest. He looked younger, despite the fading bruises about his face. He had also lost weight and the loose-fitting blue prison overall was hanging off him. He remained seated as his visitors crowded into the cramped room. Yuri showed little interest other than to briefly greet Marina in his native tongue. His visitors sat in front of him across a wide concrete table covered in blue vinyl that separated the imprisoned from the free. Blair was in the middle with Marina to his right.

'My name is Blair Armstrong and I'm a senior counsel. Dermot has asked me to do your case and I want to ask you a few questions.'

Marina translated Blair's somewhat formal introduction.

'Did we keep you waiting?' Blair asked.

Yuri shrugged his shoulders, even after the translation, as though he didn't understand.

'I am sure that you have awaited this visit with some anxiety,' Blair said, sympathetically.

Yuri nodded.

'And have probably tossed and turned at night in your cell not knowing what to say, how to present yourself, or what questions to ask.'

Yuri nodded again in appreciation at this insight into his predicament. These were the very thoughts that visited him every night when the lights went out and he was alone in his cell.

'Are you sleeping OK?'

Yuri put his head down and muttered, 'No.'

'Are you eating?'

'No.' Yuri seemed defensive and unwilling to engage with his visitors.

Blair sat back and sighed. He noticed the bruising on Yuri's face but didn't enquire how it had happened.

'Well, that's not good, Yuri, you must build up your strength. We must both be strong to face the trial.'

Marina looked at Blair. His eyes were fixed on Yuri and there was sincerity in his voice. The reference to *we* at once identified him as part of Yuri's cause and she was impressed by his compassion. Dermot smiled, it was clear that Blair was now on board. The pretty interpreter had won him over after all, he thought.

'We will talk to the prison doctor and see if we can get you some sleeping tablets, if you think that would help.'

'Thank you, sir,' Yuri replied.

'Are there any other inmates here from Russia?'

Yuri lowered his head and started fidgeting nervously. 'No, I'm alone, sir.'

'Have you family living here?'

Yuri hesitated and looked at Marina and then spoke to her at some length.

Eventually she translated his words. 'No, my mother and I moved here three years ago from Rostov, after the fire.'

Dermot looked at Marina, expecting some further information, but she shrugged her shoulders, indicating that that was it.

'Sorry, did I understand you to say that there were no other members of your family living here?' Blair enquired, with a quizzical look on his face.

'Yes, that's right, sir.'

'No aunts, uncles or cousins?' Blair continued.

'I told you I have none, sir.'

'I must know something before we go any further: did you have anything to gain financially from your mother's death?'

Yuri shrugged his shoulders. 'I don't understand, sir.'

'Had your mother any money that you hoped to inherit?'

'My mother had a bank account, but I think she only had a small amount of money in it; we were not rich people.'

Blair looked at Marina as she translated Yuri's words. The sadness in her eyes was all too evident to him.

'I must be absolutely sure of your reply: are you sure your mother was not well off.'

'No, she wasn't, sir.'

'And had nothing that might be considered valuable?'

'That's right.'

Blair looked at Marina and appeared deep in thought.

'Why did you come to Ireland?'

'My father and twin brother, my aunt, uncle and cousin were killed in a fire in our family home in Russia. My father was a distinguished man, a colonel in the army and highly respected. My mother was devastated by the deaths and decided to seek refuge in this country from the memory of what had happened, and I came with her to look after her.'

'Have you any friends here in Dublin?'

'No, sir, I haven't. Except maybe ...' He hesitated.

'Except who, Yuri?'

'Maybe Liz.'

'Who is Liz?'

'She is the nurse who looked after me in the infirmary, she was very kind to me. I like her a lot and I hope she likes me.'

'And what have you done in this country since you arrived?'

'I worked as a gardener in the local park. I kept myself to myself.'

'So you have not spoken to anyone in your native tongue since you came into prison?'

A tear slowly entered Yuri's eye, which he quickly wiped away. He appeared fragile and vulnerable. 'Do you not want to know about my case, sir?' he said, changing the tone and direction of the conversation.

'This I already know from Dermot, and I have also read the Book of Evidence, the forensic and pathology reports. Correct me if I am wrong, on the night of your mother's death you had too much to drink, had a smoke and fell asleep. You awoke the following morning with the gardai in your house. They told you that you murdered your mother and showed you the knife, but you remembered nothing and still don't.'

'Yes, that's right, sir.'

'Well, that is all I need to know for the moment.'

'Do you believe this, sir?' Yuri asked.

There was a long pause as Yuri searched Blair's eyes. Eventually Blair answered.

'Yuri, I have no reason to disbelieve you.'

Yuri leant forward, his elbows on the table and his hands clasped. 'I loved my mother, sir, more than anything in the whole world. I would never have done anything to hurt her.'

Marina hoped she had not lost the mood of Yuri's declaration in the translation and she hadn't. There was a long silence.

Blair leant forward and fixed him with his eyes. 'We will do everything we can to help you.'

Blair sensed it was time to leave and his timing was impeccable. The detail was for another day.

'A real stunner, isn't she?' Dermot said, as they waited in the reception area for Marina who had remained with Yuri in the consultation room.

Blair appeared distracted and didn't answer.

'Dermot, there is one thing troubling me.'

'What's that?'

'How come the guards arrived in such force on the morning of his arrest?'

'I thought that was a little strange too. Apparently there was an anonymous 999 call claiming there was an intruder in the house.'

'But who could have known there had been a disturbance there?'

'The guards reckon that it was a neighbour who heard something and they just got lucky.'

'Maybe,' Blair replied, but he didn't sound convinced.

Marina joined them and they walked towards the front gate. Blair stood back and held the door for her, a courtesy she wasn't accustomed to, and she bowed her head in appreciation. For reasons that weren't immediately apparent to her she didn't want to leave his company and was hoping that he would join her and Dermot on the trip back. A taxi was waiting outside the prison, but Blair looked up at the evening sky. It had stopped raining and he announced he would walk a bit, and bade them both goodbye with little ceremony.

Dermot and Marina clambered into the back of the taxi. As it moved away, she turned and looked out the window at Blair in expectation of a fleeting meeting of glances. But there was none. Blair appeared deep in thought as he turned the collar of his coat to meet the cold night air.

'Are you impressed?' enquired Dermot.

Marina gave Dermot a half smile. She took out a college book from her black leather rucksack and again sought refuge from Dermot.

'Good at the old PR, isn't he?' he persisted.

Yes, she thought, but there was a lot more to his brief interchange with Yuri than mere public relations.

Blair was walking slowly, which was his way. He tended to notice every-thing on his travels, small things others don't see. His thoughts were of Rosemary, his wife and lover for years. She had been his partner in life and they had shared everything in equal measure. Childless yet fulfilled, she had been an inspiration to him throughout his career. They often analysed some murder case together in Nico's, a cosy Italian bistro on Dame Street. After the wine had got the better of them, they giggled their way home arm-in-arm. Sought after as guests in Dublin's cocktail party circle, they preferred each other's company and seldom socialized.

Rosemary had passed away three years earlier after a short illness, and he had struggled with his grief. She had loved everything about him, and he was lonely and starved of love without her. He could see the two of them mulling over this one. There was more to this case than first appeared.

seventeen

The following morning, Blair answered the phone and was astonished to hear Marina's voice on the other end. He was taken aback when she said she wanted to meet him. He suggested lunch at Browne's on the Green.

Marina put down the phone and gave an enormous sigh of relief. It had taken courage to contact Blair. But she had a need, and surprisingly for her, a desire to see him again. And she was amazed that such an important and influential man had time for lunch with an impoverished interpreter such as her. But he did, and her confidence and self-belief soared.

She arrived on time for once, wearing the same scruffy black leather jacket, a denim mini-skirt, black wool tights and flat black suede boots. Having been told there were no vacancies by the snooty headwaiter, who mistook her for a student looking for work, she was shown to Blair's table.

Blair rose to his feet and shook hands. He looked casual in a moss-green mohair sports jacket and a light-blue open-necked shirt. He ordered a bottle of Chablis Premier Cru 1997 and mineral water without consulting her. She went to speak but he interrupted her.

'Shall we order before we talk?' This was a command and not a request, and she admired his confidence.

She felt uncomfortable with the large leather-bound menu and stared at it blankly. The waiter hovered impatiently, waiting for her decision.

'We will both have my usual, Jimmy,' Blair said to the waiter, as he handed back the menus.

'The benefit of local knowledge – I hope you don't think me arrogant, but I think you will enjoy my choice,' Blair said.

In those few moments she felt all the tension and nervousness leave her body. She looked around the opulent restaurant, admiring the elegant ladies in their sophisticated refinery engaged in quiet and no doubt intellectual conversation. Here she was with an aristocrat in his domain, yet she felt strangely at ease. She could get used to this, she thought.

'Well, Ms Petrovskaya, was there some particular reason why you wanted to see me?' Blair said in a businesslike manner.

'Yes, there was. I want you to explain Yuri's defence to me. Dermot told me a little bit about it and I find it fascinating.' She smiled at him coquettishly as she flicked back her hair.

Blair smiled. 'Well, I don't know if he has one yet, but there is the possibility of running the defence of automatism.'

'What does that mean? Dermot couldn't explain it to me.'

'There are circumstances where a person commits a crime, but their mind is not in control of their body at the time.'

'I don't understand.'

'Let me give you an example. Say you go to the dentist and he gives you a general anaesthetic and knocks you out.'

She sat upright in her chair and placed her hands on her lap.

'Right.'

'And whilst in the dentist's chair you suddenly leap up and bite his nose.'

She giggled and he gave her a withering look.

'OK.'

'Your body clearly carried out the act, but your mind was absent at the time.'

'So?'

'Well, if you were charged with assaulting the poor dentist, you could say, I am not guilty because I was incapable of forming any intent to harm him.'

'Because I was unconscious,' she observed.

'Exactly,' Blair replied.

'I think I understand what you are talking about, but what has that got to do with Yuri's case?'

Blair was conscious that ethically he shouldn't be discussing his client's case with Marina at all. But she was going to be present at the consultations and would find out one way or the other.

'Well, sleepwalking, or somnambulism as we call it, is also an example of automatism. The sleepwalker is in fact the classic automaton. During a sleepwalking episode, the body does certain things but the mind is not in control.'

'What has that got to do with Yuri?'

'Dermot has a theory that Yuri may have been asleep when he killed his mother.'

Marina put her hand to her mouth and started to giggle. 'That's crazy. He stabbed his mother, how could he do that in his sleep?'

'Marina, there have been a number of cases where people have carried out very complex acts when asleep. Let me tell you a true story. A mother, who dreamt her flat was on fire, threw her baby from a fifth-floor window, believing she was saving the child from a certain death. She woke up to find there was no fire and when she looked out her window she saw her baby lying dead in the alleyway below.'

'That sounds incredible. And all you have to do is claim you were asleep and you get off.'

Blair sat back in his chair and smiled. 'Well, it's not quite as simple as that, Marina. There are usually some clinical indicators.'

Marina frowned. 'What do you mean by clinical indicators?'

'Tell-tale signs, circumstances that suggest it might be a sleep-related crime.'

'Like what?'

'Total amnesia is the most common example. People never remember what they did when they were sleepwalking; instead they rely on other people to tell them.'

'What else?'

'Lack of motive; like in Yuri's case, an unexplained killing.'

'OK, I understand.'

'And there is often a history of sleepwalking in the accused or his family.'

'Like when he was a child?'

'Yes.'

'Which means it's more likely that it happened that way this time.'

'Yes, exactly. Also sleepwalking occurs in the first stage of sleep, so anything that promotes deep sleep, such as lack of sleep over a prolonged period, can create the right sort of conditions for a sleepwalking episode.'

'So if all these clinical indicators are present, you get off?'

'Unfortunately, it's not that simple. You see, since no one can guarantee it won't happen again, the judges, in their great wisdom, decided that the appropriate verdict is not guilty by reason of insanity. If that happens the court makes a hospital order, which means the accused is detained in a mental hospital instead of prison.'

'So why rely on the defence at all?'

'Because the accused avoids life imprisonment.'

'And if he wins his case, how long would Yuri have to stay in hospital?'

'I don't honestly know. Most psychiatrists don't agree with the judges' classification of sleepwalking as a disease of the mind, so they will probably release him after a few months.'

'And nothing else will happen to him?'

'Well, there are other problems for him.'

'Like what?'

'He is not entitled to inherit anything from his mother's estate, since the special verdict actually means that he killed her.'

Marina looked bemused.

'Please explain that to me, I don't understand.'

'If Yuri is convicted of murder he would not be entitled to inherit any money from his mother, since he had brought about her death. If the jury find that he was sleepwalking at the time, then they must bring in a special verdict of not guilty by reason of insanity. But he is still not entitled to her money.'

'So, can you get him off?'

'I don't know. The defence is very rare; annually there are only a couple of cases worldwide. The jury will take a lot of persuading to accept that he killed his mother when he was asleep. You see, it turns us all into potential monsters and that's difficult for the layman to accept.'

'Well, it makes me confident that they have the sense to be sceptical.'

Blair laughed.

Marina appeared deeply interested and so was he. As he explained it to her in simple terms he was reminded of Rosemary and how he had taught her law and she had taught him common sense.

'So what will happen next?'

'We will arrange for some experts to see Yuri and take his family history. They will dissect his past to see if there is any history of sleep disturbance. We will also have him psychiatrically assessed to see if there are any psychiatric problems that could explain why he did what he did.'

'I feel really sorry for him.' She looked at Blair through dewy eyes.

'So do I, having no family or friends, it must be very lonely for him.'

'Your work is very interesting, Blair,' she said, changing the subject.

'Yes, I tend to deal with the extremes of human behaviour and no two cases are alike.'

'You must have met a lot of strange people along the way.'

'I'm not too sure about strange. Most of my clients are actually quite ordinary people who have for one reason or another been thrown into situations not always of their own making. Very few people charged with murder have a history of violence and almost none go on to murder again.'

'What about serial killers?'

'They are rare and in a category of their own.'

'I was very impressed by your kindness to Yuri.'

'Marina, everyone deserves respect as human beings. I hope I respect others and I try very hard to understand the awful predicaments they sometimes find themselves in.'

'So you get close to your clients then?'

'My work isn't just about advocacy it's also about judgement. And if I allowed emotions to intrude, then that would inevitably affect my judgement, which could spell disaster for my client.'

Marina sat back in her chair and ran her fingers through her hair.

'I think you are going to get Yuri off,' she said confidently.

Blair laughed raucously and the women at the adjoining table looked at him disapprovingly. He lowered his voice.

'We will see. I will certainly do my best, with your help of course.'

Blair called for the bill. 'I'm afraid I have an appointment which I must attend to.'

'I enjoyed lunch, thank you very much.'

'You're very welcome, it was my pleasure.'

It was a crisp sunny day as they walked slowly along Dawson Street towards Trinity College. A weathered tramp lay huddled in a doorway, holding out a plastic cup with a few coins in it, and muttering something about being in need of money for a hostel. To Marina and the tramp's astonishment, Blair placed a fifty-euro note in the cup and walked on without saying anything. As they reached Nassau Street, Blair stopped and looked back up Dawson Street.

'What's wrong?'

'There was a guy in a black leather jacket; I thought he might be following us since we left the restaurant, but he's gone now.'

'I think you must be paranoid, Blair.'

As they were passing the front gates of Trinity College a voice called out, 'Hello, Mr Armstrong.'

A guard approached Blair.

'Hello, Jack. How are Mary and the children?' Blair said.

'They are well, Mr Armstrong, thank you.'

'Did they throw you out of the Four Courts?' Blair asked.

'No, the only reason I was down there in the first place was to listen to your eloquence.'

Blair laughed.

The guard addressed Marina. 'I could sit and listen to this man all day addressing a jury, brilliant he was, just brilliant.'

'That's very kind of you, Jack, slightly exaggerated, but kind nonetheless.'

'Seriously, Mr Armstrong, you're badly missed down there. When are you coming back?'

'Very soon.'

'We will all be looking forward to that.'

Blair and Marina walked slowly around College Green, along Westmorland Street, until the chaos and crowds of O'Connell Street came into focus.

'Why were you missing from work?' Marina asked.

'It's a long story, I will tell you about it some other time.'

They stopped on O'Connell Bridge.

'Will I see you again soon,' she asked nervously.

'Yes, I think Dermot is arranging another consultation with Yuri before Christmas, so we will see each other then.'

Marina was disappointed that Blair was restricting their next meeting to one of a professional nature. She thought that she had made it pretty obvious that she was crazy about him, and couldn't understand his apparent lack of interest in her.

'Next time, the meal is on me,' she said, knowing full well that she hadn't the finances to honour that particular commitment unless they dined in McDonald's.

'Well, let's do a little work on the case first. Take care of yourself, Marina.'

'See you later, Blair,' she said, as she watched him walk purposefully down the quays towards the Four Courts.

Sitting on the tram she took out her phone and tapped in a text message: 'Thanks 4 the best lunch I ever had & 4 making me feel like some1 important. I think u r cool and can't wait to meet with u again. is there any chance 2 meet 2morrow night 4 a drink.' She read the message twice and deleted it. She then tapped in another message. 'Thanks 4 lunch. C u soon.' And pressed the send button.

eighteen

Detective Sergeant Murphy was sitting in the detectives' office along with Ruth, preparing for a pre-trial conference with Patrick McNamara SC, who was briefed on behalf of the Director of Public Prosecutions. He had never worked with McNamara before, but knew he had a reputation for being meticulous in his preparation, if not spectacular in court. McNamara had sent his written Advice on Proofs and had specifically requested that all the deceased's personal effects should be examined thoroughly, and this task had been assigned to Barry and Ruth.

A large brown box of papers sat on Barry's desk, containing a considerable number of photographs, private letters and other documents, most of which were in Russian. He took a bundle of loose photographs, mostly black and white. He wasn't quite sure what he was looking for, but he began to inspect each one of them.

Anna Komarova's wedding pictures showed her to have been a beautiful woman in her younger years. Her husband was a tall dark man with a strong, if stern, face. There was a photograph of her and her twin sons, then in their early teens, standing by the shores of what must have been the Black Sea. She looked proud and content, smiling faces blissfully unaware of what the cruel hand of fate had in store for each of them.

There was also a photograph of the two young boys with a dark-haired girl, maybe a couple of years their junior. The girl looked vaguely familiar, probably the girl he had seen in the photograph in the sitting room on the morning of the killing; she must be the cousin who was also killed in the fire, he thought.

He moved on to the documents. They were all in Russian and made no sense to him whatsoever. Some looked like birth or marriage certificates. There was also a bundle of personal letters, again all in Russian and a letter from the Department of Justice, which granted them temporary residence on compassionate grounds.

A small brown leather folder held a number of bank statements, which Barry inspected closely. Her current account was held at the Ulster

Bank on Dame Street and the balance on the week before her death was
€655 odd. There was also a deposit book. The last balance on this
showed the sum of €14,569, hardly enough to provide a motive for her
death, he thought.

In a pocket of the folder was a small key with a number inscribed on
it. He showed it to Detective McNamara, who was seated opposite him.

'Any ideas what this is, Ruth?'

She took the key from him and inspected it closely. 'My guess is it's a
key to a safety deposit box. Should we get all these letters translated?'
Ruth asked.

'No, what's the point? But this key might be important.'

He put the papers and photographs back in the box.

'Come on, Ruth we're going to the Ulster Bank on Dame Street. Give
me back that key.'

The bank was a large building with gothic-style oak panelling reminis-
cent of a church.

'Can we see the manager?' Barry said, flashing his identity card to a
solemn-looking porter.

A small grey-haired man with sharp features wearing a brown suit
called them from behind a counter.

'This way, please.'

He led them into a large office and invited them to sit down.

'My name is Brian McNulty and I'm the manager. How can I help
you?'

Barry took the small key from his pocket and put it on the large
mahogany desk.

'Do you recognize this key, Mr McNulty?'

Mr McNulty took a pair of reading glasses from his breast pocket, put
them on and inspected the key.

'Yes, it's a key to one of our safety deposit boxes. Where did you get
it?'

'That's not important, but we need to see the contents.'

'Certainly not,' the manager said firmly. 'Client confidentiality forbids
it; you'll have to get a court order.'

Ruth gave the manager a broad smile.

'Unfortunately your client is dead, she was murdered,' she said flatly.

Mr McNulty gasped in horror, and sat back in his leather armchair.

'Oh my God, who was the client?'

'Mrs Komarova,' Ruth continued.

'Oh dear, the nice Russian lady.'

'You remember her?' Ruth sounded surprised.

'Yes, she wasn't one of our best customers, but she called into the bank at least once a fortnight and spent a great deal of time in the vault with her box and its contents. She was a charming lady.'

'Have you any idea what was in the box?' Barry asked.

'No, we always leave our clients alone in the vault, but I had the feeling it was nothing of any great worth and was merely of sentimental value.'

'What gave you that idea?' Ruth asked.

'She spent such a long time in there, and she visited us so frequently.'

Barry looked at Ruth and she winked at him. She walked around to Mr McNulty's side of the desk and flirtatiously propped herself against the desk, brushing up against him in the process.

'Mr McNulty,' she said softly, 'the trial of her killer is on soon and we suspect there may be evidence contained in that box that may be relevant to her death.'

'Really!' Mr McNulty replied.

'Yes, now we can get a court order as you suggest, but that will take time. We would appreciate it if you would save us all a great deal of time and trouble and allow us inspect the contents of the box.'

The manager thought for a moment. He looked up at Ruth and smiled.

'Well, if you think there might be evidence I will allow you to inspect the contents, but only an inspection, mind you, the contents must remain here.'

'That's all we require,' Barry intervened.

The manager led them through a maze of corridors into the bowels of the bank. Mr McNulty called a tall thin man, wearing a grey suit, to join them.

'This is our assistant manager, Mr Costello.'

They arrived at a large impressive steel door. Both men took it in turn to punch numbers into a keypad on the wall and the door of the vault opened slowly. They led the way into a dull green room dominated by rows of steel lockers.

'Number seven six eight zero, let's see, yes, over here.'

Mr Costello opened a locker with the key and removed a long narrow steel box and placed it on a table. The assistant manager took the master key from his pocket, opened the box and stood back.

'May I?' asked Barry.

'Certainly,' replied Mr McNulty, who was smiling at Ruth.

Barry looked inside and saw yellowish gauze-like material wrapped around a small object that was approximately twelve inches by nine. Cord was carefully wrapped around it, holding the gauze in place. He took the object from the box and carefully placed it on the table. Then he slowly untied the cord and removed the gauze. Inside were what appeared to be three small religious paintings. Mr McNulty clapped his hands together and raised them in the air.

'Superb!' he exclaimed. 'Icons, and early ones by the look of them, very rare indeed.'

'Are they valuable?' Ruth asked.

'I would say so.' Mr McNulty replied.

'Would you mind if we asked an expert to put a valuation on them?' Barry asked.

'Certainly, but we won't permit their removal from the bank under any circumstances.'

'We understand. Thank you very much for your help.' Ruth replied.

Mr Costello carefully placed the icons in their box and replaced them under lock and key.

'Well, that throws a spanner in the works, Barry,' Ruth said as they were driving back to the station.

'They might not be valuable at all,' Barry replied dismissively.

'Then why are they locked away?'

Barry didn't want this complication. He was confident in his own mind that the killing of the old lady was not motivated by greed. But if these icons turned out to be valuable, it was certainly going to cause a major headache for the defence team.

nineteen

It was a cold grey December morning as Blair and his old friend Robert strolled by the almost frozen waters of the pond in St Stephens Green. The park was quiet, with only the occasional jogger braving the elements. Robert, a distinguished looking man in his fifties, was a prominent heart surgeon at the Mater Hospital and had been friends with Blair for over thirty years. Both men were well wrapped up against the biting easterly wind.

'How's the family?' asked Blair.

'They're fine, Kieran is thinking of studying law.'

'Do you want me to talk to him about it? I might be able to give him some advice.'

'That would be great, Blair, he would really appreciate it.'

'I haven't seen them all in such a long while; I suppose I would hardly recognize them now.'

'It's strange the way they grow up so quickly, one day they're there and then they're gone.'

'Unfortunately I never had that privilege. Anyway get Kieran to ring me and I'll meet him for a drink and have a good chat with him.'

'Why did you ring me, Blair?'

'I need some help from an old friend.'

'What's your problem?'

'I have a big case coming up.'

Robert appeared surprised. 'I thought you had decided to retire.'

'Yes, I had, but to be honest it wasn't exactly my decision to make.'

'What do you mean?'

'After Rosemary passed away I couldn't get her out of my mind, everywhere I looked, she was there.'

'That's not such a bad thing; there's no need to bury her memory, she still has a lot to offer you.'

'I know, but I never appreciated just how much I needed her.'

They walked slowly across a small stone bridge and found a park bench draped on either side by large listless willows. They sat down looking out across the still waters of the pond where a few ducks had braved the cold morning air in search of food. Blair took a brown paper bag from the pocket of his overcoat and threw some crumbs to the ducks.

'It's a pity you didn't have children, they would have helped you deal with the grief.'

'That's a thought that's gone through my mind a million times. There's nothing left of Rosemary except the memories. We were so busy with our careers, it all passed by so quickly. I wish I could tell her now just how much I loved her.'

'I think she knew that.'

'I hope so. Why do we leave so many things unsaid?'

'I guess we fear looking a little foolish if it's not reciprocated.'

'As you say, I think she knew the way I felt about her. I find it hard to continue without her.'

'I know it's of little consolation, but you still have a lot of friends.'

Blair sighed heavily. 'I don't really. I know a great many people, but to be honest life's been pretty damn lonely for the last couple of years.'

'Lonely?' Robert sounded surprised and a little sceptical.

'Yes, I sit in my apartment most evenings drinking wine and listening to Leonard Cohen, haunted by my memories.'

'Come on Blair, Mr Cohen won't exactly lift your spirits. Why don't you get out and about more? You're a popular man – people love your company.'

'I'm not so sure about that. Sure, I get a lot of respect because I always treat people well, but the reality is that I will never be one of the boys, down at the pub talking hurling or politics. You've known me long enough to understand that.'

Robert frowned and appeared deep in thought.

'I suppose you're right, but why in God's name did you retire then?'

There was a long pause as they watched a gaggle of Japanese tourists photographing a majestic swan as it glided by under the bridge. Blair took a deep breath. 'I lost my nerve, Robert.'

'What!' Robert turned to Blair with a look of astonishment on his face.

'I lost my nerve. It's as simple as that. Blair Armstrong, the great defender, lost his bottle.'

'But in what way, I don't understand?' Robert replied.

'After Rosemary died I took a few months away from work and went to Dingle. I spent a lot of time reflecting on my life and what was left for me. After a while I thought I had got my head together, and came back to Dublin. Almost immediately I was offered a high-profile murder case and needless to say I accepted the brief. The preparation for the case ran smoothly enough and everything seemed fine until the eve of the trial.'

'What happened?'

'I am not sure. I was sitting at home working on the case when I got this strange hollow feeling in the pit of my stomach. I began to sweat and then started shaking. I went for a brisk walk, cleared my head and everything seemed OK. But as soon as I got home this feeling came over me again, a sense of panic and of impending doom. No matter how hard I tried to persuade myself everything would be all right, it got worse and worse. I didn't sleep that night.'

'And how were you the next day?'

'I felt exhausted and couldn't function. During the trial I was anxious about almost everything, even small things. I found I couldn't make any clear-cut decisions and was fretting all the time. You know me, Robert, I was always confident on my feet in court, but I lost it, all the skill deserted me.'

'And did it improve?'

'No, it got progressively worse as the case went on. I really believed it would pass and I fought it, but it won out in the end and drained me of every ounce of confidence I possessed. The night before my closing speech I rang the junior in the case and told him I wasn't well and asked him to close the case for me. I was lucky to have had such an experienced junior.'

They stood up and walked on slowly. Robert was looking for words of comfort but was struggling in his search for them.

'Everyone has a bad patch, Blair.'

'This wasn't a bad patch, Robert. We got a manslaughter verdict in the end, which was about right in the case anyway, but it could so easily have been a complete disaster. My client couldn't afford for me to have a *bad patch*, as you call it, and I knew at that moment I was finished. I refused to take on any more criminal cases and confined myself to a few civil actions. But it didn't get any better, I was settling every case, just so I wouldn't have to go into court.'

'Did you not think of seeking professional help?'

'Many times, but my pride stood in the way. I couldn't accept that the great Blair Armstrong was vulnerable, like everyone else.'

'So what did you do?'

'I left the Law Library and decided to get away from everything. And then started drinking.'

'Much?'

'Yes, far too much.'

'I'm sorry to hear all this, I wish you had phoned me earlier.'

'Look, none of us like to admit our failings, and this was perhaps the worst thing that could have happened to me: it's an advocate's worst nightmare. I know I should have shared it with someone, but I bottled it all up.'

'Why are you telling me all this now?'

'Well, a few weeks ago I got a phone call from Dermot Molloy, he was the solicitor who got me up and running.'

'Yes, I remember him. Bit of a cowboy wasn't he?'

'I suppose you could say that, but his heart was always in the right place. Anyway he said he had this interesting murder case where there was the possibility of running automatism as a defence.'

'So?'

'I hadn't heard from him in over ten years, and there he was, just when I had lost my nerve, looking for help and advice. He obviously hadn't heard the gossip about my drinking and was looking for the old Blair, the Blair he knew all those years ago. I felt it was an omen, and even though I had some serious misgivings, I agreed to do the case.'

'But why did your ignore your misgivings?'

'Because I needed to go out on a high note and I knew I had to do just one more trial, and do it right, one last great performance for myself and for Rosemary.'

'So did you do it?'

'No, it's coming up after Christmas.'

'And how do you feel about it?'

'I'm nervous, but I think I can manage it.'

'Why do you think things will be any different?'

Blair hesitated and took a deep breath. 'I have met a young Russian woman who has restored my confidence.'

Robert smiled ruefully.

'And just how young is she?'

'It's not what you think, it's not like that,' Blair protested his innocence lamely.

'How old is she, Blair?' Robert persisted.

'She's only twenty-four, but that's irrelevant.'

'And what does this twenty-four year old do for a living?'

'She's an interpreter and does some modelling.'

Robert let out a raucous laugh as he walked a little faster. Blair followed him.

'What's so funny?'

Robert stopped, turned and placed his hand on Blair's shoulder.

'There I was, beginning to feel sorry for you, and it turns out your problem is a twenty-four-year-old model. You fecker; now a problem like that I could live with.'

'No, Robert, there's no romance, we just get along that's all. For God's sake, I'm twice her age.'

'It doesn't seem to bother her, does it?' Robert patted Blair on the shoulder and walked on.

'Look, we have only met twice,' Blair protested, as he followed his friend.

'And now you're a new man.' Robert was still laughing.

'I told you it's not like that. When we first met I felt that she found me interesting. I can't really describe it, but it was like she had been waiting a long time for me, and I don't mean in a romantic way.'

'Sure, whatever you say Blair.' Robert said drily.

'No, just listen to me, will you? For some strange reason, I feel alive again, I feel young and invigorated.'

'I'm sure you do. And now you think this young model is the panacea for all your self-doubt. I hope it's that simple for you, I really do.'

Blair lowered his head. 'Unfortunately, it's far from simple, Robert.'

Robert studied his friend's face closely. 'I can see that. What is it you're not telling me? You didn't ask me to meet you just to tell me that you have fallen in love.'

'No, I didn't.'

'Then why?'

'I needed to talk, that's all. I don't know what's happening to me at the moment. I know I should be walking away from all this, but I can't.'

'Why walk away from it? She seems to have fallen for you, why not just let yourself go and enjoy it? What's your problem?'

'I can't tell you, but let me put it this way, I feel as though I am going down a road that will take me away from everything I ever knew and loved, into a world I am not familiar with and it might not be a particularly good place.'

'Listen, Blair, I haven't a clue what you're talking about. Now stop talking cryptically and spell it out,' Robert said, his impatience growing.

'I can't.'

'Is it drugs? Are you dabbling in some hard stuff with her?'

Blair laughed. 'No, it's not drugs.'

'You're not going to tell me, are you?'

'No,' Blair replied flatly.

'Are you seeing her again?'

'Yes, professionally; she is working as an interpreter in the case.'

'And what about socially?'

'To be honest, I was thinking of walking away from the whole situation, from her and the case, and going back to Dingle.'

'Look, do you want my opinion?'

'Yes, that's why I rang you.'

'From the little you have chosen to tell me, no doubt for your own good reasons, this young woman has very quickly brought you back from the brink of obscurity and given you a new lease of life. I don't know what moral dilemma has emerged for you, but do whatever makes you feel good. It sounds to me that there is a bit of magic there. It may be black magic, I don't know, but it's still magic, so just go with it.'

'Thanks, Robert.'

As they parted company, Blair embraced Robert warmly. He then strolled towards the exit at Grafton Street. He took out his mobile phone, rang Marina and asked her out for dinner the following Wednesday. She accepted without hesitation.

twenty

Marina was sure she wanted to meet Blair for dinner, but was very unsure what she was going to talk about and had spent the day in her flat trying to dream up interesting things to say. Maybe she could talk all evening about Yuri's case – at least that much they had in common, but they had exhausted that topic at lunch. She began to feel anxious. Those dreadful long pauses in conversation, which she knew would make her feel stupid and inadequate. She was also conscious that she had arrived for lunch at Browne's looking less than glamorous. So she had called around to Elena the night before the dinner date, in the hope of borrowing something suitable.

Elena, who was also Russian, worked as a translator with the same agency. She was a striking young woman in her middle twenties with long dark hair and eyes like black pearls. Marina didn't know much about her background, but she seemed to come from a respectable family, as she was well educated and had impeccable manners. Marina also got the impression from talking to Elena that there was substantial money in her family and that she was looking forward to the day when it might come her way.

Unfortunately, in the meantime, she had married Boris, a Ukrainian immigrant, who treated her badly. He worked as a security guard at an amusement arcade on O'Connell Street, but Marina thought, from the little Elena had told her, that he might have links to the Russian Mafia. She'd only met him once and he had scared her silly. He was a violent and intimidating thug who subjected Elena to continuous and brutal beatings. Eventually she had left with Kristina, her two-year-old daughter, and moved into a flat in Harold's Cross. However Boris seemed to be a constant and unwelcome caller.

Elena hardly ever socialized and seemed resigned to rearing her daughter alone. She lived an isolated existence, claiming social welfare and working for the translation agency under a false name to avoid paying tax. What little social life she enjoyed she shared with Marina and this usually consisted of sitting stoned out of her head in some grotty flat with other immigrants. As a result, her wardrobe was only marginally more interesting than Marina's, and was equally dated. However, they had picked out a pink and grey print Kenzo mini-dress and dusty pink suede boots, both of which Elena had bought in a swap shop. Marina didn't tell Elena where she was going or with whom, but Elena could see that this was an important date as she had never seen Marina put so much effort into looking good.

Marina had tried on the dress six times that day and still wasn't sure if it was appropriate. It was very short and she thought she looked a bit like a tart, but Elena persuaded her that she looked classy. Between the dress and the proposed script for the evening, she was working herself into a tizzy. The choice was stark: the black jeans and the grubby black leather jacket or the dress and the pink boots. She eventually decided on the dress and borrowed Elena's long mink coat, which her mother had given her.

Mary had been Blair's housekeeper for a number of years and was a well-nourished woman in her sixties with sparkling blue eyes and a lively expression. She was busy Hoovering the rugs in the living room when Blair emerged from the bedroom wearing a pair of denim jeans, a white shirt and a blazer. She turned off the Hoover and looked at him curiously.

'And where might you be off gallivanting this evening, Mr Armstrong?'

'Gallivanting?' Blair asked with a bemused look on his face.

'Would it be courting you might be at?'

He looked at her with a wry smile. 'Is it that obvious, Mary?'

'Well the smell of your aftershave would fell a charging rhino at a hundred paces.'

Blair laughed. 'And is there anything else you care to comment on while you're at it?'

'Well the blue jeans are fierce trendy, but will you at least let me iron the crease out of them, for you look like a tailor's dummy.'

'Since you seem to be in the mood for honesty, don't stop.'

'Stand there a minute and let me have a good look at you.'

Blair stood nervously under Mary's critical eye, as she looked him up and down. Eventually she let out a heavy sigh. 'One thing is for sure, Mr Armstrong, the good Lord blessed you with a fine physique, even though gravity is slowly returning it to mother earth.'

'Thanks for that Mary, but it was the clothes that I had hoped you might comment on.'

'Is it a young one you might be meeting or an ould one the likes of myself?'

Blair smiled at her warmly. 'Mary, I'm sure you have broken many a heart in your time and no doubt still do. You're a fine-looking woman and could never be described as an *ould one* by anyone but yourself.'

Mary blushed, turned away and set about cleaning the fire grate. She then started to chuckle. 'So it would be a young one then you'd be meeting.'

'Yes.'

'Then if you care for me advice it would be the grey cashmere sweater I left folded on the bed for you, and those jeans after I have ironed the crease out of them.'

'And what shirt should I wear?'

'No shirt,' she said emphatically. 'I already checked with me niece, she knows about these things you know, and shirts are definitely uncool.'

'*Uncool*,' enquired Blair, with a broad grin.

'That's right, Mr Armstrong, *uncool*, whatever that might mean.'

Blair vanished into the bedroom and emerged a short time later for inspection, looking decidedly uncomfortable. 'Mary, I look like a bloody American.'

She looked at him admiringly. 'And what would be so sinful about that? Wasn't President Kennedy himself a fine-looking fella? In fact, I think you look like Harrison Ford.'

Blair blushed and started laughing. 'Harrison Ford! Mary, I'm only going for dinner, I hadn't planned on going in search of the Arc of the Covenant.'

Mary looked at him seriously. 'It's nice to see you smile again, Mr Armstrong.'

'Have I been that bad?' he asked.

'Maybe not quite yourself for this long time past. I was getting a wee bit worried about you staying in all the time and all those empty whiskey bottles I have been picking up around the place.'

'I think you were right, Mary, maybe I had lost the plot for a while.'

'That's for sure. I was beginning to think you had thrown off your dancing shoes for good.'

Blair smiled. 'Not quite yet.'

'That's good to hear Mr Armstrong; the band has only just begun to warm up you know. Now I better be off. Is there anything else that needs attending to before I go on my way?'

'No Mary, everything is just great.'

She donned her hat and tweed coat and was about to leave when Blair called after her, 'By the way thanks for all the help.'

'That's grand, I hope your lady friend likes the gear.'

'No Mary, I liked the bit about the band only just warming up.'

Mary smiled and left.

*

Blair and Marina dined together in an Italian restaurant in Temple Bar. To Marina's astonishment she talked all evening about everything and anything. And Blair listened with interest to her every word. The hours flew by and she had little time to reflect on the intimacy that quickly grew between them. For the first time in her life she found a man she could trust, who didn't treat her like a bimbo and she felt strangely warm inside. As the wine flowed, so did the laughter. The restaurant emptied after midnight and they were politely prompted to make their exit by the waiter blowing out the candle on their table.

They strolled to Grafton Street, which was festooned with Christmas lights. On Nassau Street, Blair hailed a passing taxi, opened the door for her and she climbed in.

'Blair, thanks for a lovely evening.'

To her surprise, he leapt in beside her.

'It's not over yet, I'll see you safely home.'

The taxi sped off towards Rathmines. She sat close to him in the back of the taxi and crossed her long legs towards him, brushing up against him slightly. How had she left her flat? Was the washing hanging in the shower? Had she done the washing-up? Had she even made the bed? This was going to be so embarrassing.

They arrived outside the dilapidated Victorian terraced house. He jumped out and held the door for her. Against her better judgement she was about to ask him in, but he spoke first. 'Thank you for a great time, Marina.'

'I really enjoyed myself too,' she replied.

As he walked her to the door she wondered if she dared kiss him on the cheek, but before she had a chance he gently shook her hand.

'See you again soon, Marina.'

And he passed like a shadow into the night.

twenty-one

Marina called around to see Elena on her way to Dermot's office. She had no washing machine and Elena had offered to let her use hers. She noticed Elena had become increasingly friendly over the last few weeks and appeared deeply interested in Yuri's case. Marina had told her some of the background details and also foolishly told her about her dinner date with Blair. Not that there was much to tell, but enough for Elena to quiz her every time they met as to whether there were any developments on the romantic front. Marina was becoming so frustrated by Blair's apparent lack of interest in this regard that she felt like inventing a love story just to satisfy Elena's curiosity and perhaps her own imagination.

Elena opened the door. 'Hi there, Marina, come on in. I'm sorry, the place is in a bit of a mess.'

'That's OK. I can only stay a few minutes anyway. I am going to Dundrum with the lawyers to see Yuri.'

'And are you going to see the rich handsome lawyer too?' Elena teased her.

'Maybe,' she replied.

'How did I guess? I never saw you so enthusiastic about going to a consultation before.'

Marina frowned and gave Elena a withering glance.

'It's a really interesting case.'

Elena laughed.

'I don't think it's the case you're interested in. Anyway it's clear that Yuri killed his mother so he will have to plead guilty.'

'I am interested in the case, and it's not that straightforward,' Marina protested.

Elena regarded Marina closely, who was looking business-like in a black pin-stripe trouser suit and a white cotton blouse. 'Is that a new outfit?' she asked.

'Yes. I bought it in Marks & Spencers. Do you like it?'

'It's OK, but it's not really your style, is it?'

She looked down at Marina's feet and saw that she was wearing a pair of black and silver trainers and let out a heavy sigh. She opened her wardrobe and took out a pair of black high-heeled court shoes. 'Try these on. I think they might look better,' she said, handing the shoes to Marina, who grabbed them and laughed.

'I was hoping you might lend me them.'

She slipped into the shoes and strutted up and down the room. 'What do you think?' she asked.

'I think you love yourself.'

'Well, if I don't, who will?'

'Do you want a coffee?'

'No thanks, I have to fly.'

'Just before you go, tell me something, has Yuri any real chance of getting off?'

Suddenly a heavy rap on the door startled them both. Kristina, who had been asleep on the bed, started to cry. 'Who is it?' Elena called out.

'It's Boris! Open the fucking door.'

Marina looked at Elena and the fear that gripped her was all too obvious. Elena quickly grabbed her purse and slipped it under the pillow on the bed. There were two more heavy thuds on the door.

'Don't let him in,' implored Marina.

'He will break the door down if I don't.'

'Open the fucking door,' Boris roared.

Elena opened the door and a stocky man in his thirties wearing a black leather jacket and denim jeans pushed his way into the flat. He was powerfully built in a way that suggested he spent most of his time working out in the gym. His head was shaved, but he had a weak feature-less face. His eyes were glazed and he looked stoned. He glanced at Marina and, though they had met before, he didn't acknowledge her presence. He spoke in Russian. 'Where is the money?' he demanded.

'I don't have it yet,' Elena replied shakily.

He didn't ask a second time. He slapped her violently across the face with the outside of his hand, forcing her to fall backwards onto the bed. Marina moved to go to her assistance, but Boris glared at her. She froze on the spot. He turned back to Elena, who was sitting on the edge of the bed with her hands covering her head.

'Where's the money, you little bitch?' he roared.

Elena didn't answer. Boris pulled one of her hands away and landed an uppercut with his clenched fist into her unprotected face. Marina could hear the sickening sound of cracking teeth. The force of the blow lifted Elena back onto the bed and she immediately rolled herself into a protective ball in expectation of the certain onslaught.

Boris turned to Marina and pointed to the door without speaking. She left immediately. Outside on the landing, she could hear Elena crying out in pain as the assault continued. She ran out onto the street and frantically rushed up and down like a headless chicken not knowing what to do. She took her mobile phone from her bag to dial 999, but hesitated. She didn't know that much about Elena or whether she was legally in the country, and wasn't even sure if that was her real name. If she phoned the police, it could spell disaster for her friend. Deciding discretion was the better part of valour, she put away her phone and headed off to meet Dermot at his office.

Dermot was standing outside the office wearing a sheepskin coat, when Marina arrived. Yuri had been moved to the Central Mental Hospital in Dundrum so a full psychiatric assessment could be carried out. A navy-blue Range Rover pulled up alongside them and sounded the horn. Driving was Jenny Kavanagh, whom Dermot had briefed as the junior counsel in the case. She was a striking-looking dark-haired woman in her early thirties and a very successful barrister. Blair, wearing a brown tweed jacket, white shirt and a crimson red silk tie was seated beside her. Dermot and Marina climbed onto the sumptuous cream-leather rear seats. 'Hello, Dermot,' Jenny said.

'Hello, Jenny, you're looking as ravishing as ever,' Dermot replied.

Blair interrupted them. 'Manners, please. Jenny, this is our able interpreter, Marina Petrovskaya.'

'Nice to meet you,' Marina said politely.

'Yes, you too,' Jenny responded coldly.

'She also does some modelling,' Dermot added.

'Really? You don't look tall enough, must be photographic work,' Jenny observed with more than a touch of envy in her voice.

'I received the psychiatric report this morning,' Dermot said with enthusiasm.

'Well, what's the bottom line?' asked Jenny.

'Our man is as sound as a bell; psychiatrically well with no evidence of personality disorder or schizophrenia. He was also assessed by the psychologist, and his report makes interesting reading. Yuri is dyslexic and has serious learning difficulties. In the psychologist's view, he is perhaps borderline mentally handicapped and – wait for it – has the mental age of a twelve year old.'

'So, Dermot,' Blair said, 'the psychiatrist has given him a clean bill of health. It's not often I get to call a psychiatrist to give evidence that my client is normal, but that's exactly what we need in this case. An excellent start. Well done.'

'Unfortunately the bad news is that he doesn't think much of somnambulism as a defence. But he thinks Yuri's amnesia may well be genuine and was probably caused by the amount of drink he consumed on the night. He says that the levels of alcohol found in Yuri were so high he was probably in some sort of a stupor, close to unconsciousness, when he killed the old dear. He believes this could be a case where drunkenness may be a defence.'

'Even if that were so, he would still be convicted of manslaughter and could be facing ten years.' Jenny said dismissively.

Blair looked at Jenny and nodded in agreement.

'He has referred me to Professor Hindenburg,' Dermot went on, 'who is apparently the leading expert in the world on drunkenness and its effect on the mind.'

'Dermot, ask him to do a full report. I want the jury to have the best available evidence. If somnambulism falls flat on its face, pardon the pun, we need something else to throw at the jury.'

'Right, Blair, I'll get onto that straight away.'

'Any sign of a report from Professor Duncan?' Jenny asked.

'Not yet; he saw Yuri earlier in the week and wants to hold off doing even a preliminary report until he arranges a sleep EEG.'

Marina took a deep breath and, summoning up all her courage, interrupted. 'I was translating at the consultation with Professor Duncan earlier in the week and he discovered that Yuri had sleep problems when he was a child.'

Jenny glared at Marina in the rear-view mirror, and she felt like she had gate-crashed a party. Why hadn't she kept her stupid mouth shut?

'That's very helpful, Marina,' Blair responded. 'Tell us what he found out from Yuri.'

'Really, Blair!' Jenny said in a disapproving tone.

'No, Jenny,' Blair replied firmly 'Let's hear what Marina has to say, I want a sneak preview of the report.'

Marina continued shakily. 'He told the doctor he suffered from insomnia for years and when he did get to sleep he had a lot of nightmares. His parents told him that as a child he used to sleepwalk, though of course he didn't remember doing it himself. His twin brother also used to sleepwalk and Yuri remembered that himself quite clearly. During the week before the killing he was unable to sleep for nights on end and he felt very tired that evening.'

Blair turned around in his seat and faced Marina. 'That sounds encouraging. Evidence of prior episodes of sleepwalking will be very helpful, just what the doctors like. And sleep deprivation followed by a deep sleep are ideal circumstances for somnambulism.'

'Well, let's wait and see what the professor has to say about it himself before getting too excited, shall we?' Jenny retorted.

*

Yuri was seated behind a table and immediately stood up when he saw Jenny. Marina spoke briefly in friendly terms to Yuri, but he seemed more interested in Jenny. Marina took two packets of Marlborough from her bag and handed them to him.

'Yuri, this is Jenny Kavanagh, I have briefed her as junior counsel in your case. That means that she will be helping Blair at the trial,' Dermot said enthusiastically.

Marina translated and Yuri smiled and nodded in obvious approval at Dermot's choice. Jenny sat between Blair and Marina.

'Well, Yuri, it's now only four weeks to the trial. You have seen the doctors and the reports so far are very good,' Blair said.

'Are they, sir?'

'Yes, they are and I will try my best to explain exactly how we intend to run your case. That is, of course, if you agree. If you don't understand anything I say, please interrupt me and just say so.'

Yuri nodded.

'You have a number of defences open to you. Firstly, you do under-stand that the circumstantial evidence against you is overwhelming and it's clear that you killed your mother.'

Yuri shrugged his shoulders, neither confirming nor denying that this was so.

'So we must explain to the jury why you did what you did that night. The prosecution can't come up with any motive for the killing. Now, we have two ideas how to run your defence. The first of these is that at the time of the killing you were so drunk you were unable to form any intent to kill your mother. In other words, you had no control over your own actions. If the jury have a reasonable doubt and think you might have been that drunk, then they might find you not guilty of murder. However, because you brought this situation about yourself, they have to find you guilty of manslaughter.'

'What is the sentence for manslaughter?' Yuri asked.

'The maximum sentence is the same as murder, life imprisonment. There is, however, an important difference between the two. If you are convicted of murder, the judge must give you life imprisonment; he has no choice. But if you are convicted of manslaughter, he may give you a lesser sentence. In our experience, the maximum sentence in manslaughter cases is rarely handed out, but you could still get a heavy sentence.'

'How many years, sir?'

'Up to ten years, I'm afraid.'

Yuri showed no reaction, but Marina seemed taken aback by the severity of the possible sentence.

'OK, I understand. Did you say there was some other idea?'

'This is a defence called "automatism", which means you killed your mother when your mind wasn't in control of your body. In your case there is some evidence that you might have been asleep at the time of the killing. This defence is very rare, but people have killed in their sleep. We hope to be able to call expert evidence to show that this is what happened in your case.'

'But if it works would I be found guilty of manslaughter?'

'Yuri, I'm afraid it's not that simple. The law says that because the doctors can't say this will never happen again, you still pose a risk to society and in those circumstances the jury must say you are insane.'

Yuri laughed. 'But I'm not mad, sir,' he protested.

'We know that, Yuri, but the judge must make a hospital order and that means you have to be kept in hospital until a board of psychiatrists declare that you are no longer insane, and therefore no longer pose a risk to society. It's a very artificial situation, but my belief is that you won't be in hospital too long before they release you.'

'I think I understand, but maybe it would be easier if I just pleaded guilty?'

Everyone appeared surprised by his offer.

'No, Yuri, we want to make sure that you are not punished for something you had no control over, that's why we have laws. If you want to plead guilty to murder, then, of course, we can't stop you. But we don't think it's a good idea and you're much better off running the defences that I have just explained to you.'

'But, sir, if I killed my mother then I deserve to die myself.'

Blair leant forward in his seat and fixed Yuri with his gaze. 'Listen to me, Yuri, the mind is very strange and people often do things that they are not fully responsible for. Let us run these defences for you. At least then you will know yourself why you did what you did. That will be important to you in the years ahead and it may help ease the burden that you will carry on your shoulders for the rest of your life.'

Yuri sat in silence pondering his predicament. He then spoke to Marina at some length. Eventually Jenny interrupted. 'You must tell us what he is saying, it's for us to advise him, not for you,' she said curtly.

Marina was more than a little surprised by Jenny's tone. 'I'm not advising him,' she said defensively. 'He is running over his options again and I am just doing my best to explain what Mr Armstrong said to him, it's not easy.'

Blair was conscious of the friction that had developed between Jenny and Marina, and intervened.

'Does he wish to ask us any further questions before he makes his decision?'

'Yes, he wants to know if you were in his place, what would you do?'

Blair leant back in his chair. 'I would trust my lawyers, follow their advice and plead not guilty.'

Yuri placed the palms of his hands on the table. 'OK, I will do that. You are a good man and I trust you.'

Yuri stood up and shook hands with everyone except Marina, to whom he spoke briefly in Russian as the others left the room.

They all walked back to the Range Rover and Blair sat in the back with Marina.

'I was a bit surprised, Blair, that you didn't tell him that the prosecution may accept a plea of manslaughter.' Dermot declared.

'I will tell him if and when it arises,' Blair replied.

'I must say, he seemed to understand everything. What do you think, Marina?' Dermot said turning around to Marina.

'How would I know, I'm just an interpreter,' she replied.

'Fancy a spot of lunch, Blair?' Jenny asked 'There's a nice new Italian place in Temple Bar, I hear it's excellent.'

'I'd love to, Jenny, but unfortunately I have some work to do this afternoon.'

'What about dinner, then?' she persisted.

'Another time. I have a lot on my mind right now.'

Marina was delighted at his refusal and allowed herself a slight grin, which Jenny saw in her rear mirror.

'Dermot, what date is the trial set down for?' Blair asked.

'The fifteenth of January.'

'Not much will be done between now and Christmas, but could you put a bit of pressure on Professor Duncan for a report? I may have to see him in the New Year to discuss with him how we are going to present his evidence.'

'I'll do my best.'

'OK, send me the report as soon as you have it.'

They arrived outside Dermot's office on Arran Quay. Marina went to get out with Dermot but Blair leant over and placed his hand on her arm. 'Jenny, can you drop me off at Grafton Street? Marina is doing some shopping in Brown Thomas, so it would be convenient for her, too.'

Marina looked at him quizzically. Shopping in Brown Thomas, she thought? Not in her wildest dreams. He winked at her and she smiled. Jenny drove along the quays without any further conversation. She stopped the car at the bottom of Grafton Street and they both got out. 'Talk to you later, Jenny, and thanks for the lift,' Blair said, but she didn't reply.

Blair and Marina stood looking at each other on the street. He remained silent as she hopped from foot to foot in anticipation. 'Thanks for coming to my assistance, Blair.'

'That's OK, I'm sorry about Jenny, but she's like that with everyone.'

'I think she fancies you, Blair.'

Marina saw him blush. Beneath that confident exterior, he was shy after all.

'So where are we going for lunch then, sir?' she said bravely.

Blair raised an eyebrow in apparent disapproval at her presumption and for one dreadful minute Marina felt vulnerable to rejection. Then a broad mischievous grin crossed Blair's face. 'There's a nice new Italian place in Temple Bar,' he replied.

They both laughed and headed off for lunch.

twenty-two

It was 4 a.m. and Dermot was tossing and turning in his bed. The sheets beneath him were saturated in his own sweat. Fidelma turned to him and gently patted his brow. He opened an eye and looked at her. 'Are you OK, dear?' she asked.

'No, I can't sleep.'

'Are you worried about the case?'

'Yes. How did you guess?'

'It wasn't that hard; all you have done over the last few weeks is eat, sleep and drink that damn case.'

'I'm sorry, Fidelma,' he said, apologetically.

'I'm not complaining, to be honest it's good to see you interested in your work for a change. But what's wrong with you?'

'I heard a rumour today about Blair.'

'What about him?'

'One of the solicitors at Kilmainham District Court asked me who I briefed in the Russian case and when I told him that I had persuaded Blair Armstrong to take the case, he broke down laughing.'

'What did he find so funny?'

'Every solicitor in town except me knows that Blair had some sort of a breakdown during his last case. Apparently it was a complete disaster and there isn't a solicitor in Dublin who will touch him with a barge pole.'

'Christ, Dermot, what are you going to do?'

'What the hell can I do?'

'Ask him to hand back the case and get someone else in on it. I'm sure there must be other barristers who would be prepared to take it on.'

'I can't do that, Fidelma.'

'Why not?'

'Because I practically got down on my hands and knees and begged him to take it in the first place.'

'So you made a mistake, Dermot. You weren't to know about his personal problems. Be honest with him and tell him you didn't know he suffered a breakdown, I'm sure he'll understand.'

'And what do you think that will do to him?'

'That's not the real question, Dermot, and you know it.'

'What's the real question?'

'The real question is what will happen to your client if you don't.'

Dermot sighed heavily. 'I know that, but I haven't the courage to dump Blair like that. Anyway I can't believe he would have agreed to do the case if he thought he wasn't up to it.'

'That's what you want to believe, Dermot, isn't it?'

'I suppose so. But I can't dump him now and that's that. It would cripple him.'

'Is it only Blair you're worried about?'

'No, I have a really bad feeling about this case.'

'What do you mean?'

'I can't explain it, but there is something not right.'

'I don't understand, I thought you had decided to run the sleep-walking defence and everything was running smoothly.'

'We are running that defence, but to be honest I have serious doubts that Yuri killed his mother at all.'

Fidelma sat up in the bed with a look of astonishment on her face.

'But you told me that he did it in his sleep.'

'Yes I know, but I have been thinking about it and I can't get some of the forensic evidence out of my head.'

'Like what?'

'You remember I told you that there were splatters of blood on the wall behind the old lady's bed.'

'Yes, I remember.'

'And that the knife was covered in blood.'

'Yes.'

'Well the forensic people didn't find any blood on Yuri's clothes.'

'But if he did it in his sleep he was probably naked, Dermot.'

'And some of those splatters must have got on his body, or at the very least on his hands. But there was not a trace of blood found on his bedlinen and I don't understand how that could happen.'

'Did you mention your concerns to Blair?'

'Yes, but he said we couldn't have our cake and eat it.'

'What did he mean by that?'

'You see, Fidelma, if we claim he wasn't responsible at all, how can we try and persuade the jury that he killed his mother whilst sleepwalking? Blair said it had to be one or the other and our best chance was the sleep-walking defence.'

'I see what he means.'

'So do I, but I still can't get it out of my mind that the kid might actually be innocent.'

'Did you discuss any of this with Jenny?'

'Yes, and she agrees with Blair.'

'Dermot, if that's what the barristers say just accept it. After all, they are supposed to know what they are doing. And I think Blair is going to be just fine; he never let you down in the past, did he?'

'No, he didn't.'

'Well, stop worrying about stupid rumours and get some sleep.'

twenty-three

Tuesday, 9 January.

Barry accompanied Paul Hickey, a solicitor from the Chief State Solicitors' Office, along the quays as they made their way to the Distillery Building on Church Street and the offices of Patrick McNamara SC, who had been briefed on behalf of the prosecution.

'Listen, Barry, Mr McNamara has a wicked tongue so don't take anything he says too personally.' Mr Hickey had attended numerous conferences with the eminent senior counsel and knew his form well.

'You mean he's an arrogant old bastard,' replied Barry.

Mr Hickey smiled. 'Let me put it this way, he likes to run things his way and doesn't need to be told how to do his job by the likes of us.'

'I understand what you're saying, keep my thoughts to myself.'

'Unless he asks for your opinion of course, which is most unlikely.'

'Paul, you know how strongly I feel about this case.'

'That's why I'm warning you.'

'OK, I get the message.'

They entered the building and made their way through a maze of corridors to the third floor where they met Mr McNamara's secretary. She showed them into a large modern office, which was oddly decorated in crimson with dark early-Georgian furniture. A cut-glass decanter containing a rare vintage port sat on a table beside a black wig box with its owner's name engraved on the lid in gold. Patrick McNamara was seated behind a leather-covered mahogany desk and was puffing on a large Cuban cigar. He was a rotund man in his early sixties, with curly silver hair. He remained seated when they entered the room.

'Please take a seat, gentlemen.'

'Thank you,' Mr Hickey answered respectfully. 'This is Detective Sergeant Murphy, who is in charge of the case.'

McNamara grunted. 'Well, gentlemen, this shouldn't take too long. I have read the papers and everything seems to be in order. An open and shut case, I would have thought.'

'Do you foresee any problems, Mr McNamara?' Mr Hickey asked.

McNamara thought for a moment, as he flicked through the large file in front of him.

'Well, obviously the destruction of the videotapes of the interviews was a potential disaster, but I have spoken to Blair Armstrong, who is defending, and he assures me the defence aren't raising any point on it. However, had there been any sort of admission, we would have been in serious trouble.' He peered over his half-moon glasses in a disapproving manner at Barry.

'Have they any defence to it?' Mr Hickey asked.

'I hear they are relying on automatism as a defence, sleepwalking apparently – whatever next?'

'Should we get our own experts on that issue?' asked Hickey.

'Yes, ask the defence to supply us with copies of their reports and send them on to Professor Duncan. I have used him before and he is sound.'

'Unfortunately the defence have already engaged him,' Hickey said.

'Well, get someone else then. Drunkenness is also an issue, his levels were very high and no doubt the defence will try and establish that the accused was incapable of forming the necessary intent for murder. Even if they succeed, we still have our man for manslaughter.'

'And if they offer a plea to manslaughter, would you recommend it?' asked Mr Hickey.

'Certainly not,' McNamara replied flatly.

'Why not? It would certainly save a great deal of time and money.'

'I will tell you why not: all this nonsense about amnesia, I don't believe a word of it.'

'But we have no reason to doubt what the accused said to us,' Barry said.

McNamara rounded on him. 'Nonsense. I never heard such rubbish.'

'There has been a substantial development that may well change the course of the trial,' Mr Hickey said gingerly.

'And what's that?' McNamara said, leaning forward and resting his elbows on the desk.

Hickey glanced around at Barry, inviting him to take up the running, which he did.

'As you requested, we went through the personal effects of the deceased and we found some bank statements.'

'Was there anything substantial?'

'No, but we discovered a key to a safety deposit box.'

'Interesting, and did you examine it?'

'Yes, we discovered three ancient religious icons. We asked an expert from the Chester Beatty Library – they are the leading experts in this area – to inspect the icons and put a value on them.'

'And?'

'A conservative value of four million euros has been put on them, but they could be worth a lot more.'

McNamara's face lit up with enthusiasm. He stood up and walked to the window, puffing on his cigar.

'We have a motive for murder,' he said, looking out of the window, 'and a substantial one at that. Am I right in thinking our man is the sole surviving heir?'

'Yes,' Barry answered.

McNamara swung round and faced his visitors. 'Excellent. We have our man for murder, gentlemen.'

Barry interrupted. 'Mr McNamara, I appreciate your enthusiasm for a murder conviction, but I can't see this guy killing his mother for money. I thought when I interviewed him that he really had no memory of what had happened that night. I have been around a long time, and I'm sure his amnesia is genuine.'

Hickey raised his eyes to heaven.

'Which side are you on?' McNamara barked.

'It's not really a matter of taking sides. I don't believe the issue of the icons should dominate the case. Sleepwalking and drunkenness in my view are live issues.'

McNamara returned to his chair and sat forward glaring at him. 'Detective Sergeant, am I right in thinking that you asked the accused whether his mother had any money?'

'Yes, that's right, we did.'

'And he replied no.'

'That's correct.'

'So, was he suffering from amnesia when he neglected to mention that his mother was sitting on a small fortune? Or perhaps that just slipped his mind.' McNamara let out a raucous laugh.

There was a long embarrassed silence.

'I know it's important, but I don't think it should be allowed to dominate the case.' Barry said firmly.

'Well, Sergeant, regardless of your gut feeling, I am obliged to open this case to the jury on the basis that the accused murdered his mother for money, and that is exactly what I intend to do.'

Paul Hickey sensed the mounting tension between the two men and interrupted.

'This is a highly significant development and we haven't disclosed it to the defence yet. It will obviously have a bearing on how they decide to run their case. We can prepare a notice of additional evidence, but it won't be served until Friday and, as you know, the trial starts next Monday.'

'So?' McNamara snapped.

'I think in fairness to the defence we should advise them immediately of this development.'

'Certainly not; if their own client hasn't bothered to tell them, that's their tough luck. Serve it on Friday and it will give them something to think about over the weekend. Sleepwalking indeed!' McNamara chuckled to himself. 'They will be laughed out of court.'

The two men left and walked through the Four Courts yard when they bumped into Blair who was walking purposefully from the opposite direction.

'Good morning, Paul,' Blair greeted Hickey.

'Hello, Mr Armstrong, it's good to see you again. Do you know Detective Sergeant Murphy?'

Blair shook Barry's hand firmly. 'I don't believe we've met. Aren't you in the Russian case next week?'

'That's right, sir.'

Hickey interrupted. 'Actually we're just coming from a conference with Patrick McNamara.'

Blair smiled and patted Barry on the back. 'I bet you got a right grilling from the old bollocks, but don't worry, his bark is far worse than his bite.'

Barry smiled.

'I'm in a hurry so I best be off gentlemen. I'll see you both in court next week.'

As Blair walked away Paul Hickey appeared distressed.

'What's wrong?' enquired Barry.

'Did you ever meet Mr Armstrong before?'

'No, but I know of him by reputation, they say he's the best around. He seems like a really nice guy too.'

'Barry, that's a gross understatement, he is one of the finest men you are ever likely to meet.'

'But why the long face?'

'Did you know he had retired from practice?'

'No, I hadn't heard that.'

'There were all sorts of rumours circulating about him losing his bottle and hitting the booze big time.'

'Why is he doing this case then?'

'I don't know, but no one around the courts expected to see him back again.'

'He looks fine to me. In fact, I would have said he was brimming with confidence. So what are you so worried about?'

'Barry, by my silence I lied to a man I greatly respect.'

'I don't understand.'

'I should have told him that we are about to blast his defence clean out of the water.'

'He'll find out on Friday, so don't worry about it.'

'I am worried about it,' Hickey replied angrily. 'McNamara knows full well that Blair is vulnerable and that a major setback like this will force him back on the bottle. Why do you think he told us to hold back until Friday to serve the evidence about the icons?'

'I don't know.'

'There is no advantage to us at all. The motive is there and nothing the defence can do will change that. I think McNamara wants us to leave it until the last minute so that Blair panics and has a relapse.'

'That's a bit underhand, isn't it?'

'Barry, it's well below the belt and I don't like being a party to it one little bit.'

twenty-four

Wednesday 10 January.

Blair spent Christmas alone and didn't venture from his apartment. At times buried in the past, at other times despairing for his future, he was consumed by melancholy and sought refuge in the bottle. Even the frequent calls from Marina went unanswered, and her messages on his answering machine became desperate. Eventually he emerged from the haze and realized the trial was upon him. A couple of days dry, he was more focused. He decided to ring Marina, make his excuses and invite her out for dinner. As he reached for the phone it rang.

'Hello.'

'Blair, it's Dermot. We have a complete and utter disaster on our hands. You're not going to believe this, the old dear was loaded and Yuri stands to inherit a small fortune,' Dermot declared shakily.

'What the hell are you talking about?'

'Mrs Komarova was worth millions.'

'Where did you get this nugget of information from?' Blair responded calmly.

'A mole in the prosecution camp rang me a few minutes ago and told me the gardai found valuable paintings in a safety deposit box belonging to her.'

'Why were you not formally told this, if it's true?'

'They are serving us with additional evidence on Friday. The paintings are apparently worth over four million. What the hell are we going to do, Blair?'

'You're going to calm down for starters,' Blair replied firmly.

'What do you mean *calm down*?' Dermot roared down the phone. 'It's blown our case apart.'

'Why do you say that, Dermot?'

'Why do you think?'

'No, you tell me,' Blair replied evenly.

'Because our whole defence of sleepwalking is based on the crime

93

being unexplained. Now the prosecution have established a motive for the killing.'

'Please calm down. I read Professor Duncan's report and it's very helpful. I think we can still raise the sleepwalking defence.'

'But, Blair, he wrote his report on the basis that there was no motive for the killing. We have to go and see Yuri before the trial.'

'Why?'

'To find out why he lied to us and the guards about the existence of the paintings.'

'I don't think that's a good idea.'

Dermot couldn't believe how calmly Blair was taking this damning piece of evidence, and his reluctance to confront the client with it mystified him. 'Blair, will you explain to me why you don't think it's a good idea to get our client's instructions on this?'

'Because our client has the mental age of a twelve year old and twelve year olds don't murder for money. In my view we should treat this new information with the contempt it deserves.'

'Are you serious about this?' Dermot found it hard to fathom where Blair was coming from.

'I am very serious. If we treat this new evidence as a big issue, then it becomes one. 'Now, let's remain focused and get on with the real work.'

Dermot thought that Blair was one hell of a cool customer, or else he had lost the plot completely. He pressed on, 'I don't agree, we have to confront Yuri.'

'No, I will not see him and I forbid you to discuss this with him either. Do I make myself clear?' Blair's tone was closed to further argument.

'Ok, whatever you say, Blair.'

'I will see you on Monday morning.'

'I don't understand where you're coming from but if you change your mind about seeing him, let me know, as I will have to arrange to have the interpreter present.'

Blair put down the phone. It rang again almost immediately. 'What now, Dermot?' Blair barked into the phone.

'Blair, it's me, Marina.'

'Oh, hello, Marina, I was just about to ring you. Did you have a good Christmas?'

'It was OK. Where were you? I was trying to contact you.'

'I decided to take some time out and needed to be alone.'

'I see.'

'Marina, Dermot has just been on the phone in a dreadful panic.'

'About what?'

'The prosecution have discovered that Yuri's mother had some paintings which are worth a small fortune.'

'Oh Christ!' she responded.

There was a long pause. 'Marina, you're almost as bad as Dermot. It's not the end of the world.'

'What are you going to do?'

'Absolutely nothing; in my view the case hasn't changed.'

'You seem to know what you're doing. Are we going to meet up then?'

'Look, I need to do a little work right now, can I ring you at the weekend?'

'Sure, whatever you say,' she replied.

'I'll talk to you then.'

'OK, but don't forget me. I was worried about you the last few weeks.'

He laughed. 'I won't forget you, Marina, that's for sure.'

Blair put down the phone, headed straight to the drinks cabinet and poured himself a large whiskey. How the hell was he going to deal with all this? He poured himself another and felt himself sliding down a familiar slope.

twenty-five

Sunday morning, 14 January.

The church on Clarendon Street was less than half full for ten o'clock mass. All that was left of the once full congregation were the elderly and the infirm. The priest monotonously delivered a meaningless sermon from a raised stone-carved pulpit to an audience that had long since stopped listening. When the mass ended the congregation slowly filed out, leaving a lone figure kneeling in a pew silhouetted against the light of burning candles. His head was bowed, the large knuckles of his hands supporting his forehead.

The priest checked the pews for any property left by his flock and then went to the back of the church. There he emptied the paltry few coins from the collection box into a green felt bag. He then walked purposely up the nave, the sound of his leather soles against the stone floor echoing around the church. At the altar he extinguished the candles. A scented smell lingered in the air. He checked the two confession boxes and then returned to the back of the church. The sound of one of the heavy double doors being closed and bolted shattered the silence. He stood impatiently at the remaining open door, waiting for the last worshipper to leave. He stood there thumbing a set of rosary beads for what seemed an eternity and then walked towards the silent figure. The priest gently placed his hand on the man's shoulder.

'I am sorry my son, but the church is closing.'

The man turned and looked up at the priest. His eyes were bloodshot and full of tears. There was a strong smell of alcohol from his breath. It was Blair.

'Are you all right?' the priest asked.

Blair nodded and wiped the tears from his eyes. He heaved himself to his feet and staggered in silence from the peaceful sanctuary of the church.

*

Damien Dunne had asked Jenny to meet him at the Porter House on Parliament Street. Damien was a handsome young criminal lawyer who had been close to Jenny since their days in UCD. She arrived wearing a leather jacket over a skimpy taupe cashmere jumper and denim jeans. 'Hi, Jenny, you're looking great,' he said, as he stood up and kissed her on the cheek.

She sat down opposite him at a small circular table. 'Thanks, Damien, I hear you're really doing well these days.'

'Yes, trade has been good for the last couple of years. But as you know yourself, you're only as good as your last case.'

Jenny noted the look of concern on Damien's face. 'Why did you ring me, Damien?'

Damien frowned. 'It's about Blair,' he replied cautiously.

She appeared surprised. 'What about him?'

'I heard on the grapevine he is leading you in a murder next week.'

'So?'

'Look, Jenny, this isn't for general consumption, but he led me in his last case before he vanished off the scene.'

'Yes, I know; I heard Blair was unwell and you did a great job in his absence.'

'Thanks, but Blair wasn't sick.'

Damien looked around the bar for eavesdroppers and in a hushed tone declared, 'He lost it.'

'What do you mean *lost it*?'

'He was all over the place in the trial and rang me the night before he was due to close the case with some cock-and-bull story about not feeling well.'

'You think he lost his nerve?'

'I am sure of it.'

'So what's that got to do with me?'

'He hasn't done a case since, and I want you to be prepared to take up the running if he bottles out again.'

'Do you think that's likely?'

'Jenny, this isn't easy. You know I was Blair's devil and I always looked up to him. We both know he is a living legend, but I don't think he should have taken on this brief.'

'I really appreciate you telling me this, Damien. I have been secretly worried about him for other reasons.'

'What other reasons?'

Jenny considered telling Damien about her fears that Blair had been distracted by the attentions of a young admirer, but decided against it.

'It doesn't matter.'

'It matters to the client,' Damien said angrily.

'I know that, but it's about his personal life and I don't want to spread more gossip.'

'Is he drinking again?'

'What do you mean *again*?'

'He was drinking heavily during the last case, I could smell it off him every day in court.'

She shook her head. 'I haven't noticed him drinking, but there again I haven't seen that much of him recently.'

'Rumour down in the Law Library has it he has hit the bottle again, and big time.'

Jenny appeared seriously worried and shifted nervously in her seat. 'Damien, do you mind if I skip lunch? I'd better go off to the library and do some preparation.'

Damien smiled. 'That's what I was hoping you would say. And, Jenny, don't worry: if needs be, you're well up to it.'

Jenny hailed a taxi. Things were bad enough with that little Russian bitch on the scene, but she hadn't known that Blair had a drink problem. She had never addressed a jury before in a murder trial and the thought sent a shiver down her spine. She decided to ring Blair to see if he needed help in his preparation and to make sure that he was on the ball. There was no reply and she left a message on his answering machine, asking him to ring her urgently.

Marina had patched things up with Angela and was preparing to strut her stuff at a fashion show in the Shelbourne Hotel later that evening. She sat in front of the mirror in her gloomy bedsit debating whether to go blonde or brunette. Better leave it the way it had been at the casting, she thought, or the client might go mad. She glanced down at her breasts, bathed in the warm glow of a solitary candle perched on the dressing table. She leant forward towards the mirror, resting her chin on her hands and regarded herself closely. Her reflection appeared distant, almost unfamiliar. Her mood darkened and a chill ran down her spine as she felt a rough hand reach from behind and move menacingly towards her breasts. She glanced up and saw her father's face, twisted with lust, ghost from the darkness. Her mother's face was barely visible in the shadows behind him. She closed her eyes and buried her head in her hands. Her body shook, as though with fever, as she rocked back and forth, wrestling with the demons from her past.

After what seemed like an eternity to her, she felt a hand on her shoulder. But it was warm and comforting. She raised her head, cautiously opened her eyes, and looked in the mirror. Blair's brown eyes carried more than a hint of her own sadness. She tentatively reached out to touch his reflection, but it faded into the darkness. Blair Armstrong, who the hell are you? she thought. Why have you come into my life at this time? A tear ran down her cheek. Nobody had ever treated her with such respect. She wondered what such a rich and powerful man could possibly see in her. He exuded class and sophistication, and she had neither. Yet he listened intently to her every word, and appeared happy to be close to her. But why had he shown no physical interest in her? For sure, when the trial was over, he would leave her life as quickly as he had arrived and return to his privileged lifestyle, perhaps fall in love with some elegant lady. She brushed back her hair, looked with satisfaction in the mirror and smiled inwardly. She wasn't going to let him off the hook that easily, she thought.

twenty-six

Blair was slumped in his leather armchair drinking whiskey. A bundle of papers lay on the floor beside him. He glanced down at the empty glass in his unsteady hand and realized he had been drinking all day. He had almost persuaded himself that once he was back on centre stage the old brilliance would return naturally. But was it really going to be that simple? Robert had prescribed him some beta-blockers, which apparently lowered the blood pressure and were often used by public speakers to disguise some of the more obvious signs of nervousness. But he was reluctant to use them, as he feared they might slow down his thought processes, and he knew he needed to be razor-sharp. The quandary he found himself in, to take the drugs or not, was in itself creating anxiety, and he was conscious that anxiety had led to his prolonged panic attack in his last case. His thoughts were interrupted by the sound of the phone ringing.

'Hi, stranger,' Marina said.

'Hello, how are you?' Blair replied.

'I'm fine, but you never rang me as you promised,' she said crossly.

'I'm sorry, but I have been working on the case.'

'Look, I'm in the Shelbourne doing a fashion show and I was just wondering if you are alone right now?'

'Yes I am, why?'

'I will be finished at ten, and' – she hesitated – 'you live near here don't you?'

'I'm not too far away.'

'I was thinking of calling in to wish you luck for tomorrow.'

Blair hesitated. 'I don't know, Marina, I had intended to get an early night.'

'Just for a short time,' she said, toying with him.

'Marina, it's late, and I need to get a good night's sleep.'

'I won't keep you from your bed for long.'

'Do you promise?'

'Yes, I promise you'll be under the covers nice and early.'

'OK, you win,' he replied.

Blair staggered to his feet, clumsily gathered the papers and put them in his briefcase. He stood looking around the apartment. There were photographs of Rosemary everywhere. He thought of putting them away. Finally, he compromised, and left one on the mantelshelf. He put on some jazz music and dimmed the lights then went to the kitchen and brewed a strong coffee, returned to the living room and sat down.

Marina was the most beautiful woman he had ever seen, he thought. But there was much more beneath the surface. Yes they had become friends quickly, and at times she reminded him of a young Rosemary. And she certainly floated into his thoughts with an ease and grace that quelled his melancholy, and replaced it with wild dreams of passion and intrigue. But he feared where this odyssey would end, in which unfamiliar and far off place she would eventually leave him stranded? He smiled inwardly as his imagination galloped on, unbridled by reality or any sense of responsibility. His thoughts were interrupted by the sound of the buzzer. It was Marina.

He waited nervously in the spacious hallway of the apartment. The lift doors opened and he took one step back. Marina was standing in the small lift, looking sensational.

'Do I get to come in?' she asked, pouting her full lips.

Blair blushed as he realized he had been staring at her. 'I'm sorry, please do.'

He stood aside as she breezed by him. She barely wore a tiny black short-sleeved mini dress that caressed every curve of her lithe body. She sashayed around the hall as though on the catwalk. Her long slender legs, sheathed in black silk stockings, flowed down into a pair of black suede shoes with razor-sharp high heels that clicked rhythmically on the white marble floor. She removed a pair of soft black leather gloves and handed them to him, together with her leather jacket, which she carried over her shoulder. 'Can you put them somewhere for me?'

He took them from her and opened a panel in the wall that concealed a small cloakroom and hung up her jacket, placing her gloves in one of the pockets. As he turned to show her the way, she was already gliding through the double doors that led to the living room.

'This is a cool apartment,' she said, as she swayed around the room to the rhythm of the music, vaguely inspecting his many *objets d'art*.

'Thank you. Can I get you a drink?' he asked.

'Yes, please, vodka and coke,' she said with an assuredness he hadn't heard before.

He walked into the kitchen adjacent to the living room and poured her a drink. 'Can I get you anything to eat?' he shouted from the kitchen.

She didn't reply.

When he returned to the living room Marina was stretched out on the sofa, her legs seductively crossed, as she inspected the photograph of Rosemary. 'Do you still miss her?' she asked.

'Sometimes.'

Her top lip curled upwards in a half smile. He handed her the glass and she handed him the photograph without commenting on it. He placed it face down on the mantelshelf.

'How was the fashion show?'

'Same as always, overweight middle-aged women looking enviously, as their husbands strip me with their eyes.'

Blair blushed again. He sat back into his leather chair rather than beside her on the sofa.

'Do you mind if I smoke?' she asked, opening a small black suede bag lying beside her.

'No, go ahead by all means.'

She took out a packet of Rizla papers and expertly rolled herself a joint. It wasn't exactly what he had had in mind and she didn't offer him one.

'You look stressed, Blair, are you worrying about the case?' she said, as she lit her joint.

'Yes, just a little.'

'I thought you would be working on it.' She looked around the room noting the absence of paperwork.

'At this stage the work is done, I usually concentrate the night before on strategy.'

She laughed. 'You sound like a general going to war.'

'I suppose it's a bit like that, you have to have a plan.'

'Your work is so interesting, it must be really rewarding.'

He was distracted as she ran the dark red long nail of her middle finger along the top of her thigh. She drew heavily on her joint and then knocked back the vodka in one gulp. Blair was amazed by her demeanour. She had utterly changed. The quirkiness was gone, and she appeared confident and in control.

'Can I get you another drink?' he asked.

'It's OK, I will get it myself.'

She stood up and teetered into the kitchen in a way that presumed Blair's eyes were following her. She emerged seconds later and stood at the doorway, drink in hand, her willowy figure silhouetted against the bright lights of the kitchen. She paused, untied her hair and shook her head, allowing her long blonde hair to cascade down her neck and settle on her narrow shoulders. She took another sip of her drink and walked slowly to a small circular Georgian table next to him. She brushed her hand over a marble bust from ancient Greece that Rosemary had bought him for their twentieth wedding anniversary. Then she placed her glass on the table, slid behind Blair's chair and gently placed her hands on his shoulders from behind.

'Don't be nervous, Blair,' she whispered softly.

Was she talking about the case? Blair thought. Or did she sense his unease about her?

He struggled for words. 'I hope you haven't been drinking all night?' he asked, in a protective fatherly way.

She didn't answer, but continued to gently massage his shoulders. 'Say nothing, Blair, just relax.'

She ran her fingers through his hair, as she slinked to his side. He felt himself slowly sinking into relaxation as he closed his eyes and allowed the scent of her perfume consume him. Was this really happening to him, or was this a drunken dream?

'It's OK, Blair,' she whispered. 'Everything is OK; I'll look after you.'

twenty-seven

Monday, 15 January.

It was a bitterly cold morning and was snowing heavily. An armoured prison van escorted by two garda cars pulled into the courtyard of the Four Courts. Yuri, his head covered with a blanket, was rushed into the courthouse, as press cameras flashed. The barristers' robing room in the bowels of the Law Library was busy with lawyers donning their ceremonial garb. Blair was putting on his frock coat and silk gown when McNamara walked into the room.

'Good morning, Armstrong, it's good to see you back with us,' McNamara said.

'Thanks, Patrick.'

'When were you with us last?'

Blair thought for a moment. He knew exactly what McNamara was up to. 'I actually don't remember when it was, and would you believe, I can't even remember what the case was about.'

A look of disappointment crossed McNamara's face as he studded his crisp white wing collars together. 'You're not going to be awkward with me on this one, are you?'

'What's there to be awkward about? It's pretty straightforward, isn't it?'

'Well, there are a couple of things I'm not that happy about myself.'

Blair smiled inwardly. McNamara was such a stickler for detail and never really saw the bigger picture. 'Like what, Patrick?'

McNamara raised an eyebrow and smiled. 'I don't want to be giving you any ideas, now, do I?' he said, only half jokingly.

'It wouldn't be the sloppy DNA analysis by any chance, would it?' Blair replied.

McNamara frowned as he put on his gown. 'Armstrong, old boy, you know me too well.'

Blair laughed.

'Well, have you a problem with the forensics, or not?' McNamara said impatiently.

'You will be glad to hear I don't.'

McNamara breathed a sigh of relief. 'So you're still running the sleep-walking defence then?'

'Yes.'

'Despite our excellent work in discovering the icons.'

'That's right.'

McNamara adjusted his wig in the mirror and walked to the door where he turned and faced him. 'I hope you don't mind me saying this, old boy, but this sleepwalking business – it's a bit of a long shot, isn't it?'

Blair was still looking out of the window. The bastard was trying to psyche him out and a bit of reverse psychology was in order. He turned around and gave McNamara a broad grin. 'You're absolutely right, Patrick, it's complete and utter nonsense, but I'm afraid it's all we have. You couldn't lose this one in your sleep, pardon the pun.'

McNamara grunted and left the room.

Blair sat down on a chair and stretched out his right hand. Steady as a rock, he thought. He took the small bottle of pills prescribed by Robert from his breast pocket. He looked closely at the label. Beta-blockers, indeed! He shook his head and discarded them into a wastepaper bin. A night of passion with Marina had been the perfect antidote for his dwindling confidence. He stood up, looked in the mirror and smiled at his reflection. He then strode out of the room, seemingly walking on air.

The courtroom had a distinctly Victorian feel to it, with heavily panelled oak walls and furnishings. On the right hand side, and slightly elevated, sat the jury box. At a higher level again and facing into the body of the court was the judge's throne. Below, the registrar was busily checking his paperwork. Directly below him, a long bench was reserved for solicitors, who sat directly across a wide table from senior counsel. Behind them were several rows of benches, which were reserved for junior counsel and devils. The public sat all around and, unusually, the upper gallery had been opened for the occasion and was thronged with press reporters and spectators.

Dermot and Jenny were busily arranging a large number of legal text-books and leather-bound law reports. Yuri, dressed smartly in his only suit, white shirt and black tie, was seated to the left of the court in a small area set aside for defendants. He was surveying the scene when McNamara barrelled into court wearing his wig and gown. McNamara glanced across at the fresh-faced young man. Yuri, thinking he might be the judge, smiled over at him, but McNamara didn't return the courtesy.

Marina was late as always. Hurrying in the door of the courtroom she bumped into Elena, who was looking elegant in a black pin-stripe suit and white blouse. Marina looked surprised to see her.

'What the hell are you doing here?' she demanded.

Elena stepped back and raised a hand defensively.

'Take it easy, Marina, I couldn't resist coming to see this charmer of yours. Where is he?' she asked as she peered in the door to the court-room.

'Elena, please don't go into court, I don't want Blair to see you staring at him. We have a very private relationship.'

'Don't worry,' Elena said jokingly, 'I'll keep my hands off him.'

'No, Elena, I am serious, I don't want you here and that's that.'

'Can I go in for five minutes? He won't even notice me and if he does he won't know who I am anyway.'

'OK, just five minutes,' Marina relented, 'and then get lost.'

Marina hurried into the crowded courtroom, sat beside Yuri and greeted him in Russian. Dermot was looking at her from the solicitors' bench. She really was beautiful, he thought, and Blair was such a lucky bastard.

He then noticed a striking dark-haired young woman dressed in black enter the public gallery. Yuri looked over at her and smiled. She smiled back and appeared to give him a wave. Curious, thought Dermot.

The barristers' benches slowly filled, and the jury assembled in the jury box, looking around at the unfamiliar surroundings. An air of antic-ipation hung in the air. Dermot looked nervously at his watch. Where the hell was Blair?

Blair was the last to arrive, which was his way, and all eyes were upon him. He looked impressive in his frock coat, silk gown, crisp white winged collars and tabs. He carried his wig casually in his hand and appeared relaxed as he greeted the court staff individually. There was always a sense of anticipation when Blair was defending, and they were glad to see him back after such a long time. He was unaware of the dark-haired young Russian woman who was scrutinizing his every move.

Everyone stood as the judge, Mr Justice Frederick Canning, arrived with great ceremony. A rotund, distinguished-looking man in his mid-sixties, he had a reputation for fairness. He also had an open and enquiring mind.

The registrar called the case with some degree of pomposity: 'The People at the suit of the Director of Public versus Yuri Komarov.'

McNamara rose to his feet. 'May it please your lordship, I appear with Mr Brendan Walshe on behalf of the prosecution.'

Blair then rose to his feet. 'I appear with Ms Jenny Kavanagh, instructed by Mr Dermot Molloy, on behalf of the defendant.'

'Thank you, Mr Armstrong, it's good to see you back with us,' the judge said warmly.

The indictment was then read over to Yuri: 'Yuri Komarov, on the twelfth day of November 2008 within the State murdered Anna Komarova. How do you plead, guilty or not guilty?'

There was a long pause as Marina translated his words.

'Not guilty, sir.'

McNamara rose to his feet and commenced his opening speech. As he did so, Dermot noticed the dark-haired young woman leave the public gallery as discreetly as she had arrived. As she did, she looked over at Yuri and smiled.

Leabharlanna Poibli Chathair Bhaile Átha Cliath
Dublin City Public Libraries

twenty-eight

McNamara opened the case to the jury in a level tone. After outlining the principles of law that applied to the case he carefully set the scene. This he argued was a straightforward case. The jury would hear evidence that the police arrived in numbers to a gruesome scene. Mrs Komorova had been brutally stabbed to death in her own home and all the circumstantial evidence pointed to her son being the killer. He was found asleep in bed with the murder weapon lying beside him and the DNA evidence was overwhelming. He continued.

'You may well wish to know why he killed her. What was his motive? Motive, of course, may be relevant, but the absence of motive is not necessarily significant. Many murders are in fact motiveless, crimes of passion carried out in the heat of the moment; hatred or anger lying dormant for years surfacing in a violent rage. So, motive is not really important. But it may well be hugely significant in this case. And I will explain the reason why. This young man had every reason to murder his mother. She was, in fact, a wealthy woman, and he is the only surviving member of the family who stands to gain from her death. I can see that you are interested in this, and I will tell you a little about it.

'When the accused was being questioned in the garda station, the detectives were obviously looking for a motive for the killing. And the most obvious and common one is greed. So they asked him whether he stood to gain financially from her death. And he replied no and claimed she was not well off. But he lied to them, ladies and gentlemen of the jury. That's right, he told them a blatant lie, and hoped to get away with it.

'You see, outwardly at least they lived in fairly modest circumstances. There were a few nice antiques in the flat, but it was rented and these were merely a few family heirlooms brought with them from Russia. So on the surface, money didn't appear to be an issue. She had very little money in the bank and no life insurance policies that we know of. But, by excellent detective work, the guards discovered a key amongst her personal belongings. And they traced that key to a safety deposit box in a bank in Dame Street. On inspection they found three very rare religious icons valued at in excess of four million euros. I see the shock in your eyes. That's right, four million euros. So there's the motive, plain and simple. And the important point is that he lied about it.

'So, you will hear of a killing and a motive. There is actually nothing strange or peculiar about this case at all; nothing unique, as will be strongly argued by the defence. The accused killed his mother for greed. And then got drunk – either because he regretted having done such a dreadful thing, or else he was celebrating. Who knows? He wasn't expecting the guards to arrive that morning and that's why he didn't let them in, because he had no opportunity to cover his tracks. So what does he do when caught effectively red-handed by the guards? He feigns sleep and then claims amnesia. How convenient for him, ladies and gentlemen! How often have we heard or used those words when confronted with some embarrassing evidence of wrongdoing: "I don't remember". Magic words, conjured up in the innocent belief that in some way, simply because we don't remember, we can't be held responsible.

'Finally, as I say, the onus is on the prosecution to prove its case beyond reasonable doubt. When you have heard all the evidence you will be left in no doubt that Mrs Anna Komarova was killed by her son. The defence is going to call experts in relation to the effects of drink on the mind and in relation to sleep disorders as possible explanations of what happened that fateful night. Listen to that evidence and give it your most careful consideration. But, most importantly, I urge you not to lose sight of your common sense.

'Thank you for your patience. My junior will call the first witness, who is the photographer.'

'We will do that after lunch, Mr McNamara,' the judge intervened. 'I will rise until two o'clock.'

Marina was on her way out of the court when Dermot called to her.

'Do you know who that good-looking young woman was sitting in the public gallery?'

She let out a loud laugh.

'You never give up, Dermot, do you?'

'No, it's not like that. I am curious; she seemed to know Yuri.'

'Why do you think that?'

'Because I saw him smiling at her.'

'Well, he is a man too, Dermot.'

'Stop being smart, Marina. They definitely seemed to know each other. Do you know who she is?'

'Yes, she is an interpreter with my agency.'

'But how does he know her?'

'I don't know. Maybe the agency sent her down to one of the medical consultations when I was busy modelling.'

'Will you ask him after lunch how he knows her?'
'Sure, no problem.'

Blair, Jenny and Dermot sat together around a small table in the Tilted
Wig Bar across the road from the Four Courts. The case wasn't going as
well as Dermot had hoped, and it showed on his downcast face.
McNamara's opening speech had been very strong. He had adopted a
daring tactic of opening the defence case to the jury and had already cast
serious doubts over it. Dermot appeared gravely unsettled whilst Blair,
who seemed in a world of his own, was reading a copy of *The Irish
Times*.

'McNamara did a real hatchet job on us,' Dermot said despondently.

Blair didn't reply. Dermot was concerned that, outwardly at least,
Blair was showing little interest in the morning's hearing. He looked
across at Jenny with a bemused look on his face, inviting her to join in,
and she duly obliged.

'He has really thrown a spanner in the works. I always assumed that
Yuri had been drunk at the time of the killing even if he wasn't asleep,'
Jenny said, trying to provoke Blair into some sort of debate.

Dermot joined in enthusiastically. 'And the way that McNamara linked
that in with amnesia was really quite clever. If he killed her deliberately
and then got drunk, that may account for his lack of memory rather than
any notion that he was asleep. Unfortunately for us it makes sense.'

Jenny rose further to the debate. 'But he has also cast a serious doubt
over whether Yuri's amnesia is genuine at all.'

She was looking intently at Blair as she spoke, but he seemed uninter-
ested.

'By pointing to the icons as a possible motive for the killing, and then
pointing out that Yuri lied to the guards about their existence, he has
made Yuri out to be quite a devious character,' she went on.

Blair continued to read his newspaper and Dermot was becoming
infuriated by his attitude. Eventually he rounded on him. 'Blair, are you
not worried by all this? We seem to have a serious uphill battle on our
hands and it's beginning to look like murder.'

Blair folded his newspaper and placed it on the table. He then took
out a pocket diary and started flicking through it.

'Come on, Blair, what do you think?' Jenny said.

Blair didn't respond and appeared distracted. Dermot looked at Jenny,
and shook his head in disbelief. What the hell was wrong with him?

Eventually he put away his diary. 'For heavens sake, will you two calm
down and stop panicking. The case has only begun and you already have
our client convicted of murder.'

'But it's not looking great, Blair,' Dermot responded quickly.

'Don't get so excited because it doesn't appear to be going to plan. Remember, those twelve jurors are watching your every reaction in that courtroom, and if they pick up negative vibes from his legal team, what chance has poor old Yuri?'

Dermot glanced at Jenny. She nodded. She had seen Blair many times in courtroom dramas and had never seen him flustered or excited.

'Blair, Detective Sergeant Murphy will be giving evidence this afternoon and in my view he is vital to our case,' Dermot said firmly.

'And why is that?' Blair replied with interest.

'I happen to know that he is sympathetic to our case.'

'And how do you know that, Dermot?'

'You know we got some advance notice that the icons were going to be introduced as a motive for the killing?'

'Yes, last Wednesday, when you rang me in a panic.'

'That came, off the record of course, from the sergeant. Apparently McNamara wanted to delay telling us until Friday.'

'That sounds like McNamara's style all right, but what point are you trying to make?'

'It clearly shows he's on Yuri's side, doesn't it?'

'All it shows is that he believes in fair play, and for that I admire him.'

'I don't agree. In the district court, he told me to get a good silk for Yuri, and I got the distinct impression that he thought there was some merit in Yuri's case.'

'Don't read too much into it, Dermot. He's a decent man, that's all,' Blair replied dismissively.

'Well, I think you should ask him if he believes Yuri's amnesia is genuine,' Dermot replied firmly.

Blair let out a raucous laugh. 'Just like that?'

'Yes,' Dermot replied, brushing aside Blair's condescending attitude.

'And what if your hunch is wrong? And he says he thinks our client is a cunning liar.'

Jenny joined in. 'Dermot, Blair's right. You never ask a question in a criminal trial unless you are almost certain of the reply. It's the golden rule of cross-examination.'

'I am pretty sure he will help us out,' Dermot responded.

'Pretty sure isn't good enough,' Blair replied bluntly. 'One loose question like that could bring the whole pack of cards down, and I don't intend to ask it.'

'But, Blair—'

'But nothing, that's my decision and it's mine alone to make.' Blair sat back and folded his arms, his expression closed to further argument. Dermot went a deep shade of scarlet and rose to his feet.

'I will see you back in the courtroom, Jenny. I have some calls to make.'

He put on his sheepskin coat and walked out the door. Blair turned to Jenny and sighed. 'Follow him, Jenny, and try to explain the dangers involved.'

Jenny grabbed her coat and scarf, ran after Dermot and caught up with him on the street. 'Dermot, don't be angry. Blair is right about this. You can't expect him to ask a loose question like that.'

Dermot turned and faced her, his face contorted with rage.

'Look Jenny, he is sitting in there as though he doesn't give two hoots about our case.'

'Do you really believe that?'

Dermot shrugged his shoulders and walked on. 'I don't want to believe it, but he seems distracted at the moment, as though his mind isn't on the case at all.'

'I know what you're thinking.'

'What am I thinking?' Dermot asked.

'That he has fallen for that Russian girl and can think of nothing else.'

Dermot stopped in his tracks and turned to her. 'You've noticed it too, then.'

'I think it's been pretty obvious from the beginning.'

'Have they been seeing each other?'

'I don't know for sure, but my intuition says yes.'

'Christ, I hope we are both wrong about this. We need Blair at his best; otherwise we have no chance. And McNamara seems determined to get a murder conviction.'

They returned to the hallway outside court number one and waited amongst the crowds for the doors to be unlocked after the luncheon recess. Blair came walking towards them with his wig in hand and Marina at his side. They looked relaxed and happy together.

'What are you two looking so worried about?' Blair asked, as they approached Dermot and Jenny.

'Nothing, Blair,' replied Dermot, 'absolutely nothing.'

Just then the doors of the courtroom were opened and Blair strode inside. Marina sidled up to Jenny.

'He looks so cute in his wig and gown, doesn't he?' Marina said, looking at Blair as he resumed his seat.

Jenny glared at her and didn't answer. She sat in behind Blair and looked across at Dermot. He was looking even more worried. Blair turned around to her. 'Will you cross-examine the scenes-of-crime people? I don't think there's anything of interest to us, but if you can think of something, feel free to fire away.'

She was amazed by his cavalier approach and now seriously shared Dermot's concerns.

Dermot approached Marina. 'Did you ask Yuri who the young woman was?'

'Yes, it's as I thought, she was at one of the medical consultations in Dundrum, so that's how he knows her.'

'That solves that mystery then. Thanks, Marina.'

'You're welcome,' she replied.

The jury returned to court and the hearing resumed.

twenty-nine

A number of witnesses were called by the prosecution. The scenes-of-crime examiner had prepared a map of the interior layout of the flat and marked various relevant locations. A photographer had taken photographs of the inside of the flat and close-up photographs of the various blood deposits. He had also photographed the knife lying beside Yuri's bed. He attended the post-mortem and had photographed the deceased and taken close-up photographs of her injuries. The stab wounds were obvious and spoke for themselves. A photograph of the deceased's frail right hand clearly showed the bruising to her wrist. He also had photographed the back of the woman's scalp. There were tufts of hair missing from her scalp and the area beneath was red and raw looking.

Jenny couldn't think of any useful questions to ask.

The guards who were first at the scene recounted how they had forced their way into the flat and found the deceased lying in her bed. Two officers had gone to Yuri's bedroom, where they found him apparently asleep. Garda Reddy, who was first to find Yuri, stated that he found him asleep in bed. He had considerable difficulty rousing him and was eventually joined in the room by Detective Sergeant Murphy.

Extensive evidence was given concerning the detention of the accused in the garda station. All the legal requirements were complied with, and the prisoner had no complaints concerning the manner in which he was treated. He was fingerprinted and photographed. Samples of blood and urine were taken from him, and he consented to all these procedures. Dr Zuharry, who examined him, stated that he conducted a cursory examination and found no injuries on the suspect.

The next witness was Detective Sergeant Barry Murphy. Detective Sergeant Murphy gave evidence to the jury about how he had been one of the first officers to arrive at the scene and how he had discovered the corpse. He said that whilst he was examining the body, he heard screaming coming from the back bedroom. He went down and found the prisoner in the company of two of his colleagues. He also discovered a bloodstained knife lying beside his bed. The knife was then produced, still covered in dried blood, and he identified it as the knife he had found at the scene. McNamara suggested that the knife be handed to the jury so they could examine it. The jury passed the knife around gingerly, as though it were a grenade. Detective Sergeant Murphy then pointed to various locations on the map and in the photographs that the jury had been supplied with. He described how he had arrested Yuri and his violent outburst when he was being led from the scene and how he and other officers had had to restrain the prisoner and handcuff him.

McNamara feigned that he was momentarily distracted when this piece of evidence was given, and asked the sergeant to repeat it. A most unfair tactic, intended to ram home Yuri's violent streak. The sergeant repeated his evidence. He then gave evidence about the interviews. He read from the original notes that he had taken at all three interviews. These notes, he said, were read over to the prisoner, and he agreed they were correct and had signed them. The jury was provided with a typed copy of the handwritten notes. Very little turned on the interviews, and McNamara brought the witness quickly through the evidence. Lastly, and most significantly, he gave evidence concerning the discovery of the safety deposit key amongst the personal items belonging to the deceased. He had gone to the bank and discovered the icons.

'I think I forgot to ask you this, Detective Sergeant,' McNamara observed. 'During your questioning of the prisoner whilst he was in custody, did you at any time ask him if his mother had anything valuable that he might inherit?'

He had in fact asked this question already and had received a positive reply. He was again reminding the jury of the more sinister evidence against Yuri. Jenny tapped Blair on the shoulder, prompting him to object at these unfair tactics, but he didn't stir.

'Yes, we did ask him that. I think I already gave that evidence earlier and it is contained in the body of the notes of interviews that were handed in as exhibit forty-three.'

'Indeed. The jury will have those signed notes when they retire to consider their verdict, but remind me of his answer.'

'He said she only had a small amount of money in the bank. Those were his exact words. Or should I say the words as translated by the interpreter.'

'So,' continued McNamara, 'when you went to the bank, were you surprised to find such a hoard of valuables in his mother's safety deposit box?'

'I suppose I was.'

'It would appear he told you a deliberate lie about that.'

'Yes, so it would seem.'

'Did he even give you the slightest hint during the three interviews that his mother was such a wealthy woman?'

'No he didn't. But, to be honest, we didn't focus greatly on that issue.'

'But it was an issue?' McNamara pressed.

'Yes, it was.'

'And an important one.'

'Yes, I accept that.'

'And he was given every opportunity to tell you the truth about their existence and how valuable they were?'

'Yes.'

'So it seems that he deliberately concealed the existence of what was clearly a motive for her murder.'

'Yes, that's one interpretation.'

'Tell me, Detective Sergeant, during the course of the interviews did he display any aggression or violence similar to that which you encountered when leaving the flat?'

Jenny again tapped Blair on the shoulder, prompting him to object. He didn't respond. However, thankfully the judge did.

'Really, Mr McNamara, in none of the papers before me, or in the evidence I have heard so far, is there any hint of violence on the part of the prisoner during the course of the interviews.'

'I know that, my lord. I was just trying to be fair to the prisoner.'

'I know exactly what you were doing Mr McNamara. Now, move on.'

'Tell me, from your dealings with the prisoner, did you form a view as to whether this young man had a violent nature?'

Jenny pushed Blair in the back aggressively, but he still didn't intervene. What was wrong with him? This evidence was clearly inadmissible and highly improper. Why was Blair letting McNamara get away with all this?

'Mr Armstrong,' the judge intervened again, 'are you not going to object to this witness giving evidence of opinion on such a crucial point as this?'

Blair rose slowly to his feet. It was the first time he had spoken at the trial.

'Perhaps Mr McNamara could state the basis on which he seeks to introduce evidence of opinion from this particular officer.'

'Well, my lord, I say he is very well placed indeed to give this evidence. He was in the company of the prisoner from the moment of his arrest until he was subsequently charged with the offence. He had every opportunity to assess whether he was dealing with a man of violent propensity.'

The judge waved his hand dismissively. 'You know the rules, Mr McNamara. I won't allow the witness answer, and I am a little surprised

you asked such an unfair question in the first place. The accused is entitled to fairness. Now, have you any more questions for this witness?'

It was clear that the judge's patience was wearing thin. Jenny was
pleased that they had such a fair-minded judge presiding. He was
compensating for the apparent lack of interest of her senior counsel.

'I have no more questions,' McNamara said as he sat down.

'We will take a short break,' the judge announced, and he rose from
the bench.

The jury filed out to the sanctuary of the jury room. Some of them
looked across at Yuri as they left. Sympathy wasn't etched on their faces.

Blair left the courtroom and met Marina outside. They headed off
together for a short walk. Dermot and Jenny stood together looking
worried.

The court resumed after fifteen minutes.

'Mr Armstrong, have you any questions of this witness?' the judge
asked.

'Yes just a few, your lordship.' Blair rose to his feet and turned to the
witness.

'Detective Sergeant, how long are you in the Guards?'

'Twenty-seven years.'

'And how many murder investigations have you been involved in?'

'Upwards of fifty, sir.'

'Did a suspect ever so readily fall into your lap?'

'No, I don't believe so.'

'Was a crime ever so quickly and easily solved?'

'No, sir.'

'So in that regard, this case is unique in your experience.'

'Yes.'

'The culprit didn't make any effort to flee the crime scene, although
he had hours to do so?'

'No, he didn't.'

'Or, indeed, cover his tracks?'

'No.'

'It would appear quite the opposite is the case.'

'That's what's so strange about it.'

'And there does not appear to have been any plan?'

'No, sir.'

'Would it be reasonable to conclude that this wasn't thought out
before the event?'

'I would agree with that.'

Jenny could see where Blair was going. He had asked a short series of
questions and had received no resistance from the witness. In fact quite
the opposite – he seemed more than happy to agree with Blair. If he had

resisted in any way, Blair would have taken him apart. The few propositions he had put forward were logical and didn't need the witness's support at all. Blair was merely testing the water. And it appeared warm.

'When interviewing him, you advised him that he was not obliged to answer your questions?'

'Yes, we advised him of that.'

'That was, of course, his right.'

'Yes.'

'If he chose, he could have sat in silence and ignored you.'

'Yes, the accused has a right to silence.'

'A position adopted by many suspects?'

'Yes, some prisoners can be very difficult.'

'And what of a solicitor, did you tell him he could consult with a solicitor?'

'Yes, we did. As you know that is also a suspect's right.'

'And no doubt solicitors too can be obstructive at times.'

Blair looked across at Dermot and then at Barry and smiled.

'Yes, sometimes they can be more difficult than the criminals.'

A ripple of laughter went around the courtroom over McNamara's stern face. Blair smiled.

'My own experience also, Sergeant,' Blair responded.

A wave of laughter swept the courtroom, this time engulfing McNamara, who reluctantly joined in. Jenny relaxed, put down her pen and stopped taking notes. She sat back, looking up at Blair with admiration. His face had come to light. Somehow, in a few short moments, he had built up a relationship with the witness, and she knew the road he was taking.

'But I think he declined the offer of a solicitor.'

'That's correct.'

'And said he was innocent and had nothing to hide.'

'That's right, sir.'

'Mr McNamara made great play of the fact that when he was being led from the flat my client became violent. At what exact moment did he display this so-called violence?'

'As we reached the door of his mother's bedroom.'

'Was he trying to flee the scene?'

'No, in my view he was trying to get into his mother's room.'

'At that stage her lifeless body was clearly in view.'

'Yes.'

'And up until that moment, what had been his demeanour?'

'Most agreeable, sir.'

Jenny couldn't believe how well this was going. How far was Blair going to push this line of questioning? When was the moment to back off?

'Something, or someone, and I don't suggest for one moment it was you Sergeant, seems to have provoked this sudden and dramatic change in his demeanour.'

'It would appear so.'

'Was it perhaps the sight of his mother lying dead in her bed?'

'I believe it was.'

'But surely then, it must have also have come as a shock to him, if it provoked such a response?'

'I believe it did.'

'As though he didn't know his mother was dead until he arrived at that point in the hall?'

'Yes.'

'Did you think his response contrived or genuine?'

McNamara leapt to his feet. Blair immediately sat down and looked around at Jenny. He was attempting without success to hide the smirk on his face. 'Now, listen to this,' he whispered to her.

'Really, my lord,' spluttered McNamara, 'it would be improper for this witness to express any view on this matter.'

'And why is that?' the judge asked.

'Because this is mere opinion evidence.'

'I thought you advanced an argument just before the break in support of this witness's unique position to give us his insight into the events. What's changed since then?'

'Well, your lordship ruled against me.'

'I will reverse that ruling and allow you to ask your question in re-examination of the witness. It seems to me, however, that you may not get the answer you were so eagerly looking for. Now, Mr Armstrong, please continue.'

The judge was clearly interested in the line of questioning, as were the jury. This certainly was not the case opened by McNamara. Jenny now understood why Blair had remained silent earlier. He had set the trap perfectly. He knew the judge would never have allowed McNamara to ask the question about Yuri's violent nature, but he also knew that if he had entered the debate and objected, he would have debarred himself from his current line of cross-examination.

'Sorry Sergeant, before we were interrupted by Mr McNamara, I asked you did you think his response genuine.'

'I think it was.'

'But surely that would be bizarre. It would mean that in your view my client didn't know he had killed his mother.'

'Well, that's just my own view.'

The judge sat back in his seat, removed his wig and scratched his head. 'I am sorry to interrupt you, Mr Armstrong,' he said apologetically, 'but I want to clear something up.'

The judge looked over his half-moon glasses at Barry. 'Detective Sergeant, have I got this right? You, as an experienced detective, thought that the accused was unaware that his mother had been killed until he saw her body lying on the bed?'

'Yes, my lord.'

'Thank you, Sergeant, I just wanted to be sure of your evidence. Please continue, Mr Armstrong.'

'And the violence Mr McNamara has spoken of so often, was not directed at you at all, but was merely an effort by my client to get to his mother's side?'

'Yes, I believe so.'

'Then you interviewed him in the garda station.'

'Yes, we had three interviews with him.'

'And even though the evidence at the scene clearly pointed to him, did he claim to have no recall of having killed her?'

'That's right; he said he couldn't remember anything that happened that night other than watching a football match on the television.'

'But did you believe him?'

McNamara again objected, but was abruptly over-ruled by the judge. Jenny wondered whether this was one question too far. She could see McNamara glaring at the witness.

'Did you believe him, Sergeant?' Blair pressed the witness.

The sergeant paused before answering. He was fully aware the impact his reply would have on the case. Eventually he answered. 'Yes I did, sir.'

Blair immediately honed in on the answer. 'But, Sergeant, you were wrong. You were clearly deceived by my client.'

The declaration took everyone in the courtroom by surprise, and a murmur rippled around the public gallery. Blair had controlled the witness up until this point with questions that demanded a yes or no answer. He had now opened the door for the witness to say what he liked, which was always dangerous. Jenny knew, however, that the web had been spun and the sergeant was now firmly tied into the defence case.

'Well, it was a gut feeling. His response in the flat was out of keeping with the notion he had killed his mother.'

'What else forces you to conclude my client was sincere?'

'During the interviews, he didn't seem to know what had happened. I have interviewed a lot of murderers in my time and he just didn't seem to fit the bill.'

'And?'

'He said he loved her, and for some reason I believed him.'

'Assuming you're right, Detective Sergeant, that his amnesia was genuine, that he was shocked by her death and that he in fact loved his mother, is that why the discovery of the icons came as such a shock to you?'

'Yes, when I found out I was taken aback.'

'Because it meant your judgement that hadn't let you down in twenty-seven years was flawed after all?'

'No, I don't believe it was,' the sergeant said defensively.

'But you clearly got it wrong, Sergeant. Yuri Komorov murdered his mother for money. This young man, with the mental age of a twelve year old, killed for greed. Then he pulled the wool over your eyes and managed to deceive you completely. He is no more than a cunning murderer.'

There was a concerted gasp from the public gallery and the registrar called for silence. The jurors looked over at Yuri to observe his response to the accusation levelled against him by his own counsel.

'Well, what do you say to that, Sergeant?' Blair persisted.

'I don't believe you're right, sir.'

'Please, Detective Sergeant, tell us why not.'

'Look Mr Armstrong, you pointed out yourself that this was a unique crime scene, that he fell into our hands too easily. Clearly there was no planning, no attempt at escape, and no cover up. And his reactions – they were genuine I know they were. I don't believe he remembered doing any of this. I don't believe for one moment that he killed his own mother for money.'

Blair paused so that the full impact of his answer could settle on the jury.

'So, in your view, the icons whilst capable of being a motive, in fact weren't?'

'That's right.'

Blair wasn't quite finished yet. He looked directly at Murphy.

'But, he lied to you about them. If you're correct in your beliefs, how can you possibly explain that?'

Jenny couldn't believe just how skilful Blair was. This was all merely opinion evidence and almost valueless, but somehow Blair was giving it greater significance than it deserved. Now, having got Barry to agree in the first place that Yuri seemed genuine, he was vigorously cross-examining him in the certain knowledge that the witness would bend over backwards to stand over his expressed view. The more he sought to undermine Barry, the stronger Barry's evidence would become.

'I don't know why.'

'Perhaps because of the language difficulty, he didn't understand the significance of your question,' Blair prompted gently.

'Yes, that's quite possible, in fact probable. My memory is that we discussed life insurance policies and neither your client nor the interpreter fully understood our questions. The true meaning may have been lost in translation.'

'Or he may simply not have known these icons existed at all. There is no evidence that he did.'

'That's also true. His mother appears to have been quite secretive about them and they were locked away in the bowels of the bank. The manager or staff at the bank had no recall of your client ever being in the bank.'

'And even if he knew they existed, he might not have known of their enormous value.'

'That's also another possibility.'

'Sergeant, if my client didn't kill for money, what was his motive?'

There was a long expectant silence. Barry thought long and hard about his answer.

'Sir, in my view that is a mystery. I can put it no further than that.'

Blair sat down.

'Have you any re-examination, Mr McNamara?' asked the judge.

'No, my lord.'

'Then we will rise now and resume the hearing tomorrow morning. Ladies and gentlemen, I must warn you not to talk to anyone about this case. You are, of course, free to discuss it amongst yourselves, but don't even speak to your own family about it.'

The jury left the jury box. The open hostility that had been so evident at lunchtime had left their faces. There wasn't warmth, but the hostility had gone.

'Fancy a drink, Blair?' Dermot asked sheepishly.

'No thanks, Dermot.'

'Oh, come on,' Jenny said.

'No, you two go on, I have an appointment. I'll see you both in the morning.'

Dermot carried Jenny's papers as they left the building. Outside it was bitterly cold and still snowing heavily. They hailed a taxi and, as they climbed in, they caught a glimpse of Blair and Marina leaving the building together.

thirty

The following morning, the trial resumed. A number of gardai gave formal evidence covering the preservation of the scene and the body of the unfortunate Mrs Komarova. Whilst the jury listened intently to the evidence, it was rather tedious. The most important witness of the morning was the scenes-of-crime examiner.

Detective Sergeant Collins was an officer with more than twenty years' experience in the examination of serious crime scenes. With the aid of the location maps and the photographs he pointed out the areas of interest.

He had examined the front door. The lock was intact but the frame of the door was splintered and severely damaged. The door being forced open by the guards had caused this. There was no other evidence suggesting that the door had been interfered with prior to their arrival.

He had examined the windows and found them all to be locked and intact. He concluded that there was no evidence of forced entry. Then he had examined the front bedroom. The most obvious evidence of a violent assault was the heavily bloodstained sheets and quilt covering the bed. The blood had seeped into the mattress. On the wall behind the bed he had observed a number of tiny splatters of blood, which extended to ceiling height. These splatters were most likely cast onto the wall as the knife, which would have been covered in blood after the first stab wound was inflicted, was raised up and down repeatedly. There were also spots of blood on the carpet around the bed; the same process probably deposited these. A number of small spots of blood were also found on the carpet in the bedroom between the bed and the door. These small spots were probably caused by blood dripping from the knife as the assailant left the room.

The examination of the hall had revealed on the right-hand side as one goes towards the bathroom, three spots of blood on the skirting-board opposite the door to Yuri's bedroom, and on the wall nearest the bedroom a small smear of blood on the wallpaper at waist height.

He had then examined Yuri's bedroom. Of greatest note was a small hunting knife lying on the carpet beside the single bed. The blade and handle were both heavily bloodstained. He had carefully lifted the knife and placed it in a clear plastic evidence bag. Subsequently fingerprint analysis was carried out on the knife, but no identifiable prints were found. The carpet beneath the knife was also bloodstained. He had examined the sheets, pillowcase and quilt for the presence of blood. None was visible to the naked eye, but the items were removed for microscopic examination back at the laboratory. This was subsequently done and no blood was detected on any of the items. He also observed a glass ashtray with the remnants of what appeared to be two cannabis joints, a bottle of Jack Daniel's and an empty glass. All these items were examined for the presence of blood, but none was detected.

On the floor beside the bed he observed an old alarm clock lying on its side. The clock had stopped at 11.30. He later stripped the clock and examined its mechanism. It was in good working order, but a small cog had become dislodged, and this might have been caused by the shock of impact with the floor if it had fallen from the bedside table. This, in his view, had possibly caused the clock to stop at the stated time.

He had then left the flat and examined the landing and staircase leading down to the front door. He located a tiny smear of dried blood on the wall halfway down the stairs. Unfortunately there was an insufficient amount for analysis. In any event, it was impossible to say how long it had been there.

Blair didn't cross-examine the witness.

Dr Mary Hancock was called next. She was a forensic scientist and had also been trained in DNA analysis. She examined all the samples taken from the flat together with a sample of human hair, some human tissue and a sample of blood all found in the nail scrapings taken from the fingernails of the deceased. The investigation team had informed her that the accused was the only surviving relative of the deceased and, with that in mind, she constructed DNA profiles of each of the samples she had received.

The samples taken from the bedlinen, the quilt, the carpet, the wall behind the bed all matched that of the deceased. The samples taken from the skirting-board in the hall also matched her blood, as did the sample from the carpet in Yuri's bedroom.

The blood on the knife had been compared with the blood of the deceased. It also matched.

The samples taken from the smear of blood in the hallway and from the nail scrapings along with DNA extracted from the hair did not match that of the deceased. However, it did match the sample taken from Yuri, and the chance of someone other than a close relative sharing the same DNA profile was one in seven million. Reference to a close relative did not include his mother. Though they shared similar profiles, the differences observed between the two profiles allowed for her to be excluded as a possible source. As there were no known relatives this had also been excluded from the equation.

The court then adjourned for lunch. Blair called Dermot and Jenny over and they remained on in a huddle after the court had cleared. 'The prosecution will finish this afternoon and we have to decide whether we should call our client to give evidence, so what are your views?' Blair asked intently.

'I think we have to,' Dermot immediately rushed in. 'The jury will want to hear his side of the story.'

Blair turned to Jenny. 'What do you think?'

'I don't know, Blair; it's always a risky business putting a client in the witness box.'

'That's my feeling precisely.'

Dermot intervened. 'Hang on, Blair. If he doesn't give evidence the jury is bound to speculate that he has something to hide. Surely he has to explain what he knew or didn't know about the icons?'

'I don't agree, Dermot. First you must appreciate that all his evidence will be given through the interpreter and it's bound to be somewhat disjointed. Because of the lengthy pauses between the questions and the answers he will appear to have too much time to think and the jury may well perceive he has an unfair advantage over McNamara. Secondly, he has too many embarrassing questions to answer.'

'Like what?' Dermot asked.

'The most obvious is why his amnesia is selective.'

'What do you mean?'

'Well, he seems to remember the football match, what he had to drink, smoking two joints and then going off to sleep.'

'But that's consistent with our case, isn't it?'

'Then why doesn't he remember where his mother was, and whether he spoke to her or not? The picture he painted to the guards was that of a loving son who looked after his mother's every need. Remember. Bringing her hot chocolate in bed and her reading to him. But when it comes to the night of the killing he remembers absolutely nothing of what she was doing, and that doesn't make sense if he remembers everything he was doing. It's as though she has been airbrushed from the picture.'

'I hadn't thought of that,' Jenny joined in.

'Precisely,' continued Blair, 'and if McNamara has noticed it, the first question he will ask is, "Why didn't you check on your mother on this particular night of all nights, and why didn't you even bid her good night?" And it's going to look very strange that he didn't do that.'

'You think he's vulnerable, Blair, don't you?' Dermot asked.

'Yes, I do. And how is he going to explain his lies about the icons? As the evidence stands, Detective Sergeant Murphy has provided a possible explanation for that: "The meaning may have been lost in translation" are the words he used, and that's quite plausible. But if Yuri is pressed on the point in cross-examination he may well blurt out something damaging.'

'There is also another problem,' Jenny pointed out. 'I have been watching Marina throughout the trial and she appears to be an extremely competent interpreter. It's difficult to believe there was any misunderstanding during those interviews. That will become even more obvious if she were to sit next to Yuri in the witness box translating everything with ease.'

'That's an excellent point, Jenny.' Blair responded. 'Are we all agreed then?'

Jenny and Dermot nodded.

'Dermot, will you go and tell Yuri that he has the right to give evidence, but we are advising him strongly against it? I know he will follow our advice.'

Dermot headed off, looking for Marina, so he could go down to the cells and explain to Yuri what was going on.

The court resumed after lunch and the State Pathologist was first into the witness box. Dr Carmel Hudson was a petite, attractive woman in her early forties, if not younger. She described how she had visited the scene of the crime on the morning of the killing. She had conducted a cursory examination of the corpse and then arranged for the removal of the body to the morgue, where she subsequently carried out a full and thorough post-mortem. Before leaving the scene she measured the temperature of the body and the room. She formed the opinion that the time of death was sometime between 11 p.m. and 1 a.m. During the course of her internal examination of the body she discovered that Mrs Komarova's liver was riddled with cancerous tumours. This had in no way contributed to her death, but Dr Hudson commented that even with treatment her life expectancy, had she not met her death violently, was only a matter of months if not weeks. A look of dismay crossed Yuri's face when Marina translated this.

External examination of the body revealed that the deceased had received four stab wounds to her chest in an area close to her heart. The wounds were all approximately two inches in width. Examination of these entry wounds revealed that they were similar in nature and shared a common distinct feature. With the aid of an enlarged close up photograph of one of the wounds, she pointed to its edges. One side was clearly V-shaped and the cut to the underlying skin was clean. The other side appeared to have an uneven jagged appearance. This she concluded was clear evidence that the murder weapon had been a single-edged knife. She had tracked the wounds to determine the depth and direction of penetration into the underlying tissues. The deepest wound was nearly four inches whilst the other three were all approximately three and half inches deep. The direction of the wounds varied slightly but, assuming the deceased was lying down at the time of the killing, they were all inflicted from above.

McNamara then asked for the knife to be produced, and the court usher handed it to the witness. She removed it from the clear plastic evidence bag it was preserved in. Dark-brown dried blood was still visible on the blade. The pathologist described the knife as being a small single-edged hunting knife. The blade was three and a half inches in length and one and three quarter inches at its widest point. She was asked her opinion as to whether or not this was the murder weapon. She replied it was consistent with the size and type of weapon used. Although the track of the deepest wound was four inches and the blade was half an inch shorter, this was accounted for by compression of the rib cage and the surrounding area. McNamara asked her to explain what she meant by this. She described how when a knife is thrust with force into this area, the rib cage compresses, allowing for a deeper penetration. When the knife is removed and thereby the pressure on the ribs released, they expand again and the depth of the wound is commonly longer than the knife that inflicted the injury. Despite this, she felt the amount of force required to inflict these injuries was only moderate, since the tip of the knife was very sharp.

Death, in her opinion, resulted from shock and asphyxia, due to internal bleeding into the lungs. She also noted bruising around the deceased's right wrist, which may have been caused by her attacker holding her down. She was elderly and would bruise easily, so a minimum amount of force was required. More significantly there were three lacerations to the outer palm of her left hand. Two of these lacerations were deep and the underlying bone was clearly visible. In Dr Hudson's opinion, these were classic defensive injuries often encountered in knife attacks. Naturally the victim would try and ward off the attacker and these injuries would have deflected the knife, as the assailant was thrusting it down. As a result there were at least seven thrusts in total. The four that met their target close to the heart, and a further three that were warded off.

On examination of the head and scalp, she noted that there were tufts of hair missing and some underlying redness of the scalp. This, in Dr Hudson's view, strongly suggested that the deceased had been grabbed violently by the hair during the attack.

Nail scrapings were taken from underneath the deceased's fingernails and the scrapings from her right hand uncovered some blood and human tissue. A hair approximately two inches in length was also found. These were sent to the laboratory for analysis.

In answer to a question from McNamara, she advanced the opinion that the accuracy with which the knife wounds were inflicted, all in an area the size of a small orange, would be inconsistent with them being inflicted by someone who was labouring heavily under the influence of alcohol.

Blair had no questions of the witness.

'That concludes the prosecution case, my lord,' declared McNamara.

'Are you calling any evidence, Mr Armstrong?' asked the judge.

'Yes, my lord, we will be calling four expert witnesses.'

'It has been a long day,' concluded the judge. 'We will hear from them tomorrow morning, same time, same place, ladies and gentlemen of the jury.'

Marina approached Blair as he was leaving the courtroom.

'Do you fancy going for a drink, stranger?' she asked.

Blair noticed tears in her eyes.

'What's the matter with you?' he asked with concern.

'It all seems so pointless.'

'What do you mean?'

'Blair, she was going to die anyway.'

'Yes, she was.'

'Another few weeks and none of this would have happened, and we wouldn't be here now.'

'But we would never have met,' he said, trying to lift her spirits.

She smiled. 'So it was fate that brought us together.'

Blair stopped and turned to her, gently placing his hands on her shoulders. 'Marina, I'm sorry I haven't had much time for you the last couple of days, but I have to put all my efforts into this. You understand that, don't you?'

'I suppose so, but I miss you.'

'I miss you too, and I will make it up to you when this is all over.'

'Do you promise?'

'Yes, of course.'

'Can we just go for one drink, Blair? I need to be with you right now, I feel so down.' She looked at him with sad eyes.

'OK, but only one.'

Marina linked arms with him and rested her head on his shoulder as they left the courthouse.

thirty-one

The court resumed the following morning and the first witness for the defence was Dr Elizabeth Greene, a forensic psychiatrist attached to the Central Mental Hospital. She had been requested by the defence to conduct a full psychiatric assessment on Yuri to see if he suffered from any mental abnormality that might explain why he had killed his mother. In her opinion, having examined him over a period of two weeks, he was completely sane and was a pleasant, well-adjusted young man. There wasn't even a hint of psychosis, schizophrenia or any of the many identifiable personality disorders known to psychiatry. She was at a complete loss to understand why he did what he did. The psychologist, Mr Kidd, had carried out a psychological assessment, but the only thing of significance that emerged was that Yuri was slow and socially underdeveloped, with the mental age of a twelve year old. But in Dr Greene's opinion, this fact was irrelevant and couldn't in her view account for his actions on the night in question.

The next witness was Professor Hindenburg, a large, portly man with white curly hair and a bushy beard. He carried himself with confidence and spoke with enormous authority and a booming voice. Blair decided to give him centre stage and examined him in a quiet and almost subservient tone.

'Professor Hindenburg, would you please outline your qualifications for the benefit of the ladies and gentlemen of the jury?'

'I have a first class honours degree in psychology, a doctorate in electrophysiology, and I am a fellow of the British Psychological Society. I am also a member of the American Society of Psychiatry and am at present Professor of Human Psychopharmacology at the University of Kent.'

'And what is your particular area of expertise?'

'I have studied the effects of drugs, including alcohol, on the human brain for the last twenty-five years and have published over seven hundred and fifty papers in learned journals and periodicals. I have also written twelve books on the subject.'

The jury looked suitably impressed and he clearly had their undivided attention.

'And do you take a drink yourself, Professor?'

The witness seemed surprised by the question. 'Yes, I have been known to partake on occasions.'

Most of the jurors and the judge smiled. Blair had cleverly removed any notion of arrogance and had humanized the witness in the minds of the jury.

'You have been requested by my instructing solicitor, Mr Molloy, to provide expert evidence on the possible effects of alcohol on the mind of the accused at the time of the commission of the offence.'

'Yes, that is correct.'

'And what documents did you have to assist in you in arriving at the conclusions you are about to give?'

'I had all the garda statements in the case, the reports of the various medical witnesses and, most importantly, a report from the forensic toxicology department which indicated the blood levels of alcohol that were found in the samples taken from the accused whilst he was in custody.'

'Those samples, I think, were taken at eight o'clock on the morning of his arrest.'

'That's correct.'

'Remind us of the level of alcohol found in the blood of the accused at that time.'

'Let me just check my notes, if I may.'

The witness fumbled through a much-travelled notebook. 'Yes, I have it now; it was a reading of two hundred and four.'

'Is that a high reading?'

'Yes, it is high, well over twice the legal limit at which one is allowed in law to drive a motor car.'

'I think you were advised that the accused told the guards whilst he was being questioned that he drank a full bottle of bourbon before retiring to bed sometime shortly after eleven o'clock the previous night.'

'Yes, I am aware of that fact from reading the notes of the interviews. And he stated that he drank it over a remarkably short period of time. I also understand that a clock beside his bed had been knocked over and the mechanism had stopped at thirty minutes past eleven.'

'Is it possible to determine scientifically the level of alcohol in his blood at eleven p.m. from the reading taken the following morning at eight?'

'Yes it is.'

'Please explain to the jury how that is possible.'

'Scientifically we know the rate at which alcohol leaves the body. It is eighteen milligrams per cent.'

'I certainly don't understand that and some of the jurors may also struggle with it.'

'It's really quite simple. Eighteen milligrams of alcohol per one hundred millilitres of blood leaves the body every hour. It leaves through natural processes, such as urination or even by sweating. It is therefore possible to do a back-calculation. Now, the rate at which alcohol leaves a body of course, varies from person to person. Anywhere from fifteen to twenty per cent per hour are acceptable levels. However, eighteen per cent is the internationally recognized average level.'

'Please carry on, Professor.'

'Assuming he had his last drink at eleven, and I understand he knocked the bottle back in a very short time indeed, that means that eight hours at least elapsed before the samples were taken the following morning. Therefore at around midnight his reading would have been three hundred and sixty-eight.'

'Why do you say midnight rather than eleven, or indeed eleven thirty, when the alarm clock appears to have been knocked over?'

'Alcohol is not absorbed into the body immediately. I will return to this later in my evidence. It normally takes between forty-five minutes and an hour to be absorbed. For that reason I have taken midnight as the appropriate time at which the alcohol level would have peaked.'

'The level of three hundred and sixty-eight, is that high or low?'

'It is exceptionally high.'

'Perhaps you could describe for the jury the effects that alcohol has on the brain.'

'Well, as everyone knows, alcohol is a poison and is very toxic for the nervous system. The best way to describe it and its effects on the brain is to call it a top-down drug.'

'What do you mean by that?'

'The effects are first evident at the top of the brain, in the cortex, which is that part of the brain where one has thought, sensation and reason. This is where events that are happening around you are registered and assimilated. So the first thing that happens when people take alcohol is that they lose their ability for critical thought. Initially this is quite discrete, but as the levels increase the effects become more profound. Then as the alcohol moves deeper into the brain it begins to impact on other functions.'

'Such as?'

'Co-ordinated movements become more difficult, and people are no longer able to control their motor functions. Speech and balance become seriously impaired. Even the ability to focus on objects becomes increasingly more difficult. If one keeps administering alcohol it will eventually reach the brain stem and the process of respiration, that is breathing, will be affected. That is why people die from over-doses of alcohol.'

'At what levels does one expect to see these various effects?'

'At concentrations of between a hundred and eighty and two hundred and fifty milligrams per cent, co-ordinated movement is really not possible. We talk about a behaviour known as "wall banging". People within this range stagger very noticeably, often banging against walls as they attempt to walk. They certainly would be unable to place pieces in a jigsaw, for example. Speech is slurred and the person is often inco-herent.'

'And what about levels between two hundred and fifty and three hundred and fifty?'

'We scientists call this stupor. At the higher levels within the range you speak of, people are moving into a state of unconsciousness. The higher mental functions are totally absent. People are unable to reason and have very little thought. Amnesia is very common during and after.'

'And above three hundred and fifty, what are the effects?'

'The top of the range is in or around four hundred and fifty, and this invariably results in death. Below this, people are in a coma and are unconscious. They are completely unaware of anything that is happening around them and are incapable of any structured thought. If they are still capable of speech, it has no meaning. For example, they may start off a sentence and their memory is so impaired that midway through, they forget what they are talking about. Sleep is almost inevitable at these levels, and often saves people from a certain death because they are no longer able to continue the ingestion of the drug.'

'At those sort of levels are people capable of forming any intent?'

'Because alcohol is an inhibitor, it stops the brain working. At these higher levels the effects are profound. People are incapable of rational thought, decision-making and reasoning. In my view, they are effectively acting on automatic pilot. I do not believe that, scientifically, people are capable of forming any real intent. Whether legally they are is, of course, a matter for the court.'

'You mentioned the onset of sleep as being a natural consequence. Please explain.'

'At these higher levels someone would be unable to resist sleep and complete unconsciousness.'

'In all your experience, have you ever encountered a case such as this where due to drink alone a person seemingly without any reason murdered someone close to them?'

'It is completely outside my experience. In maybe thirty per cent of cases drink makes people prone to violence, even at much lower levels than we are talking about here. It is, as I am sure the jury is well aware, an unfortunate fact of life: drink breaks down our inhibitions. The normal social restraints are removed and the violent nature of the individual is released. But drink itself does not produce violence – it is already within the individual. From what I have been told of this young man, he has no known history of violence and, in the absence of such a history, I have never known alcohol to provide the sole explanation for murder. I might add, at these high levels, even if alcohol is the only factor, it is my considered opinion that the accused was so intoxicated so as to be unable to form any real intent.'

'And his amnesia, is that consistent with the very high levels that you have calculated?'

'Yes, absolutely; it fits into the overall picture perfectly. As I said, there can be amnesia at the time, but also after the drinking episode.'

'Thank you very much, Professor. Would you please answer any questions my learned friend may have?'

Dermot was delighted with the evidence. He sensed that a murder verdict was now unlikely. Manslaughter was certainly a real option for the jury.

McNamara rose slowly to his feet. There was a long pause. He then began his cross-examination, with his hands clasped firmly behind his back.

'Professor, your very learned opinion is based entirely on the history given by the accused to the gardai, is it not?'

'I don't understand.'

'The whole premise of your argument is based on an assumption that the accused had consumed all the bourbon prior to eleven thirty.'

'Yes, I suppose that is correct.'

'He may, for all you know, have consumed his last drink at say four in the morning.'

'Yes, that is a possibility.'

'In which case, all your theories and estimates, fine though they may be, are absolutely worthless.'

'Yes, I agree. As I say, my starting point is the reading at eight the following morning, and it is based on the assumption that he stopped drinking at some time before midnight. But then there is the evidence of the stopped clock and that supports the version given by the accused in that regard.'

'Nonsense, Professor. For all we know, the clock could have stopped the morning before and he may simply never have rewound it, or it may not have been used for days or even months.'

'Yes, I suppose that is true.'

'So you are simply relying on the accused being an honest historian.'

'Yes.'

'I am sure you would have preferred, as a scientist, to have had the benefit of some objective evidence.'

'Yes, this is true. Counsel is quite right, my lord.'

'Now, if I put the following theory to you: he killed his mother after a couple of drinks and then polished off the rest of the bourbon much later – you would have nothing to counter that other than what you are told by the accused himself?'

'Yes, I must agree.'

'And if his amnesia is in fact genuine, and I underline if, that would be equally consistent with my theory?'

'Yes, I would have to agree with what you say. Amnesia would also arise in that scenario.'

'In fact, I must suggest to you, there are compelling reasons why your theory is in fact wrong.'

'Why do you say that?'

'You see, we know from the pathologist that the deceased was stabbed four times in a very precise area near her heart. If my memory is right, the stab wounds were confined to an area the size of an orange.'

'Yes, I heard that evidence.'

'So it naturally follows if the accused was as drunk as you seem to suggest and his motor functions were severely impaired, he would have been incapable of carrying out precise and deliberate movements.'

'I see what Counsel is getting at, and to some extent I must agree.'

'In fact, if your estimated readings are correct, he would have been more of a danger to himself.'

'Yes, that is so; he probably couldn't have used the knife effectively.'

McNamara raised his hands in apparent frustration. 'Professor, he was either drunk or he wasn't.'

'It is not, with all due respect, quite that simple. As I said in my direct evidence, it takes approximately an hour for alcohol to be fully absorbed into the system. The accused said he drank the bottle of bourbon quickly. As a result, there would have been a period of time when the alcohol was present in his system, but had yet to be absorbed.'

McNamara glared at the witness. 'And how does that get around the point I am making?'

'During this initial timeframe, the full effects of the alcohol would not be felt. It is likely that he was still capable of the finer actions necessary to inflict the injuries you describe.'

'So, what is the point you are trying to make?'

'During this period, before the effects had fully kicked in, I am saying he was capable of inflicting the fatal injuries, since his motor functions were not significantly impaired.'

McNamara grinned and sighed heavily. 'Therefore, all your evidence in relation to the accused not having the ability to form any real intent, of him being in a stupor, close to unconsciousness at the time of the killing, simply do not apply to this case at all. You see, Professor, you can't have it both ways, can you?'

There was silence in court as the professor considered his reply. He fumbled nervously through his notebook as though looking for inspiration. Whilst he did so, some of the jurors sat back in their seats. It was obvious that McNamara was right. Checkmate.

'Well, Professor?' McNamara pressed the witness.

'I must confess, I had never thought of it from that angle. I had never given close thought to the pathologist's report.'

'So, can the jury take it, from your evidence, that in order to be capable of inflicting these fine movements we have agreed were necessary for him to inflict the injuries, he must have been at the lower levels that you spoke of earlier in your evidence?'

'Yes.'

'And at those levels he would have been capable of rational thought and decision-making?'

'Yes.'

'So it would appear that by the time he reached the very high levels you speak of, the killing was already history?'

'It would certainly appear so.'

'Thank you very much, Professor. I am sure the jury have found your evidence most helpful.'

McNamara turned to the jury and smiled before resuming his seat.

'We will rise now for lunch,' the judge declared.

Professor Hindenburg nervously gathered his papers as he left the witness box. He looked across the courtroom as McNamara was leaving his seat grinning like a Cheshire cat. He then looked up at Yuri who was being led away by the prison warders to the cells below. Disappointment was etched on his face and he was shaking his head from side to side. The professor was acutely aware of the damage he had done to Yuri's case.

Blair approached the professor, who was clearly feeling isolated. The hero turned villain. 'Thank you for your time and effort, Professor, your evidence is greatly appreciated.'

He shook his head. 'I fear I have done more harm than good.'

'Maybe not, indeed, as I will explain later, you may have done the defence an enormous service.'

'If I have, I certainly can't see it.'

'You gave your evidence honestly and within the parameters of your expertise and we can ask no more than that. I am most grateful to you.'

Hindenburg looked at Blair and admired his generosity. He was not to be scapegoated for the obvious disaster.

'I should have alluded to the obvious pitfalls before you gave your evidence. If there be any error it is mine, not yours, Professor.'

Dermot and Jenny were waiting outside in the hallway.

'Well, Blair, he was a complete disaster. That's manslaughter removed as a possible verdict,' Dermot said angrily.

Jenny nodded in agreement. Blair smiled at them. 'Will you two never learn? You both look as though you are on the *Titanic* after it struck the iceberg,'

'I don't understand. What in God's name are you up to?' Dermot replied, unable to disguise his frustration.

'Do you really think for one moment that McNamara's reasoning and probable line of questioning hadn't occurred to me before Professor Hindenburg gave evidence? I would have thought it was pretty obvious, and I can assure you we are riding the crest of a wave, not drowning in the cold Atlantic. Go off and have a good lunch and I will see you back here at two o'clock.'

thirty-two

The court resumed after lunch. The next witness called on behalf of the defence was Professor Duncan. He was a smartly dressed handsome man in his mid fifties and spoke with great authority.

'Would it be fair to say that you are regarded as the leading authority on sleep disorders?' Blair asked.

'Well, I don't know, Mr Armstrong, but I certainly would like to think so.'

'To start with, Professor, I will ask you to explain exactly what sleep is.'

'There is actually no scientific definition of sleep. We doctors talk in terms of the process of sleep and then identify its physiological effects on the body. Its function in respect of the mind, though much researched, is not fully understood.'

'Perhaps you could describe the various stages of sleep in the first instance.'

'The first physical act is that of lying down or sitting, which places the body in a relaxed state which is essential for the onset of sleep.'

'Once so prepared what happens then?'

'There is an initial short period when the body relaxes. Slowly the muscles and the central nervous system begin to operate at very low levels. There is then what is sometimes described as a hypnic jerk. I am sure the members of the juror have encountered this. It is often a jerking movement of the body from a very relaxed state, which is followed almost immediately by a sensation of falling. We can literally feel our bodies falling into a state of total relaxation.'

'What happens next?'

'The body then enters a phase of what is referred to as slow-wave or deep sleep.'

'Is this when dreaming occurs?'

'No. Studies indicate that there is little or no thought process during this period of time. If dreaming does occur it is primitive and is not recalled on waking.'

'And then what?'

'You then enter the first cycle of REM sleep. That is rapid eye movement sleep, generally known as "dream sleep". Dreams can be complex with strong visual images and intense thought processes. Normally one would act out one's dreams, but nature has provided a mechanism whereby our muscles are paralysed during this phase of sleep. This paralysis keeps you in bed so, for instance, if you are dreaming of running along a beach you do not get out of bed and start running around the room. The mind is permitted to function in a complex way but the body is physically prevented from reacting to the direction of the mind.'

'Do we recall our dreams?'

'Sometimes dreams are recalled, more so in some individuals than others. The reason for this is as yet unknown.'

'And how long does the REM period of sleep last?'

'There are normally four sleep cycles. Initially deep sleep may last for one and half hours, followed by a much shorter period of REM sleep. Then we return to deep sleep, but this period is shorter and less deep than in the first cycle. This is followed by a longer period of REM sleep. By the time we reach the fourth cycle, there is very little deep sleep but the REM period is much longer and dreaming is at a peak. These dreams can be complex with well-developed storylines and are most likely to be partially recalled.'

'Why are dreams only partially recalled?'

'That is an interesting question. If we remembered our dreams in detail it would be like remembering everything we did since we got up this morning. Such detailed recall of our dreams would lead to a situation where we would find it nearly impossible to separate reality from our dream world. The two would be fused and you would have chaos.'

'Am I correct in thinking that the essential difference between slow-wave sleep and REM sleep is that during slow-wave sleep the mind is largely inactive so the body though relaxed is not paralysed?'

'Yes.'

'But during REM sleep the mind is very active, but the body is effectively paralysed?'

'Yes, that's right.'

'Are there any disorders that are associated with sleep?'

'Yes, there are, we call these parasomnias. These are unwelcome phenomena occurring during sleep and they are divided into different groups. Confusional arousals, night terrors, sleepwalking, REM sleep behaviour disorders and sleep related epileptic seizures. The first three occur during deep sleep.'

'Perhaps you could explain each of these.'

'Firstly there are night terrors. I must stress that we are not talking here about nightmares, which are quite different and occur during REM or dream sleep. It is a condition quite common in children and approximately ten per cent of children suffer from them at some time or another. The condition is also present in adults, but to a lesser extent. They occur during deep sleep. Clinical studies indicate that they occur in the first period of deep sleep that is within the first hour and a half of sleep.'

'What happens?'

'The onset of night terrors is abrupt and the episodes are brief, between one and four minutes. They are accompanied by a sudden and dramatic increase in the heart rate and respiratory amplitude. Screaming, and massive bodily movements, with profuse sweating, often follows them. If any of the jury has children, they may have actually observed this. A child will suddenly call out and sit bolt upright in the bed shaking, sweating and maybe talking incoherently. The episode lasts for a short period of time and the child returns to deep sleep. It can be quite terrifying to observe.'

'During this episode is the subject conscious of his environment?'

'Absolutely not, the subject is totally out of contact with everything going on around him. Where there is recall of the episode, and this is rare, the recall is very vague and obscure, but is always associated with feelings of extreme fear, of being trapped with a desire to escape from danger. The images are vague but terribly frightening.'

'During such an episode is someone capable of rational thought?'

'No. The mind is detached from reality and the real environment. Reason and logic are absent.'

'Professor, when I was a child I saw my little sister behave in the manner you describe. I wanted to intervene to help her but was actually scared to do so, why was that?'

'If a parent or someone close to the subject intervenes to comfort their child, the child would be unaware of their presence or who was trying to help them. The person is unresponsive to any external stimuli. If any mental functions are present they are primitive in the extreme. The behaviour is truly automatic.'

'But was my fear justified?'

'Yes; your sister would not have understood what was happening to her; she would not have known who you were, or that your motives were in fact good. What feelings she would have had in this state were ones of extreme fear so there is every possibility that she would have reacted violently towards you.'

'Would you now tell the jury about sleepwalking.'

'There is a close and overlapping relationship between sleepwalking and night terrors. They share a common physiological substrate and form a continuum with sleepwalking being the less intense and night terrors being the more intense disturbance. A significant number of subjects who suffer night terrors also suffer from what we call somnambulistic episodes. Where this is so, the sleepwalking episodes are more vigorous and frantic than normal sleepwalking episodes.'

'Does sleepwalking also occur during slow-wave or deep sleep?'

'Yes, it does. The normal sleepwalker that the jury maybe familiar with is the one who rises from the bed and walks to the toilet, performs functions there, and then returns to bed. Often their eyes are open but they are oblivious to any external stimuli. They are working on automatic pilot and appear in a zombie-like state. If you call their name they will not answer. There is normally no recall of the event afterwards.'

'That is a fairly primitive function, going to the bathroom. Are sleepwalkers capable of more purposeful actions?'

'Purposeful is an unfortunate word, Mr Armstrong. There is actually no purpose at all since the subject is effectively unconscious at the time. If, however, you mean are they capable of more elaborate actions, the answer is most definitely yes. The varieties of actions encountered are numerous and many people will either know of persons who sleepwalk, or who themselves do.'

'Professor, can sleepwalkers become violent?'

'Yes, there are many well-documented cases of violent acts, even homicidal acts being carried out by sleepwalkers. I will give the jury examples later in my evidence when the picture is perhaps a little clearer. But I should say that people are very reluctant to discuss these incidents, they often feel that they will in some way be stigmatized as being evil.'

'Perhaps you could deal with confusional arousal or what I think is termed "sleep drunkenness"?'

'The term "sleep drunkenness" was coined in a trial in Germany in 1791. It is, in fact, unrelated to drink and because drink looms large in this case I prefer to use the term "confusional arousal". This also occurs during slow-wave or deep sleep, but occurs on waking from sleep and not during it. The waking is normally prompted by some external factor, since the natural pattern is that slow-wave sleep moves into the next stage of REM sleep and is not interrupted naturally.'

'What sort of external factor could prompt it?'

'Sometimes the need to urinate may interrupt the normal cycle and force arousal. Or it could be a loud noise or a sudden change in temperature. Whatever the cause, the subject is suddenly awoken from deep sleep.'

'Is the person fully awake?'

'No. The body is unprepared for waking during slow-wave sleep and there follows a period of up to ten minutes when the person is confused and incapable of any rational thought. He is in a state close to unconsciousness and is unaware of his actions.'

'Is he awake at all?'

'During the episode the subject awakens only partially and exhibits marked confusion, disorientation of time and place, perceptual impairment and the behaviour is often inappropriate. Cognition is typically altered from full wakefulness with confused thinking, misunderstandings, errors of logic and sometimes aggressive behaviour is observed.'

'Could you put that in simple terms Professor?'

'In other words, he has no idea what is going on or what he is doing. A classic case is that of Bernard Schidmaizig. He was awakened from deep sleep by a loud noise some time around midnight. He saw the dim shape of a figure and grabbed an axe he kept beside his bed. He struck out, hitting the terrifying figure, and by doing so he killed his wife. When his mind eventually cleared he was found by his son embracing his wife crying "Susanne, wake up". They were happily married and there was no motive for the killing. He had absolutely no recall of killing her.'

'That sounds quite incredible.'

'There are many well-documented cases of violence committed in this state. Another one is the case of Simon Frazer in 1878. He was awakened from deep sleep and saw an image of a wild beast jump on his bed and attack his child. In great excitement and in an effort to save his child he seized the animal and dashed it against the wall. In reality he killed his eighteen-month-old son. He was in a state of sleep drunkenness at the time.'

'Had any of these people a history of violence or psychiatric illness?'

'No, they were ordinary people like you and I.'

'So, could any one of us in this courtroom be capable of killing someone close to us if we found ourselves in this state of confusional arousal?'

'I am afraid the answer to that is yes.'

McNamara, who busily whispered to an expert commissioned by the prosecution, momentarily distracted Blair who was conscious that the judge would allow them to call evidence in rebuttal if Professor Duncan slipped up on any scientific fact. But he was quietly confident that this was most unlikely.

'Professor do you have any more examples that might help explain this to the jury?'

'Yes. There are more than forty relevant examples, but perhaps I could confine myself to giving a further two or three.'

'Please carry on, Professor.'

'In 1931 a fireman who was happily married, woke to find himself battering his wife who was in bed beside him, with a shovel. The shock was so great he fainted. Later, when he found his wife dead, he attempted suicide. He had no recollection of getting up and going down to the kitchen where the shovel was kept. There was absolutely no motive for the killing and he never recovered from the guilt of what he had done. He eventually succeeded in killing himself.

'There was a famous case in 1879 from Kentucky. A man called Fain was staying in a hotel. The night porter went to his room approximately an hour after Fain went to sleep. The porter had an urgent message for Fain and woke him from deep sleep. In his confused state Fain shot the porter three times and then went back to sleep. He, too, had no history of violent behaviour and had absolutely no recall of killing the porter.

'Then there was the case of Esther Griggs in 1859. She was having a dream that the house was on fire. She picked up her baby daughter and dropped her from a third-floor window, believing that she was saving her from the flames. Unfortunately the young baby died from the fall. A police officer who was on the street below and witnessed the entire incident, gave a graphic account of seeing the mother in a confused dream-like state.

'Finally, the most recent and well-documented case is that of a Canadian man called Kenneth Parkes. He was a twenty-three-year-old man who worked in the electronics trade. After an uneventful day he watched television with his wife until midnight, when she went to bed. He fell asleep at approximately half past one on the couch watching Saturday Night Live. In a state of sleepwalking, he drove fifteen miles to his mother-in-law's house and stabbed her to death and attacked his father-in-law but not fatally. He then drove to a police station and seems to have come out of his confusion. He told the police he thought he had killed some people. He suffered partial amnesia, which covered the time of the attack. He got on very well with his in-laws and there was absolutely no motive for his actions. A barrage of tests was carried out on him and some very learned psychiatric evidence was given at his trial. It was determined by the court that he was not responsible for his actions because he was sleepwalking at the time. What is so interesting about this case is that he carried out seemingly purposeful actions, taking a knife and driving some distance. It is also relevant that he had a prior history of sleep disturbance.'

'If I could just stop you there, Professor, I think you have examined the facts of this case very closely.'

'Yes, I have.'

'And you interviewed the accused at some length in the Central Mental Hospital?'

'Yes. When I received all the statements and reports in this case, I thought it was important to see the accused and take a history from him. It was clear to me from reading the psychiatric report that this young man had no psychiatric history and was not psychotic. I consulted at length with Dr Greene and we decided to look elsewhere for possible causes, as to why he killed his mother.'

'What possible causes did you explore?'

'Well, obviously intoxication was very prominent in our enquiry. There was also the possibility that he had a sleep-related event. I arranged for him to undergo a sleep EEG which proved negative for any abnormality.'

'Did anything arise from your interviews with him that you considered significant?'

'Yes. Firstly I had to satisfy myself that his claimed amnesia was genuine. I went over the history of the events with him several times and he showed a remarkable consistency in his account of what happened. He had a fairly unremarkable evening watching a football match on television. His favourite team, I think it was Chelsea, won the match and he was very happy about this. He then drank a large amount of bourbon and smoked some cannabis and following this went to bed in good form.'

'Are you happy that his amnesia is genuine?'

'I have a lot of experience of exploring this with patients and in this case, though originally sceptical, I was satisfied that he was genuine.'

'What, if any, effect would alcohol and cannabis have had on him?'

'They would both induce sleep. Deep sleep is found to be more prominent after alcohol. It is highly probable in my view that he fell very quickly into a deep sleep.'

'Did you discover anything else of relevance?'

'Yes, and this is highly significant. He gave a history of sleepwalking in his childhood. He also told me his twin brother frequently suffered from night terrors. He actually observed these at first hand and recounted them in graphic detail.'

'Why is that relevant, Professor?'

'A history of sleepwalking strongly suggests that this event was sleep-related.'

'Did you find anything else of importance?'

'Yes. In the days leading up to that night he had found sleeping very difficult.'

'Why is that relevant?'

'From a clinical point of view, it is significant because sleep deprivation promotes deep sleep, and the case histories suggest it is a factor giving rise to sleepwalking or night terrors.'

'What about the fact that the garda officers found it so difficult to wake him the following morning?'

'This could also be important. At that hour in the morning he ought to have come out of REM sleep quite easily. As I have already indicated, the normal cycles of sleep lead to a situation where the body effectively prepares the mind for consciousness the following morning. The fact that he appears to have been still in a cycle of slow-wave sleep and was confused when he emerged from it suggests that his sleep that night was abnormal.'

'What is your scientific opinion of what happened that night, Professor?'

'I am of the view that there are two reasonable possibilities that may explain why he killed his mother. Firstly, that his violence was due to a night terror or sleepwalking. Secondly, there is in my view a greater likelihood that something woke him from deep sleep and he was in a state of confusional arousal and in consequence his actions were done without full consciousness.'

'Why do you think that?'

'Guidelines were published by Professor Alexander Bonkola in 1974 for the clinical and forensic evaluation of cases of suspected confusional arousal after the study of twenty murder cases associated with this condition. Those guidelines are internationally accepted since. In my view, the facts of this case appear to meet almost all the clinical guidelines and I believe this is a classic case of confusional arousal, and I hold a very firm view that his actions that night were done in an unconscious state.'

'Thank you, Professor. Would you stay there and answer any questions that Mr McNamara may have?'

McNamara was talking to his expert who was sitting behind him. They appeared to be arguing. After some time the judge intervened. 'Mr McNamara, are you ready, or do you need a short break?'

'No, I am ready, my lord. Professor, did you carry out any objective tests on the accused?'

'Yes, in order to rule out epilepsy as a possible cause, I arranged for him to undergo an EEG. The results of this were negative. We also arranged an MRI scan, which showed no abnormalities.'

'Why did you carry out those particular tests?'

'There have been cases where tumours in the frontal region of the brain have been implicated in violent automatic behaviour and I was anxious to exclude this as a possibility in this case.'

'And were there any abnormalities in the scans?'

'No.'

'Did you carry out any other objective scientific tests?'

'Yes, a nocturnal polysomnograph was performed.'

'Was that normal?'

'Yes, it was.'

'So it would seem all the objective scientific tests were completely normal?'

'Yes.'

'Therefore your findings are based on subjective material emanating from the accused?'

'I don't fully understand your question.'

'The accused provided all the information on which you base your conclusions.'

'Yes, but I am trained to test these accounts very thoroughly, which I did in this case. I was satisfied with the answers the accused gave me.'

'You rely heavily in your final opinion on two matters. Firstly, the accused had a history of sleepwalking, as did his brother.'

'Yes, this evidence I consider lends a great deal of weight to my final conclusions.'

'Secondly, that in the days prior to the killing he was deprived of sleep, which I understand, would have made the deep sleep particularly profound.'

'Yes, that's right.'

'But the accused may simply have been making all that up in order to back up his case.'

'I don't agree with that proposition.'

'Why not?'

'The psychologist found that he had a mental age of a twelve year old and I can't imagine that he would know what was relevant to his defence from a clinical point of view.'

'But someone might have told him.'

Blair immediately leapt to his feet, but the judge waved him to his seat. 'It's all right, Mr Armstrong. I know what you are going to say. Mr McNamara, are you suggesting that someone on the defence team prompted the accused to give a false account to the doctors?'

'I am not going that far, my lord,' McNamara replied.

The judge leant forward, his face flushed with anger. 'That is not an answer to my question. Either you are making that suggestion or you're not. I will not allow you to implant something so sinister in the jurors' minds and leave it there to contaminate their thinking unless you have some evidence to support it.'

'I am unable to lead any evidence.'

'I regard the manner you are approaching this as most unsatisfactory. Mr Armstrong, I may tell you, enjoys the highest respect in these courts and his integrity has never once been called into question. It seems to me that you are trying to deliberately implant in the minds of the jury an idea that there may have been collusion between the defence legal team and the accused in providing false information to the doctors in order to add substance to the defence case. Now, I take a very dim view of that, so I insist you withdraw that suggestion or call evidence to substantiate it.'

'In those circumstances, your lordship, I withdraw the suggestion.'

The judge turned to the members of the jury. He was clearly trying to contain his anger. 'Ladies and gentlemen, I try not to interfere if at all possible in the conduct of the trial. But it seems to me that what you have heard is most unfair to the accused. It was deliberately done to cast a shadow over the defence that is being relied on by him. And it was done subtly to produce a prejudice in your minds. I am very disappointed that this has happened. Please disregard this suggestion, not for the sake of the defence team who are thick-skinned, but out of fairness to the accused, who is vulnerable. Carry on with your questioning, Mr McNamara, and focus on relevant matters.'

'In obtaining a personal history from a patient,' observed McNamara, 'would I be correct in thinking that a doctor would often consult other members of the family in order to corroborate that history?'

'That, of course, would be the ideal situation. Unfortunately it wasn't possible here.'

'Were you able to consult with any medical records that existed in Russia?'

'No, that was not possible, either.'

'So, for all we know, he may have been diagnosed previously as a psychopath in his home country.'

'Yes, but that is pure speculation on your part.'

'But speculation is exactly what I suggest to you that you have engaged in. Your evidence, Professor, is no more than mere conjecture.'

Professor Duncan shook his head defiantly. 'I cannot agree with that observation. I have looked at the known facts and drawn what I believe are reasonable inferences from the evidence. I do not say this was definitely a sleep-related event but suggest that it is a reasonable possibility that it was.'

'With respect, Professor, you seem to have given the accused the benefit of the doubt on every point?'

The judge leant forward towards McNamara and intervened. 'Don't answer that, Professor,' he said. 'Mr McNamara, am I right in thinking that the law requires me at the end of the case to instruct the jury that they are obliged to give the accused the benefit of the doubt on any of the evidence?'

'Yes, that's correct, my lord.'

'So what is your complaint in relation to this witness? Are you suggesting that he is biased in favour of the defence and has lost his impartiality? Before you answer that, I should indicate in the strongest possible terms that Professor Duncan is a witness who has given evidence in court on numerous occasions. Indeed, if my memory serves me correctly, you yourself have used his services on behalf of the prosecution on more than one occasion. His independence as an expert witness is well established. Now, do you suggest bias on his part?'

'No, my lord, I don't.'

'Do you suggest he is not adequately qualified to give his expert opinion on these matters?'

'No, my lord.'

'And you have an expert yourself, present in court, who can contradict the professor on any scientific fact that he has given evidence about?'

'Yes.'

'Well, then, please start asking relevant questions and let's get on with this case.'

McNamara was clearly thrown off his stride by the judge's continuous interruptions, but continued. 'You are aware that in this case there was a substantial motive for the killing.'

'I understand that is very much open to debate.'

'We know the accused went to the sitting room and procured his knife from its pouch. Do you ask the jury to accept that he did so whilst he was asleep?'

'Yes, it is very possible. I have already indicated people are capable of complex and seemingly purposeful acts but they are not conscious when they carry them out.'

'Doctor, sorry, Professor, I have a copy of the report you sent to the defence solicitor, Mr Molloy. I will hand it over to you and ask you to read the last paragraph, headed "Final Opinion".'

The court usher handed a copy of the report to the witness.

The witness read from the report. 'I have considered the issues of whether your client was at the time of the killing in a state of automatism arising from some sleep disturbance. The most likely culprits in my view are night terrors, sleepwalking or confusional arousal. However, I have also had to consider very carefully the exceptionally high levels of alcohol reported to be in his system. This in my view clouds the issue considerably and introduces the distinct possibility that this was in fact a drink-induced psychotic episode as opposed to a case of automatism arising from a sleep event. I wish I could be more helpful.'

'What do you mean by "a drink-induced psychotic episode"?'

'Well, drink reduces our inhibitions, and if someone has a history of violence, then there is the possibility that the killing could be due to a psychotic episode brought about by drink.'

'But I thought the accused had no known history of violence?'

'As you have already pointed out, he was the only historian we had. I found him to be a very mild-mannered, placid person when I interviewed him. But I was conscious that he might have been playing up his passive nature. I think I was being particularly cautious when dealing with that aspect of the case. And that is reflected in my report.'

'But in your direct evidence, you didn't mention the possible role of drink in this case other than to point out that it would encourage the accused to go into a deep sleep more quickly.'

'Yes, and cannabis was also relevant in that regard.'

'But, Professor, why have you altered your original somewhat guarded diagnosis set out in that report sent to Mr Molloy only two weeks ago, and now come down so heavily in favour of sleepwalking as an explanation?'

'There is a very simple explanation.'

'Well, please tell us, Professor, what has changed your mind.'

'I was present in court for the evidence of Professor Hindenburg and in particular for your excellent cross-examination. You were, of course, correct in pointing out that the very high levels of alcohol reported by toxicology couldn't be correct since the very precise and accurate nature of the assault was totally inconsistent with the slobbering movements of a drunk. I, along with Professor Hindenburg, hadn't allowed for the period of nearly an hour before the full effects of the alcohol kicked in.'

'So?'

'Put simply, drink is not the cause of this killing. That is a scientific fact based on the evidence of your own forensic pathologist. That means sleep is now a much more likely explanation for this strange and bizarre killing than it was when I wrote that report. You see, if he were sleepwalking before the effects of the drink were apparent, then he would be quite capable of the accuracy you so eloquently describe as being necessary to carry out the crime.'

McNamara turned around and whispered to his own expert who was shaking his head from side to side. 'I have no more questions, my lord,' McNamara concluded.

'Very well, is your client going into evidence, Mr Armstrong?'

'No, my lord.'

'Ladies and gentlemen of the jury, that concludes all the evidence that you are going to hear in this case. Tomorrow, Mr McNamara will deliver his closing speech on behalf of the prosecution, and Mr Armstrong will address you on behalf of his client. It will then be my job to sum up the evidence and explain the principles of law that you must apply in the jury room when considering your verdict. Feel free to discuss the evidence amongst yourselves but don't discuss it with anyone else. See you tomorrow morning at ten-thirty, and in the meantime have a pleasant evening and a good night's sleep.'

Blair was hurriedly leaving the courtroom when Marina caught up with him.

'Where are you rushing off to?'

'I'm heading home to do some work on the case.'

'Do you fancy a drink? It's on me.'

'Marina, I am really sorry, but I can't tonight.'

'What do you mean, you can't?' She sounded disappointed that she was being dismissed so easily.

'I can't go and have a drink with you because I have a closing speech to make tomorrow and I must prepare it.'

She frowned, unable to disguise her disappointment.

'You don't seem to have any time for me these days.'

'I have to work on the case, you must understand that.'

'I suppose so, but are you at least going to get yourself something to eat? You can't work on an empty stomach.'

'I will get something back at my place.'

'Can I come?' she asked sheepishly.

Blair laughed. 'No, Marina, you can't come and you know you can't, so stop teasing me, will you?'

Marina looked up at him coyly. 'Even if I promise I won't get in the way of your work?'

'Look what happened the last time you promised me that.'

'OK, but at least let me cook you a good meal. You've never tasted my cooking, have you?'

'No, I haven't.' Blair looked sympathetically at her plaintive face. 'OK, you win, but you must leave after dinner. Is that a promise?'

'I promise, an hour after dinner and I'm history.'

Blair laughed as he hailed a taxi. 'And where did you get the hour from?'

'Well, we have to have some time together and I might be able to give you some ideas for your speech.'

He looked at her and smiled.

thirty-three

Blair was stretched out on the sofa in front of a roaring fire, his notes of the trial scattered around him. The smell of a lamb curry wafted from the kitchen where Marina was busy demonstrating her culinary skills. After dinner she dimmed the lights and sat on the floor at his feet sipping a glass of red wine. The flickering flames danced across her angelic features and she appeared mesmerized by their unsung melody. Blair was gently stroking her hair from behind as they sat together in silence.

'Blair, I need to tell you something,' she whispered nervously.

'About what?'

'It's about my past.'

'Marina,' he said, shaking his head, 'there is a time to think and a time to talk.'

'What do you mean?'

'Now is a time for thoughts and not for words.'

Marina paused. 'You mean you just want to think about the case, is that it?'

'No, my thoughts about the case, are all done.'

'Then what do you mean?' she asked.

'Whatever you need to tell me is perhaps best left to another day. I don't need any distractions right now.'

'But this is really important to me. I need to tell you something.'

Blair continued to stroke her hair without answering.

'Well, can I tell you about my past?' she pressed.

There was a long silence. Blair then spoke softly. 'Is it about your father?'

She turned around and looked up at him in astonishment. 'What about my father?'

Blair hesitated.

'What do you know about my father?' she pressed.

'I know that the guilt you feel deep down inside is not yours, but his.'

She sat up and looked into his eyes. 'How do you know this? How do you know about my father? I don't understand.'

'Do you think, after all my years of working with victims, that I can't recognize the symptoms of abuse, or that I can't hear your demons crying out to be relieved of the dreadful burden you carry?'

'But ...'

He lowered himself to the floor beside her, and drew her close. 'Do you think for one moment that I can't see the sorrow and pain when I look deep into your eyes?'

She lowered her head in shame. 'Is it so obvious?' she whispered.

He gently lifted her chin with his hand. 'Only to someone who cares to see.'

'But why didn't you ask me about it before?'

'A famous poet called Keats once wrote that beauty is truth and truth beauty, that is all ye need to know.'

'I don't understand.'

'The truth for you is that you are not responsible for the things your father did. Accept that truth, take it into your heart and hold it there forever.'

She started to cry and he took her in his arms. 'But the pain has been terrible.'

'Only because you persuaded yourself to accept the blame.'

'Maybe I am to blame.'

'That's crazy. How can a child ever take the blame for the pain inflicted by a parent?'

'Do you really believe that, Blair?'

'Yes, I do.'

'So I did nothing wrong then?'

'Marina, the only thing you did wrong was to allow yourself to feel a guilt that was never yours to feel.'

There was a long silence as his words settled. 'Blair, I have never told anyone about this before.'

'I am pleased that you decided to confide in me.'

'So am I.'

'You know, sometimes it's good to drop your guard and share your soul.'

'But only with someone I can trust.'

'And do you really trust me, Marina?'

'One hundred per cent, Blair.'

He laughed.

'What's so funny?' she said indignantly.

'I guess you must be the only person I ever met who trusted a lawyer.'

She smiled and took a gulp of her wine. 'I need to tell you something else.'

He stood up, walked to the fireplace and stood with his back to her.

A brass French carriage clock on the mantelpiece chimed softly. 'I think your hour is up,' he said abruptly. 'We have talked enough for tonight.'

'No, I need to tell you something else,' she insisted.

'Well, it will have to wait until another time. I'm tired and need to get some sleep.'

'Are you serious?' she asked incredulously.

Blair turned and faced her. 'Yes, I am very serious. I promise we will talk about whatever it is that you want to tell me, but not tonight.'

'It's really important,' she protested.

'And my closing speech is important to Yuri.'

'But I need to tell you right now: it can't wait.'

'Well, it's just going to have to wait,' he replied firmly, his expression closed to further argument.

She stood up and went to the hall to get her jacket. Blair followed her.

'I am sorry, Marina. You know I have to be ready for tomorrow.'

She turned to him. 'I suppose so. You have your own priorities.'

She gave him a peck on the cheek and left.

thirty-four

The court resumed at 10 a.m. on Thursday, and a sense of anticipation hung in the air. McNamara's closing speech was brief and relied heavily on the motive that emerged when the icons were discovered. He made light of the sleepwalking defence describing it as 'nonsense', bordering on 'fantasy'. Blair sat dispassionately throughout.

When McNamara finished, Blair rose slowly to his feet. Looking around the courtroom he cast his eye on the public gallery thronged with alert spectators perched awkwardly on the edge of their seats awaiting his every word with interest. His gaze moved slowly over the row of benches packed with young barristers eager to learn from the great master, until it eventually settled on Yuri, sitting in the dock, ashen-faced and looking frightened.

He then turned to face the jury. 'Ladies and gentlemen, there are those in our society who advocate the abolition of juries and you may well wonder why. The reason is that these people fear the impartiality and sense of justice that intelligent and fair-minded people like you bring to these proceedings.'

He turned to the press box. 'The media, if they had their way, would simply convict or acquit depending on which was the more sensational verdict, merely so that they could sell more newspapers.'

His gaze then settled on McNamara. 'The law and order lobby would convict whoever was unfortunate enough to occupy the dock. And some prosecutors see the democratic right to be judged by one's peers as an obstacle to the speedy conviction of those they have singled out to charge.'

He looked up at Mr Justice Canning. 'On the other hand, there are lawyers and eminent judges who recognize the strengths and integrity that you, as jurors, collectively bring to the administration of justice and believe the system far richer for it.'

He rested his hand on the bench in front of him and lowered his large frame towards the jury. 'We all carry some burden of responsibility on our shoulders through life, as parents, as children, as wives, husbands or friends. The decision you are about to make is the most important decision you will ever make in your lives, for it will decide the destiny of one of your peers. And it is a decision that is final and cannot be altered.'

Blair paused for a moment.

'That's right, ladies and gentlemen. In years to come this day may come back to you. You might have second thoughts about the evidence you have heard over the last few days, and you might begin to doubt the correctness of your decision. And if that happens, you will be helpless, ladies and gentlemen, unable to right the wrong you might feel you have done, and it will haunt you night and day for the rest of your days.'

Blair heard McNamara cough, and raised his voice slightly to drown the deliberate distraction. 'The only way to avoid such an appalling scenario is to approach your deliberations in a fair-minded way and never lose sight of the fundamental principle that the burden rests on the prosecution to prove its case beyond reasonable doubt.'

'You may well ask, why does the prosecution carry such a heavy burden? The answer is simple: to protect the innocent. Yes, it may well be that many guilty persons walk free from these courts because of what is perceived by some as an over-generous concession to the accused. But the thought of the innocent being wrongly condemned is truly horrific. Surely we would prefer ten guilty men to go free than see one innocent man languish for the rest of his life in a prison cell.

'What is a fair-minded way to approach your deliberations? It is certainly without prejudice. But unfortunately prejudice is endemic in the world we live in. It can be racial, ethnic, religious, social – the list is endless. It is the most primitive and repulsive of all human emotions and yet, unfortunately, it is also the most powerful, driving normal people to conflict and even war. It has no logic, no reason, and therefore difficult to combat. Often, it is so deeply hidden in our hearts, others can't see it festering there. And sometimes it is so ingrained within us, we are even blind to it ourselves.

'What prejudices might surface in this case? The most obvious one, of course, is racial. My client is a foreigner, from Russia. What do you know of Russians outside the news and the usual stereotype portrayed in the movies? Do you consider Russians to be cold, with perhaps a lesser moral code than us? Ask yourselves, does that cause you any difficulty? Do you feel my client is cold and heartless? Ask yourselves why you feel that way.

'He is also an immigrant. Do you disagree with our immigration laws? Are you hostile to him because he should have stayed in his homeland, instead of burdening the taxpayer here?

'He is also young. Is he therefore deemed to be reckless and irresponsible? And unfortunately, he is also slow. Does that lead you to believe in some way that he is less worthy of a place in our society? That he is in some way less important than others?

'Forgive, me, ladies and gentlemen, for pointing out these matters to you. I mean no insult. But I mention them at the outset merely to alert you to the possibility that prejudice might creep into this case. I ask you to look deep into your hearts and if you discover some bias or pre-conception against my client, root it out and banish it from your minds. Do not pay mere lip service to the principle of fairness, but give it real meaning by the manner you approach this case.

'Ladies and gentlemen, Mr McNamara opened this case to you last Monday and advised you of the principles of law that apply in a crim-inal case. He told you the accused man comes to this court enjoying the presumption of innocence and that this presumption is the golden thread that runs through our criminal justice system. He also explained, quite properly in my view, that the burden of proving the case rests fairly and squarely with the prosecution and that the burden is a weighty one. He went on to tell you that the prosecution must prove its case beyond all reasonable doubt, and I agree with everything he said last Monday.'

Blair looked around at Mr McNamara and fixed him with his hawkish dark eyes.

'But what surprised me greatly was that he failed to remind you of these principles in his closing speech. In fact, many of his arguments flew directly in the face of the very principles he so eloquently and fairly brought to your attention in his opening speech. You may well ask your-selves why he now asks you to rely on assumptions when he quite clearly told you that you must rely only on the evidence you have heard.'

Blair turned back to the jury.

'Let me give you an example of what I am referring to. Motive, or, more importantly, the lack of it, is a matter that has loomed large in this trial and no doubt it will occupy a great deal of your time in the jury room. Mr McNamara claims there was a substantial motive for murder. He tells you that the icons were that motive and that's why my client killed his mother. He also relies heavily on the supposed lies told by my client to the guards when he apparently told them his mother was not a wealthy woman. His aim in doing this was to show that he is a cunning young man capable of deception when it suits him. Now, let's break that argument down, shall we?'

Blair became more intense as he leant towards the jury.

'Where is the evidence that my client knew that the icons existed at all? That's right – where is the evidence? Well, there simply is no direct evidence that he ever did. Why should we assume he knew his mother's business? Did your parents never keep secrets from you? Did your parents confide all their financial affairs to you? Can you be satisfied beyond a reasonable doubt that my client must have known of their existence? Yes, it is likely that he did, it might even be very likely that he did know of their existence – but can you be sure? Is there a reasonable possibility that his mother kept their existence secret from him? If there is, then you are bound by law to give him the benefit of the doubt on this issue and to deal with the case on the basis that the icons are not material to this case.

'If, however, you are satisfied beyond a reasonable doubt that he was aware of their existence, then can you be sure he deliberately concealed this fact from the guards? I want to remind you of the very fair evidence of Detective Sergeant Murphy. He pointed out that there was some confusion in the interpreter's mind when the issue of my client's mother's financial affairs was being discussed. He said in evidence, and I quote what he said, "some of the words may have been lost in translation". He was there, ladies and gentlemen, and he is best placed to judge whether my client deliberately misled him. But he tells you there is a possibility that due to the nature of the questions or the manner in which they were translated, my client might have misunderstood the real meaning of those questions. If the guard who was there concedes that, how can Mr McNamara go behind the evidence of his own witness and ask you to substitute a different view? Again, it is an example of giving the benefit of the doubt to my client, and if you apply that principle, you must proceed on the basis that he did not deliberately mislead the guards about the icons. If, however, you are still sympathetic to Mr McNamara's argument, I urge you to consider the following points.'

Blair raised his hand in front of him and raised his forefinger as he made the first point.

'Firstly, if he murdered his mother for money, what was his plan? What was he going to do with her body? If he intended to dispose of it, how was he going to explain her disappearance to the authorities? And how was he going to lay claim to the money?

'Secondly, where is the evidence of any plan? Why did he go back to bed and leave the knife lying by his side? Why did he make no effort to make it look as though there had been an intruder? Ask yourselves this simple question: prior to that dreadful night, had Yuri hatched a plan to do away with his mother? There is, of course, not a scintilla of evidence in support of that proposition. I repeat, there is no evidence to suggest that there was any premeditation in this case and, in fact, all the evidence points to the contrary.

'Thirdly, is his amnesia genuine, or is he faking it as Mr McNamara implied in his closing speech? Let me remind you that the officer in charge of this case gave his opinion on the matter. Of course, that opinion is not binding on you, but he is again uniquely placed to offer it and he is a very experienced guard. He firmly believes that my client had no memory of having killed his mother, and he bases that opinion largely on his reactions in the flat that morning when he saw his mother's lifeless body lying in her bed. I want you to concentrate your minds on those reactions. The guards arrived and rang the bell three times. Mr McNamara again implied that Yuri might well have been awake and refused to let them in. But how did he know it was the guards? There is no evidence that he did. If he did, why did he not seek to escape from a crime scene that so clearly pointed to him being the killer? One would perhaps have expected him to climb from a window in an effort to escape or, at the very least, to dispose of the murder weapon lying next to him. But no, according to Mr McNamara he pretended to be asleep. What utter nonsense, ladies and gentlemen. Complete and utter nonsense, and it's not worthy of any further consideration. And what of the evidence of the two officers who found it so difficult to wake my client, even checking his pulse, fearing that he might be dead? Was my client just acting as Mr McNamara suggests? He seems to be the only one on the prosecution team who thinks so. And then slowly my client came round, and in the words of the officers, he looked bewildered. Bewildered and scared at these strangers in his room. And what does he do, ladies and gentlemen? What is the first reaction of this cunning murderer who did away with his mother only hours earlier so he could inherit her fortune? What does he do?'

Blair paused and looked at each of the jurors individually.

'He called out for his mother. That's right, he called out for his mother, over and over again.'

Blair leant down and picked up the photograph that Detective Sergeant Murphy had taken from Yuri's room. He looked at it, noting the mother's smiling face as she hugged an adoring son. He then asked the usher to hand it to the jury. They passed the photograph from one to the other examining it closely.

'My client adored his mother. They spent their lives together and suffered hardships together.'

The faint sound of Yuri beginning to cry could be heard, but Blair drowned it out quickly.

'There is no evidence before you that they were anything other than happy. There is no evidence of rows or arguments. So to whom does he call out to for help when he feels threatened? His mother, of course. But why, if he knows she is dead? Ask yourselves, why does he do it? Is this all contrived to fool the garda officers, as Mr McNamara implies, or is it genuine?

'And then he was led away from the scene and he saw his mother's lifeless body lying on her bed. What does he do? Does he hang his head in shame as one might expect? Does he try and flee the scene, as Mr McNamara mistakenly suggested in his opening speech? No, ladies and gentlemen, he broke down completely and tried frantically to get to her side.'

Blair stood to his full height and folded his arms, wrapping himself in his silk gown.

'Let me briefly recap, ladies and gentlemen. You are dealing with a young man who loved his mother with no evidence of any disharmony between them. He went to bed with absolutely no evidence of any plan to kill her. He was next woken by garda officers and he called out to his mother, but she didn't respond. He then broke down completely when he saw his mother lying dead in her bed. What are we to make of all this? Well, I suppose the most obvious explanation is that he genuinely had no recall. Or else this young man is simply mad.'

Blair paused, unfolded his arms and looked around at Jenny and then at the jury.

'Ladies and gentlemen, there is a presumption in law that an accused is sane until the contrary is proved on the balance of probabilities. You may well ask why we called Dr Greene to prove our client was sane when the law presumes him to be so? But there is much more to it than that. We exposed our client to the microscope of the forensic psychiatrists to see if there was some abnormality in his mind. Maybe some psychosis would emerge that might explain why he killed his mother. Perhaps he was schizophrenic. Or perhaps was suffering from some form of personality disorder. He was examined thoroughly and we even invited the prosecution to examine him independently. Surely from all this close scrutiny some explanation for his behaviour would emerge and solve what had clearly become a mystery.'

Blair again paused. Unfolding his arms, he looked around at Yuri and fixed him with his gaze as he continued.

'Alas no! This young man sitting before you is like you and me. He is not psychotic, there are no demonic voices talking to him and he suffers no personality disorder. He is just another Joe Bloggs. Yes, of course, he is dyslexic and a slow learner. He is not the brightest of chaps either. He probably didn't even understand the subtlety of Mr McNamara's suggestion that he was a cunning individual capable of deceiving the most experienced of garda officers.

'So your task becomes more difficult, because psychiatry cannot solve this mystery. And logic defies it. Ladies and gentlemen, we have an unexplained murder. Or have we?'

Blair stood back from the jury.

'I couldn't help but notice when Mr McNamara was opening the case and first mentioned that the defence would be relying on sleepwalking as a defence, most of you smiled with incredulity. I hope the evidence that you have heard during the course of the trial and particularly the evidence from Professor Duncan has opened your minds to the reasonable possibility that my client might have killed his mother whilst he was asleep. I say "might have", and I want to stress that. There is no burden on the accused to prove anything. All that we are required to do is to raise a reasonable doubt in your minds.

'Sleep, ladies and gentlemen, has been incriminated and well documented in over forty murder cases as the reason why otherwise perfectly sane and ordinary people, like my client, killed someone close without reason or motive. This is an historical fact. It may shock, it may even frighten you, and that fear will no doubt create scepticism. It is not as Mr McNamara suggests the product of modern alternative psychiatry. Sleepwalking is real, it is observable and within the experience of many of us. Cases where a person commits homicidal acts when asleep, or in the twilight zone of waking from sleep are thankfully, rare. But they are nevertheless recognized as circumstances where the perpetrator cannot be said to have control over his or her actions. They are not accountable for what they do, because the conscious mind is absent and they act on what has been described by one witness as "auto pilot".

'The idea that we can act violently in sleep is not new. It is not, as Mr McNamara implied, some phoney defence dreamt up by defence lawyers. It has been recognized for centuries. If I may quote from Plato's Republic: "In all of us, even in good men/There is a lawless wild beast/Which peers out in sleep". Stop, ladies and gentlemen of the jury, and consider those learned words, written centuries ago, yet still relevant today in this very courtroom. In 1313 the Council of Vienne in France ruled that "A sleepwalker who kills or wounds is not culpable for his actions". In the seventeenth century Covarrubias, the famous Spanish canonist declared, and I quote, "Acts done in sleep are not sinful". And in the same century the brilliant Dutch jurist Mattheus stated that acts done in sleep were not criminal unless there was evidence of enmity. Closer to home, McKensie another great jurist in his discourse on the Law of Scotland, compared the actions of sleepwalkers to those of infants and concluded that they were therefore not punishable.

'So where does that leave Mr McNamara's argument that the idea that a person could kill in their sleep is "far-fetched and fanciful", when it is has been recognized for centuries in human affairs, in canon law and in the laws of civilized countries? No, ladies and gentlemen, what we are considering here, no matter how much we find the idea repugnant, is real.

'I agree with Mr McNamara when he tells you that if you think the accused was sleepwalking, the law in this country requires you to bring in a special verdict of not guilty by reason of insanity. That is the law and I am not entitled to quarrel with it. So, what are the possible verdicts that arise in this case?

'Firstly, you could find my client was sober and awake when he killed his mother. That his amnesia is faked, and he acted in a cold evil way, doing away with his mother, so he could profit from her death. If this is your view, then your verdict can only be one of murder.

'Secondly, you might find that he consciously and voluntarily carried out the killing, then got drunk and has no memory of it because alcohol induced his amnesia. Your verdict again would be murder.

'Thirdly, you might find that he was indeed drunk, became violent and killed his mother, but was still conscious of what he was doing. Your verdict again would be murder.

'Fourthly, you might consider my client was so drunk that he was incapable of forming the specific intent required for murder – in other words he was not conscious of what he was doing at the time of the killing. To a large degree the evidence in this regard has been undermined, but if you still consider this a reasonable possibility, your verdict would be manslaughter.

'Fifthly, you might consider that this killing is related to any of the three disorders outlined to you by Professor Duncan, and that my client was not conscious of his actions when he killed his mother. If this be the case then you must bring in the special verdict of not guilty by reason of insanity.'

Blair looked around at Yuri and fixed him with his hawkish eyes. Yuri stared at the great defender without blinking. Marina was sitting beside him and, as the jury followed Blair's eyes, she appeared uncomfortable and shifted nervously in her seat. Blair then swung around to the jury. His expression, which had been deadpan, changed dramatically.

'Ladies and gentlemen, my client is at your mercy. He is slow and dim-witted, yet he has his life ahead of him. You may well ask, what sort of life that is likely to be? Regardless of your verdict, he will have to live with the terrible reality that he killed his beloved mother. Do you think a day will pass, be it in prison, or confined in some mental hospital, or ultimately when he is set free, that he will not suffer for what he did? Even if he is found guilty of murder he will suffer, not because of his confinement, but because his mind will never be free of guilt.'

Some of the jurors noticed tears in Yuri's eyes as Marina translated these words. The more observant also detected that even the interpreter's eyes had moistened.

'This young man is no monster,' Blair boomed. 'Look at him, ladies and gentlemen. Look at the young man who cried his heart out when he discovered his mother was dead and sobbed uncontrollably when he was in the garda station. Are those the reactions of Mr McNamara's cold-hearted murderer? Are you looking at a monster, or at a confused innocent looking for the truth?'

Blair defiantly looked around the court as if to challenge anyone to rise and dare disagree with him. He then lowered his voice.

'Now he is alone in this world. Will that ever change? Is he ever going to enjoy someone's love and trust again? No, he will be haunted by what he did. In many ways your verdict is probably irrelevant to him. At least in prison he will have persons who will look after him, feed him, perhaps eventually warm to him. And then, no doubt, when he has finished his sentence, he will be deported back to his homeland. And what awaits him there? Not family or friends. Who will warm to a man who killed his own mother? I think you know the answer.

'And regardless of your verdict, he will be poor, because any one of the verdicts available to you will mean he will not be entitled to the riches that were to be his had all this not happened.'

Blair looked across at McNamara and appeared to address his remarks to him.

'If greed had been his motivation, he would have fought this case tooth and nail, right to the bitter end. He would have pointed the finger elsewhere, claiming that he was framed. He would have prayed for a benevolent jury who might have believed him. But he didn't do that. As soon as he raised the defence of sleepwalking, he gave up his millions. If greed had been his motive, do you think he would have given in so easily?'

Blair looked back at the jury.

'The strange thing, ladies and gentlemen of the jury, is that my client is not fighting for his freedom or for money. He is looking for an explanation for what happened in the same way you are. He cannot understand why he killed the one he loved. That he got drunk and killed his mother will be poor consolation to him. But that he occupies a place amongst the rare cases of sleepwalkers who kill for no reason, will in some small way help him deal with the nightmares that lie ahead for him. I ask you to give him that morsel. Not out of sympathy, but because the evidence in this case compels you to. In my respectful submission, there is not just a reasonable possibility, there is a probability that he killed his mother in his sleep.'

Blair paused momentarily. He then raised himself to his full height.

'This young man would do anything to bring his mother back to life. He would sacrifice his own life if that were possible. His was not the conscious mind behind this outrage. It was the subconscious mind in sleep, a mind he had no control over, for if he had, his mother would still be here and we would not be assembled together in this courtroom. Fact, ladies and gentlemen, may sometimes be stranger than fiction. The history of sleep-related homicides proves this truism. An open and unbiased mind will have absorbed the scientific evidence presented in this case.'

Blair leant forward and looked at each juror individually.

'Thank you for giving me your full attention, I am confident that your minds are indeed open and unbiased, that you will return a just verdict, and that verdict will be not guilty but insane.'

Blair sat down and there was a long silence, which was eventually broken by the judge.

'Ladies and gentlemen of the jury, I will rise for fifteen minutes and then commence my charge.'

Blair sat motionless in his seat. A strange silence descended on the courtroom. A short time later the judge returned and delivered his charge. His summary of the facts was fair to both sides and his directions to the jury on the law impeccable.

The jury gathered their notebooks and slowly filed out of the jury box to consider their verdict.

thirty-five

Marina was standing alone in the cold air outside on the quays having a smoke as she found the tension hard to bear. Blair, Jenny and Dermot emerged onto the street. Leaving the other two, Blair approached Marina.

'We are all going over the road to have a coffee. The registrar will send for us if there is any news. Would you like to join us?'

'No, thanks, I brought a book with me and I will do some studying.'

'Look, Marina, don't pay any attention to Jenny. I know she can be a bit frosty, but she doesn't mean any harm.'

'No, it's not her, I really do have some studying to catch up on.'

But, of course, the problem was Jenny. Ever since that day in Dundrum, Jenny had ignored her, and Marina felt uncomfortable in her company. Marina knew that she would talk law or politics, anything to exclude her from the conversation. And she didn't want to feel foolish and inadequate in her company.

'OK, but you know where we are if you change your mind,' Blair replied.

As Marina watched him walk away, it was clear to her that they lived in different worlds, materially and intellectually. Yes, Blair had treated her as his equal, but his friends and colleagues – would they be so generous?

The minutes and hours ticked by slowly. In the courtroom, the jury keeper sat close to the jury room waiting for the inevitable gentle knock on the door that would signal the jury were ready to announce their verdict. The anticipation grew, and even casual observers began to feel uneasy. The longer the wait, the quieter the courtroom became.

The sound of a door opening caused acute interest. It was the court clerk. He had already sent for Blair and McNamara, as the judge had indicated he intended to direct the jury that they were now entitled to bring in a majority verdict.

Quickly the court reassembled, the lawyers took up their positions, and Yuri was brought up from the cells and nervously took up his place. Marina sat beside him in the dock and whispered something to him in

Russian. Dermot observed Yuri place his hand in Marina's, looking for some comfort, but she pulled it away gently.

The judge entered centre stage. Then the jury filed into court and took their seats. All eyes were upon them.

'Mr Foreman,' the registrar enquired, 'have you reached a verdict on which you are all agreed?'

'Yes, we have.'

Members of the public leant forward in their seats. The word that the jury was back with a verdict filtered out into the hallway and there was a rush of spectators into the public gallery. The foreman handed the issue paper to the registrar, who in turn handed it to the judge. The judge folded back the paper, looked at it and without any expression handed it back to the registrar. He waited for the audience to settle and then slowly and somewhat theatrically read the issue paper.

'Your verdict on count one on the indictment is unanimous?'

'Yes,' replied the foreman.

Blair felt a rush of blood to his head as Yuri buried his head in his hands in anticipation.

'You say the accused is not guilty by reason of insanity.'

'Yes.'

Yuri looked at Marina as she translated the words. He asked her to repeat them. Blair sat back and breathed an enormous sigh of relief as Jenny gently patted him on the shoulder. Dermot was unable to disguise his relief and appeared close to tears.

'Mr Armstrong, I will make the relevant hospital order. Thank you all for your assistance in this difficult case,' the judge said as he gathered his papers.

He then rose from the bench. McNamara leant across and shook Blair's hand.

'Well done, Armstrong.'

Blair slowly removed his wig; conscious that it would be the last time he did so. What he really felt like doing was throwing it in the air. The three lawyers went over to a bench at the back of the court where Yuri was sitting with Marina, awaiting the arrival of the hospital staff, having left the clutches of the prison officers. As Blair approached, Yuri stood up. There were tears in his eyes. At first he shook Blair's hand, then he put his arms awkwardly around Blair's large frame and hugged him. Blair appeared embarrassed, but allowed Yuri this moment.

'Thank you, sir, thank you,' Yuri blubbered, in a manner suggesting he had rehearsed those few words of English over and over again. Perhaps Marina had helped him.

Blair looked at Marina. There were tears in her eyes also. He smiled down at Yuri.

'It has been my pleasure, Mr Komarov.'

He then turned and walked away, as Yuri thanked Dermot and Jenny in turn.

Blair returned to the front bench to collect his papers and, as he did so, Marina approached him.

'That was brilliant, well done.'

Blair smiled, then placed a hand on her shoulder. 'I am bringing Dermot and Jenny for dinner to Shanahan's, I would love you to come.'

'I don't know, Blair, we can celebrate on our own later.'

Just then Jenny approached and interrupted them. 'Blair, I booked the table for eight, so we'd better get a move on.'

She looked at Marina and spoke warmly. 'It's booked for the four of us and we would love you to join us.'

Blair looked at Jenny and smiled. It was a kind gesture and he appreciated it. 'Right,' he said with enthusiasm. 'We will all meet up at eight o'clock, then. I had better go and change.'

He hurried off, but, as he reached the door of the courtroom, Barry was waiting for him.

'Congratulations, Mr Armstrong. I have been around a long time and never saw a performance quite like that.'

Blair acknowledged the compliment and smiled. 'I think he has more than me to thank for the result, Detective Sergeant.'

Blair stood at the door and looked back into the body of court number two. He felt like a gladiator looking at the arena that he had ruled over for so many years. Images of the many great dramas flashed before his eyes. He could hear his own powerful voice echo around the walls of the famous chamber. For one moment he thought he saw Rosemary's face smiling down at him from the public gallery. He closed his eyes, fought back the tears; then he turned and walked briskly away.

They dined at Shanahan's, drank champagne and fine wines, and discussed courtroom strategies and where the truth in the case really lay. Jenny declared that she never doubted that Blair would carry it off. Dermot proclaimed that it was he who had first suggested the sleep-walking defence and the glory was his. There was laughter and relief as the stress of the trial receded. Marina never turned up.

thirty-six

One month later.

Marina's mobile phone rang. It was Elena. Kristina could be heard crying in the background.

'Hi, Elena. What's up?'

'Marina, I am ringing to say goodbye.'

'What do you mean, *goodbye*?' There was shock in Marina's voice.

'That bastard beat me up again. I can't take any more and am getting the hell out of here.'

Marina detected sadness in Elena's voice.

'Where are you going to go?'

'Back to Russia.'

'You must be joking.'

'No, I am serious.'

'But Russia! You're crazy to go back there.'

'Maybe, but I can't stay in this country any longer. I have to go.'

'When are you leaving?'

'Tonight.'

There was a long silence.

'I will miss you, Elena,' she said at last, and she sounded as though she meant it.

'And I will miss you. I am ringing to say thank you for all your help and for your friendship. I don't think I could have lasted here so long without your shoulder to cry on.'

Marina felt strangely emotional.

'Don't make a speech now. You make it sound as though we will never see each other again.'

'You know we probably won't. But I will send you an e-mail and let you know how I am getting along.'

'Please stay in touch, Elena, I will be worrying about you.'

'How's the romance going?' Elena asked.

'It's on ice at the moment, but you never know what the future holds.'

'He's a good man. Don't go cold on him. If I had a man like that, I would never let him go. And not because he is rich and famous as I said before, but because he seems to have a heart of gold.'

'Thanks for that, Elena, and you're right, but it's not that simple. I will let you know how we get on.'

'And don't neglect your studies.'

'You sound like my mother now.' Marina's voice began to quiver.

'I have to go, look after yourself.'

'Take care, and give some kisses from me to Kristina.'

'*Paca.*'

'*Paca*,' Marina responded, but Elena had already hung up.

Marina was trembling as she slumped down on her bed. It all seemed so sudden. Elena had been in a good mood recently and this was a bolt out of the blue, she thought.

thirty-seven

Six weeks later.

Dermot was enjoying his newfound reputation as a serious solicitor and the Solicitors' Golfing Society had invited him to an outing at Powerscourt Golf Club. Though Dermot didn't play much golf, he wasn't going to miss the opportunity to bask in glory. He had taken a few lessons in advance and was feeling lucky.

He arrived at the club early for an eleven o'clock tee-off and decided to have a light breakfast in the clubhouse. Entering the bar, he spotted a group of colleagues who chatted energetically at a table by a window overlooking the practice green. One of the men spotted Dermot and immediately stood up and walked towards him. It was Bill Clancy who had qualified at the same time as Dermot but had gone on to specialize in personal injury law.

'Dermot, it's good to see you. Come on over and join us. I want to introduce you to some sharks.'

'Hello, Bill, it's been a long time, you look as fit as ever.'

'This is Charles Watson, Bernard Williams and Alan Costello. They make up the rest of your fourball; and I can tell you they are a shower of bandits, so watch out.'

They all laughed.

'We were just discussing your famous victory,' Alan said.

'Yes, it was one against the head all right,' Dermot replied, using a rugby parlance he knew these sporting types would understand.

'It certainly was. Alan was just wondering what sort of fees you got out of the case on legal aid.'

'I suppose it's probably worth about thirty grand, but I put a lot of work into it.'

'I am sure you did. Alan was saying he probably made five times that out of the administration of the estate.'

Dermot felt this was yet another swipe at him by high fliers who measured everything in terms of fee income rather than job satisfaction.

What he didn't understand was the reference to the administration of the estate.

He sat down beside Alan. 'It's a lovely day for golf, Dermot, there's a real touch of spring in the air.'

'At long last, it was a hard winter,' Dermot replied.

'We are paired together. What do you play off?'

'Sorry?' Dermot had been taken aback by the earlier comment and appeared distracted.

'What's your handicap?'

'I am a poor twenty-one. And you?'

'Nine.'

'That's impressive, maybe I can learn a little from you out on the course.'

Alan turned to speak to Charles, but Dermot interrupted him. 'Exactly what estate were you talking about, Alan?' he enquired, trying to make his interest seem casual.

'The one arising out of your case, of course. I thought you knew about it.'

'I didn't know you were handling that,' Dermot replied, the surprise in his voice thinly veiled.

'Yes, that's why Bill paired us today.' Alan looked at his watch. 'We had better make our way to the first tee.'

Bernard, Alan and Charles all drove off the tee with confidence and accuracy. Dermot took a few practice swings, closed his eyes, and hoped for the best.

'Good shot, partner!' Alan exclaimed, as Dermot's ball luckily flew off down the fairway.

They all wandered down the fairway. The smell of freshly cut grass filled the still morning air as Dermot and Alan headed towards the semi-rough on the right. Dermot was first to play. He took a seven iron from his bag.

'The estate must be a total mess, but it's worth well over four million with those icons,' Dermot said, and then took his shot.

'It was a total mess you mean.' Alan took his shot and nailed the ball to within a foot of the pin.

'What do you mean, *was*?'

'We wrapped it up quickly and the estate is closed, everything has been paid out, and my fees are in the bank,' Alan declared.

Dermot stopped in his tracks and stood staring at him. 'I hope you didn't pay out to the son. Although he was technically acquitted, he was still disinherited by the insanity verdict.'

'I know that. I got an opinion on that very point from John McBride SC.'

They waited for the other two to take their shots from the far side of the fairway and then walked on.

'I am relieved to hear it. So, who was the lucky beneficiary? The State, I suppose.'

'No, it was the niece; other than your client she was the only surviving heir to her aunt's estate.'

'What?' Dermot exclaimed.

'Her niece, Uliana Komarova,' Alan said in a hushed tone.

Dermot was stunned. He knew for a fact that Yuri was the sole surviving member of the family. What fraud had been perpetrated here? 'Please explain, Alan, I don't understand.'

'Mrs Komarova died without a will, so all of her estate automatically passed to her only surviving son. The other son, as you know, was killed in a fire along with his father, aunt and uncle.'

'But their daughter also died in the fire,' Dermot said firmly.

'No, she survived the fire and came here with her aunt and your client.'

Alan looked puzzled.

'Surely you know about her.'

'Go on,' Dermot demanded.

'Because there was a suspicion that the deaths might have been deliberate – your client's father was a top military man, you know, or maybe you didn't – all three of them were granted temporary residence here on compassionate grounds.'

'And?' Dermot couldn't believe what he was hearing.

'And the niece presented herself after the trial and made a claim on the estate.'

'You paid out without checking everything?' Dermot said accusingly, convinced that whoever this woman was she had made a false claim.

'Of course not, Dermot, everything was checked and found to be in order: birth certificates, marriage certificates, death certificates and the most important certificate of all, your client's certificate of conviction; it was all kosher, believe me. How did you not know this?'

Dermot looked away embarrassed as his mind raced.

'Are you OK, Dermot? You don't look too good.' Alan asked.

Dermot broke into a cold sweat and felt weak. Why hadn't Yuri told him about his cousin? Why had he lied to them about the icons? What the hell was going on?

Dermot stood on the edge of the green and waited for his playing partners to finish out the hole.

'Listen, guys, I'm really sorry, but I have to go. I forgot about an urgent meeting.'

They looked at Dermot and then at each other in bewilderment.

Dermot collected his clubs and hurried back towards the clubhouse. Reaching his car, he threw his golf bag into the boot and sped out the gates of the golf club, the tyres of his car skidding on the gravel driveway.

He picked up his mobile phone with an unsteady hand and dialled his office. 'Tracy, dig out the file on Yuri and get me an address for the O'Connors, you know, the couple who lived below Yuri. Also get onto the Chief State Solicitors Office and ask them for copies of all the personal papers belonging to his mother.'

'I will do it right away. What's up, Mr Molloy?'

'Just do as I say,' he snapped.

Dermot pulled into a lay-by and turned off the engine. He rubbed his eyes and let out an enormous sigh. What did all this mean?

Tracy rang him back a few minutes later. 'The O'Connors are now living in Greystones, number thirty-one, Meadow Crescent. I also rang the Chief State Solicitors Office and they have some personal letters and photographs. They are sending them over right away.'

Dermot drove furiously along the motorway towards Greystones, his thoughts hazy and confused. He fervently hoped that this was a fraud that had been perpetrated against the estate and had nothing to do with Yuri, but serious doubts were raised in his mind.

He arrived at the O'Connors' home, a small, neat bungalow with leaded windows and a tidy garden. He rang the doorbell and a frail, elderly woman answered the door.

'Hello, my name is Dermot Molloy. I'm sorry to disturb you.'

'Yes, how can I help you?'

'I am a solicitor,' he said, handing her his card, which the woman inspected closely with the aid of her spectacles.

'I acted on behalf of your neighbour in Sandymount, Yuri Komarov.'

The woman took a step back and closed the door slightly.

'It's OK, the case is finished. I don't mean to upset you in any way. I'm wondering if you could help me with a few matters; it will only take a couple of minutes.'

She looked at him again and he noticed her glance down at his feet. He was still wearing his golfing attire.

'I don't know,' she said suspiciously.

'Sorry about my clothes,' he said feeling a little foolish. 'I've just come from the golf course.'

A hand pulled back the door and a tall, thin, elderly man appeared behind the tiny woman. 'I am Michael O'Connor, and this is my wife, Barbara. Please come in.'

'Thanks I will.'

Dermot was brought into a small brightly decorated living room and was offered tea, which he declined. The couple sat together holding hands opposite him on a sofa.

'We read about the case in the papers,' the woman said.

'Yes, it got a lot of media coverage,' added her husband.

'Can you tell me anything about his mother?' Dermot asked.

'Oh, she was a nice woman, very educated, you know, and spoke good English too,' Mrs O'Connor said. Her husband nodded in agreement.

'Were you friendly with her?'

'Well, yes, of course we were. They were both very friendly people.'

'Did she ever discuss how she came to be in Ireland?'

'No, we never asked. It wasn't our business,' Mrs O'Connor replied.

'And what about Yuri?'

'He was a happy lad, always smiling and laughing. We thought he was a bit simple, you know. But he didn't speak any English, so we didn't know for sure.'

'Did they ever argue?'

'No, quite the opposite, they got on really well. He was very caring towards her and also to us; he used to collect coal for us in the winter. He was a decent lad. Who could have guessed?'

'Did they have any friends or visitors?'

'Only one, she was a pretty, dark-haired girl. She used to call about once a week and always late at night.'

'Do you know who she was?'

'She looked like she might be Russian, too. I thought she was related to them, because she had a key and used to let herself in. Michael thought she was Yuri's girlfriend, but I thought she looked too sophisticated for him.'

Mr O'Connor interjected, 'They were always fighting, you know, the girl and the mother. We often heard raised voices late at night and she would leave, slamming the door behind her. I don't think she ever left without slamming that bloody door; it drove us mad.'

'Did the mother ever mention what they were fighting over?'

'No, and we wouldn't ask. We just minded our own business.'

'Can you think of anything else that might help me?'

'No, that's really all we know about them.'

'You have been very helpful, thank you both very much.'

As they reached the hall door, Mrs O'Connor looked saddened. 'I never thought he would do such a thing to his mother. They were so close. Was he really asleep when he did it, Mr Molloy? It sounds incredible.'

'That's what the jury decided,' Dermot replied.

He sat back in his car and his mobile phone rang. It was Tracy.

'Mr Molloy, those letters have arrived, but they are in Russian.'

'Well, that's not much good to me.'

'Two of the envelopes are postmarked here in Dublin.'

'That's interesting.'

'Will I go on the internet and get them translated?'

'That's a great idea, Tracy. I will be back in the office in about an hour.'

Dermot then dialled Blair's number. He didn't really know how to break the news to him. 'Blair, it's Dermot. I need to see you urgently.'

'What's wrong?'

'I can't talk on the phone.'

Blair laughed at Dermot's paranoia.

'Can I call around this evening?'

'Is it urgent?'

'Very.'

'I am going out to dinner, Dermot. Could you meet me in the Shelbourne beforehand, say at seven?'

'That's great. See you then, Blair.'

As Dermot drove back towards his office, it started to rain heavily. He was trying to make sense of the developments. A niece, no one knew about except Yuri, runs off with all the money! And she fought regularly with the old dear. Why had this girl never come forward? Why had Yuri not told them about her? Is it possible that he was covering for her in some way? But what had she done? Had she killed the old lady? If she had, then why was he covering for her? None of it made any sense. If there was some innocent explanation, why had she not come to the trial? His thoughts galloped on. He frowned, remembering the dark-haired girl in the public gallery, who had waved over to Yuri and smiled at him. Could that have been her? Yuri said she had translated at one of the medical consultations in Dundrum. Was he lying?

On the way back to the office, Dermot called into Pearse Street Garda Station where he spoke to the sergeant in charge at the front desk.

'Is Barry about?'

'Sure, Mr Molloy, I'll get him straight away.'

Barry walked down the stairs from the detective's office and appeared surprised to see Dermot.

'Fancy a coffee, Barry?'

'Sure.'

They went to O'Neill's Bar on Pearse Street and sat down at a table near the window.

'You did a great job for Yuri, Dermot.'

'Thanks, we did everything we could.'

'No, really, I was delighted with the result. I knew that kid couldn't have been in his right mind when he did it.'

'I need a favour, Barry,' Dermot said, dismissing Barry's observation.

'Yeah, sure.'

'I need to know who phoned the guards on the morning the body was found.'

'Why do you want to know that?'

'Please don't ask questions, Barry. Do you know who made the call or not?'

'It was an anonymous call.'

'Was the caller male or female?'

'I don't know, but I can check it for you. Those calls are taped.'

'Have you any idea who it might have been?'

'No, it could have been the milkman, or someone out for an early morning stroll who heard the disturbance.'

'What disturbance, Barry?'

'Well, I'm sure the mother screamed out for help; you don't have to be Sherlock Holmes to deduce that.'

'What time was the call logged at?'

'I think around six forty-five in the morning, we responded pretty quickly to the disturbance.'

'What disturbance are you talking about then?'

'I told you.'

'No, Barry, that simply cannot be right.'

'What do you mean?'

'The time of death was before one o'clock in the morning at the latest.'

Barry sat back and scratched his head.

'I'd forgotten about that. Now you come to mention it, we wondered about that at the time, but guessed we struck it lucky.' He shrugged his shoulders. 'What's the point to all this?'

'I need to know who phoned the guards, and why.'

'What exactly are you driving at?'

'I don't know, but something's not right.'

'Dermot, are you suggesting someone else is in on this?'

'I can't say.'

Barry looked intensely at him. 'You obviously know something I don't; are you going to share it with me?'

Dermot stared blankly out the window at the heavy traffic for a few minutes, and then turned to Barry. 'Did you know there was another member of the family who survived the fire in Russia?'

'No, you've got that wrong, Yuri and his mother were the sole survivors.'

'Did you ever check it out?'

'There was no need; Yuri was caught red-handed, so there was no need to look any further into his background,' Barry said, defensively.

'Barry, there is a cousin, her name is Uliana Komarova and she surfaced after the trial and ran off with all the money.'

The astonishment on Barry's face was all too obvious. 'Christ, Dermot, you're not serious?'

'I'm very serious.'

Barry sat back and appeared deep in thought. Eventually he leant forward, hands resting on the table. 'Don't tell me this sleepwalking defence was a set-up.'

'I can't exclude that possibility.'

'And the bastard will be out in no time, to share the money no doubt,' Barry said angrily.

A look of anxiety crossed Dermot's face. 'He's still my client, so this is off the record – right?'

'No problem.'

Tracy scanned the first letter into the computer and e-mailed it to the translation service. It read as follows.

Dear Auntie
I am sorry for losing my head again last night but you must under-
stand how frustrated I am. I am under a lot of pressure to get the
icons. What I told you is the truth but you just won't believe me.
We are all in danger and you must hand them over now. I don't
want to go to court in this country to get them but you leave me no
choice. I am not joking I will do it. I don't want to go to court
because people might ask questions about where you got them. I
beg you to change your mind or at least give me my share.
Uliana

Tracy didn't understand the significance of the letter, but left it on Dermot's desk and went for a late lunch.

thirty-eight

Blair was waiting in the Horseshoe Bar wearing a dinner jacket and sipping a gin and tonic when Dermot came barrelling in.

'What will you have to drink, Dermot?'

'Whatever you're having, only make it a double.'

'What are you looking so worried about?' Blair asked.

'We have a problem, a really big problem,' Dermot replied, looking around the bar furtively.

The waiter arrived and Blair ordered the drinks.

'Are you going to let me in on the secret?' Blair asked.

'This is going to come as an enormous shock to you, and I don't really know how to tell you.'

'Just come to the point, and tell me what's up.'

Dermot took a deep breath. 'Our client isn't quite as stupid as we thought.'

'What the hell are you talking about?'

'I think they killed the old lady in cold blood.'

Blair raised an eyebrow and looked intently at him. 'Have you been drinking this evening, or what?'

'No, just listen to me, will you, there was another person in on the murder?'

Both men remained silent as the waiter returned with the drinks and placed them on the table. The word *murder* hung in the air. After the waiter departed, Blair leant forward in his chair. 'Dermot, will you stop beating around the bush and tell me what this is all about?'

'I have discovered that Yuri wasn't alone. He has a cousin who has been lurking in the background all along, and I believe she was in on the murder.'

'You're talking nonsense?'

Dermot looked curiously at Blair.

'Are you not surprised that he has a cousin?

'Shocked,' Blair replied sarcastically. 'Just get on with it will you.'

'The cousin – Uliana is her name – survived the fire in Russia, and came to Dublin with Yuri and Mrs Komarova, but didn't live with them. She called frequently to the house and had serious rows with her aunt about the icons. I believe she was under some sort of pressure, and needed the money badly.'

'This sounds crazy.' Blair observed, coldly.

Dermot, undaunted by Blair's apparent lack of interest, pressed on. 'A week before the murder, Uliana wrote to the old dear demanding she hand over the icons. She claimed their lives were in some sort of danger and threatened to go to court if the old lady didn't give them to her.'

Dermot took out a copy of the letter from his pocket and handed it over.

'That's a copy of the letter; Tracy got it translated on the internet. The translation may not be completely accurate, but the gist is pretty clear.'

Blair picked up the letter and examined it. After a minute he folded it carefully, and passed it back. 'What else is there?' he asked.

'What else do you want? I can't think of any explanation why Yuri didn't tell us about Uliana. And why didn't she come to court and support him? What was she hiding from?'

'Probably from suspicious folks like you,' Blair replied flippantly.

'This is serious, Blair; it gets worse.'

Dermot took another gulp from his gin and tonic, leant forward, and spoke in a hushed tone. 'The letter clearly reveals a motive for the murder.'

Blair shook his head defiantly. 'Dermot, this is all conjecture. We fought the case and got a really good result for your client. Why are you digging all this up now?'

'Because I think it's important – though you clearly are unimpressed, for whatever reason.'

Dermot sat back in his chair and faced sideways towards the bar.

'Come on, Dermot; don't be like that. It's not that I'm unimpressed. I just don't know where you're heading with all this. What are you trying to prove?'

Dermot sat forward in his seat and clasped his hands. 'Let's assume for the moment there was no theory about sleepwalking in this case at all.'

'All right,' Blair replied reluctantly.

'And let's suppose Uliana called around on the night of the killing, Yuri was drunk, and there was a heated argument about the icons. The old dear stubbornly refused to hand them over, and in a fit of rage Uliana, or Yuri, or perhaps both, stabbed her to death. Then Uliana panicked and left. Yuri, realizing what they had done, was overcome with grief and then finished off the bottle of bourbon, and fell asleep, only to be awoken in the morning by the guards.'

'All right, go on, what happened then?'

'He didn't know what to say to the guards, so he pretended to remember nothing, and in his naivety he hoped to get off.'

'That doesn't make any sense; the circumstantial evidence was overwhelming, he had no chance of getting off, and even a dimwit like him would have known that.'

'Well, then, suppose for a moment it was Uliana who stabbed the old dear. Yuri decided to cover for her and said nothing of her presence there that night, and decided to take all the blame on himself.'

'And why in heaven's name would he do that?'

'Because neither would get the icons if they were both in on it; if he took the blame, at least she would get them.'

'That's some theory!' Blair observed incredulously.

'There may be another explanation, if you have the time to bear me out.'

'Get on with it, Dermot, and leave out the sarcasm.'

'We were so preoccupied with the sleepwalking defence, we overlooked a whole load of relevant evidence and never even considered that someone else might have murdered her.'

'And neither did the gardai, Dermot. And I'll tell you why. Because there is absolutely no evidence that anyone else was there that night, and even your own client said he was alone with his mother.'

'That's the whole point, Blair. Can't you see, it was too simple, too neat and tidy.'

'So what did we miss, what did we overlook that was so vitally important?'

'Well, for starters, the guards relied on the fact that there was no evidence of a forced entry. I found out that Uliana had her own key and could have let herself in.'

'Go on, Dermot, and hurry up, will you?'

'Then there was the blood found by the guards on the wall in the hallway opposite Yuri's room.'

'I don't understand, it was Yuri's blood, wasn't it?'

'No, Blair, that's the point, the DNA expert didn't do a full profile on the samples because he was told by the guards that there were no surviving family members. The analysis simply showed that the sample was consistent with Yuri's blood – or that of a close relative. The close relative could be Uliana.'

'OK, I remember that.'

'And then there was the dried blood found under the old dear's fingernails. The same story: not the old lady's blood but consistent with Yuri's blood. Consistent with is not the same as saying that it was Yuri's blood, but we all understood it to be Yuri's because there was no other relative that we knew of.'

'Yes, Dermot, I do understand, I am not stupid,' Blair remarked impatiently. 'What I want to know is, where does all this get us?'

'I haven't finished. Yuri was medically examined in the garda station – do you remember the evidence?'

'No, but I'm sure you're going to remind me of it.'

'He had no injuries of any description, no scratches or grazes, absolutely nothing. So where did that blood come from, Blair? It must have come from the other close relative.'

Dermot waited to see Blair's reaction, but there was none. He continued, 'Then there was the hair under her nail too, same DNA profiling.'

'So that's him or her, isn't it? It's consistent with either of them.' Blair quickly undermined Dermot's theory.

Dermot shook his head. 'No, it has to be hers.'

'How in God's name do you arrive at that conclusion?'

Dermot reached inside his pocket and took out a mugshot of Yuri taken in the garda station on the morning of his arrest and placed it on the table. Blair picked up the photo and inspected it. He put it back on the table. 'I don't see anything.'

'That's the point; his head is almost completely shaved in that photograph. His hair had grown by the time of the trial, so nobody twigged that it couldn't have been his hair.'

Blair sat back in his seat, cushioned his chin in his hand, and looked at Dermot intently.

'So what's your theory, Holmes?'

'OK, and don't cut me short. Uliana was angry with her aunt because she desperately needed the icons. She fought continuously with the old lady, but she refused to give in. Uliana was in the habit of calling late at night and called on the night of the killing. Yuri was already in bed and was out for the count. Uliana had another row, but this time lost her temper. She then went to the lounge where she saw Yuri's knife in its pouch. In a rage she took out the knife, went back into the bedroom and stabbed her aunt. The old dear put up a struggle, clawing at Uliana and scratching her. She also pulled out some of her hair. When it was over, Uliana panicked and didn't know what to do. She decided to make it look as though Yuri had done it, so she took the bloodstained knife down to his bedroom, and dropped it on the floor beside his bed. He was still senseless. On the way down to the bedroom she brushed against the wall and deposited her own blood from a scratch on her arm or hand. She then fled the scene, turning off the lights as she went.'

'What then?'

'She didn't know what to do, so she lay doggo for a while. She was worried Yuri might come round, so she made an anonymous call and tipped off the guards. She knew Yuri was unaware that she had been there that night, so he couldn't implicate her.'

Dermot sat back in his chair proud of his reconstruction. Blair remained silent momentarily, apparently deep in thought. 'I never heard such nonsense!' Blair declared eventually.

Dermot was livid at the manner in which Blair had dismissed him, and his face turned a deep shade of purple. He felt a sudden surge of anger coupled with frustration. 'What's wrong with you, Armstrong? Are you so bloody proud that you can't admit your last great case may turn out to be a disaster? Is that it? Are you going to let your client suffer, because of your inflated ego?'

Blair stood up calmly. Dermot assumed he was leaving as he sauntered out to the foyer. He wanted to go after him to apologize, but didn't. Blair went to the reception desk and spoke for a short time on the phone. He then returned and sat in front of Dermot. He called the waiter and ordered two more drinks. The two men stared at each other, but remained silent.

'I'm sorry, Blair, I didn't mean that.'

'Forget it, Dermot. Now, what else has occurred to you that I should know about?'

'Well, Uliana must have visited Yuri in prison.'

'Why do you say that?' Blair asked.

'For whatever reason, he lied to us about her existence. That means she must have gone to see him after his arrest and discussed the whole thing. Maybe she convinced him to keep her out of the picture if she agreed to give him half the estate when the trial was over.'

'That would be pretty trusting on his part.'

'He has the mind of a twelve year old, don't forget.'

Again there was silence. 'So what do we do now?'

'What do you mean?'

'Shouldn't we go to the guards or something?'

'Are you mad?' Blair replied angrily. 'He's still our client. Whilst this theory of yours suggests he may not have been the actual killer, he has told so many lies along the way it would be reasonable to conclude that they were in on it together.'

'But at least we have to tell them that Uliana exists, and that she has made off with the money.'

Blair shook his head defiantly. 'No, Dermot, it's not your business.'

'Where's the harm to our client? He can't be tried again for murder?'

'That's right.'

'So if we can establish that Uliana did it, then surely the hospital order will be quashed?'

'Maybe, if it was straightforward, and if she came forward and confessed, but I can't see her doing that. If you dig up all this new stuff and it begins to look like they conspired together, what chance do you think there is that they will release him from the mental hospital? I can tell you – absolutely none. Yuri will not see the light of day for years.'

'Are you seriously telling me that we can't tell anyone what we know?'

'I'll get advice from the Professional Practices Committee, but I am pretty certain that not only are we under no obligation to tell the guards, but we would be prohibited from acting in any way that was to our client's detriment.'

Dermot leant forward in his seat and buried his head in his hands.

'What's wrong now?'

'It's too late, I already told Detective Sergeant Murphy about Uliana.'

'Oh, Christ, you didn't.'

There was another long silence.

'Don't worry, Dermot. They were bound to have found out anyway.'

'Do you think so?'

'Absolutely. Do you know where Uliana is now?'

'She's vanished, probably gone back to Russia.'

thirty-nine

Dermot was unable to sleep as he tossed around in his bed, his mind racing back and forth. Why had Blair been so dismissive of all his theories? He was right, of course, when he said that Yuri had lied to the guards from the very beginning and that this strongly suggested that, whatever charade was being played out, he had an interest in it. But was Yuri the actual killer? He mulled over the forensic evidence until he was confused. He got up at five, trying not to disturb Fidelma, and slipped quietly out of the house.

He sat bleary-eyed behind his desk, his heavy head cushioned in his hands. Despite Blair's advice, he picked up the phone, rang Barry, and arranged to meet him in Martha's coffee shop across the street from the garda station.

Dermot was tucking into a fry of bacon and eggs when Barry arrived.

'What's up, Barry? You look as bad as I feel.'

Barry slumped into the chair opposite Dermot, a worried look etched across his face. 'I slipped up badly on this one, Dermot.'

'What do you mean?'

'We took too many shortcuts and when all this comes out in the wash, heads will roll; unfortunately mine will be the first.'

'Look, Barry, everything I said to you yesterday was said in confidence. I told Mr Armstrong that I mentioned it to you and he nearly hit the roof; something about client confidentiality and all that.'

Barry didn't appear to be listening as he gazed out the window at the early morning traffic. After a long pause he turned to Dermot. 'You know I have to investigate what you told me. I'll say I found out from another source. I won't bring you into it in any way, and that's a promise.'

'I appreciate that; I don't want to be hauled before the Law Society.'

Barry's breakfast arrived and he also began to tuck in.

'I don't think Yuri was the killer,' Dermot declared.

Barry didn't answer immediately and appeared reluctant to hold a secret. 'It may be a bit more complex,' he replied eventually.

'What do you mean?'

'I made contact with the police in Rostov earlier this morning.'

'And?' Dermot enquired with interest.

'Yuri's father was indeed a top military man, but was also suspected of supplying arms to the Russian Mafia. The police over there believe he cheated on some deal he entered into with them. There was a major art theft at the Russian Museum in St Petersburg, which was linked to the Mafia. It was strongly rumoured at the time that Yuri's father had been paid with a number of valuable icons that were part of the haul. He supplied the Mafia with a large consignment of Kalashnikovs, and there was supposed to be a second consignment as part of the deal. The army became suspicious and Yuri's father was suspended pending a full investigation. He was unable to deliver the goods and when the Mafia came looking for the return of the icons, he foolishly held out. You don't double-cross those guys, Dermot; they're as ruthless as the Provos. Anyway, there was evidence that the house had been ransacked before it was torched. Colonel Komarov, Yuri's twin brother and his aunt and uncle were all killed in the fire. Yuri, his mother and Uliana vanished shortly afterwards, and the Russian police have been searching for them since. And so apparently have the Mafia. The Russian police had no idea they had travelled to Dublin. When I told them about the killing they immediately thought the Mafia had tracked them down and were behind it.'

Dermot sat back and rubbed his brow as he considered carefully what Barry had said.

'That doesn't make sense. It didn't bear the hallmarks of a hit.'

'My thoughts exactly,' Barry replied.

'But the Mafia may have been leaning on Uliana. She sent a letter to Mrs Komarova the week before the killing and it sounded fairly desperate. I believe she killed her and then framed Yuri. What I don't understand is, if he was innocent and knew nothing about what happened, why he lied to us.'

'Maybe he didn't,' Barry said, as though a thought had just flashed across his mind.

'What do you mean?'

'Maybe the quality of the translation during the interviews was poor. It might actually be that simple. Those translation agencies are unregulated; most of them use foreign students who are only part-timers. I doubt whether any of them are professionally qualified. We have had some dreadful experiences in the past with them.'

'Like what?'

'We had a case a few months ago that was thrown out of court. The defence challenged the confession on the basis that the interpreter had mistranslated what their client actually said whilst in custody. They got

183

a professional interpreter who checked the tapes of the interviews and it turned out over half of what was said had been mistranslated.'

'That sounds incredible. You think that might have happened here?'

'It's a possibility, but having said that, we used the same interpreter in a drugs case last summer and she seemed pretty good. Mind you, nothing was challenged in court, as the accused pleaded guilty.'

'Where can I check her qualifications?' Dermot said with enthusiasm.

'With the translation agency, Tenko Translators I think they're called.'

'I'll do that immediately. If you're right about this, it could explain a multitude.'

They parted company, and Dermot walked along the boardwalk that skirted the Liffey. He decided to ring Marina out of courtesy and ask her about her qualifications. She had been very helpful throughout, and he felt bad at having to drag her into all this. He also wanted to ask her where he could find the dark-haired woman who had been in court. He was now convinced that she was Uliana and he'd actually had a fleeting glance of the killer. If she had been under pressure from the Mafia, her life must have been hell. Where was she now? Was she even still alive?

Marina didn't answer her phone, so he left a message on her voicemail for her to contact him urgently.

forty

Blair walked to the Shelbourne, where he had arranged to meet Jenny. She was already there when he arrived, sitting in the sumptuous lounge sipping tea from delicate china and looking elegant in a cream silk trouser suit. She stood up and gave him a peck on the cheek. He sat down and ordered some coffee.

'Thanks for meeting me at such short notice, Jenny.'

'That's OK, but why the urgency?'

'Has Dermot been in contact with you yet?'

'No, should he have been?'

'He rang me yesterday with some mad theory that Yuri hadn't killed his mother after all.'

She laughed. 'How did he come up with that one?'

'He discovered that a relative made a claim on the estate.'

Jenny looked puzzled as she poured more tea. 'But I thought Yuri was the sole survivor.'

'That's the whole point; apparently there was a cousin lurking in the shadows and Dermot believes she could have murdered Yuri's mother.'

'That sounds pretty far-fetched.'

'That's exactly what it is, far-fetched, but Dermot seems determined to pursue his theory.'

Jenny appeared deep in thought. 'I wonder why Yuri didn't tell us about her.'

'I don't know, and to be honest, I don't care,' Blair said impatiently.

'But why does Dermot think that she was the killer?'

'He has some theory about her putting pressure on her aunt to sell the icons.'

'And is there any evidence of that?'

'A short letter written a couple of weeks before the murder. The letter's actually not that strong, but Dermot is making a big song and dance out of it.'

'Could he be right?'

Blair raised his hands in exasperation. 'I don't know, Jenny, and I don't give a toss. Yuri got a very good result, and if the authorities get wind of all this the whole thing will blow up and, when it does, Yuri will be kept in custody until it is resolved.'

Jenny frowned and appeared confused. 'But isn't it our duty to do something for him?'

'Christ, Jenny, you sound like bloody Dermot,' Blair said angrily.

'But if Dermot is right, what else can we do?'

'Jenny, Yuri lied to the guards and to us about the existence of his cousin and to my mind that means he must have been in on this all along. It doesn't matter whether he was the actual killer or not, he was part of the plan.'

Jenny thought for a moment. 'I suppose what you say makes sense.'

'There's no supposing about it. If it emerges that he was in on this, can you see the authorities letting him out of hospital?'

'Not for a good while anyway.'

'I firmly believe that we should let sleeping dogs lie.'

'Why are you telling me all this?' she asked.

'I am going on a long holiday, so will be away for some time. I know Dermot will start pestering you about it when I am away, and I wanted to discuss it with you before I go so we would both be on the same wavelength.'

Jenny laughed. 'So you want me to baby-sit him while you're away and keep him in check.'

'Yes, more or less. I think he's a loose cannon at the moment and I don't want him undoing all the good work we have done.'

'Don't worry, I'll look after Dermot. I have him wrapped around my little finger.'

'So I can rely on you?'

'Yes, of course you can. By the way, where are you off to on this holiday of yours?'

'Barbados; and I haven't bought a return ticket.'

'Where are you staying in case I need to contact you?'

'At the Royal Pavilion.'

'And who are you going with, or shouldn't I ask?'

'I'm going alone,' he answered emphatically.

Jenny couldn't hide her surprise.

'Why are you looking at me like that?' Blair asked defensively.

'Like what?'

'With that suspicious look on your face.'

'I'm just a little curious.'

'And why is that?'

'I thought you might have had a certain little someone to keep you company.'

'And where did you get that idea from?'

'A little birdie whispered in my ear.' She laughed.

Blair smiled. 'Well, the little birdie was very much mistaken.'

'A man like you should never be alone, it's a waste.'

Blair laughed. 'Are you flirting with me, Jenny?'

'Yes I am, and have been for years, but it never got me anywhere.'

He laughed again. 'You'll find someone a lot better than me, Jenny.'

She mustered a smile, gathered her belongings and left.

forty-one

Tenko Translations was situated in a small office above an immigration advice centre on Parnell Street. As Dermot pulled up in his Mercedes he saw a group of overweight Nigerian women wearing brightly coloured clothes talking energetically outside the centre. He climbed the narrow dingy stairs and straight ahead a sign declared the office to be that of Tenko Translations. He knocked on the door.

'Come in.'

Sitting behind a small desk was an attractive oriental woman, who appeared to be in her early thirties.

'How may I help you?'

'I am a solicitor. Dermot Molloy is my name.'

He handed her his card.

'Pleased to meet you. My name is Bushba. Are you looking for some referral business, Mr Molloy?'

'No, that's not why I'm here.'

'What is it then?'

'We used your translation firm in a case recently, Marina Petrovskaya was the translator.'

'Oh, yes, I remember – the Russian boy who killed his mother.'

'Yes, that's right. Anyway a difficulty has arisen and we think there may have been some problem with the quality of her translation work. I need to check Ms Petrovskaya's qualifications.'

Bushba let out a loud laugh.

'What's so funny?' Dermot said indignantly.

'Mr Molloy, I have a lot of interpreters on my books. Most of them are part-timers, some are students, and a lot of them are immigrants themselves. We get paid thirty euros an hour and we give ten to the interpreter. They do visits to garda stations at all hours of the day and night. They go to prisons, or spend all day down in the immigration tribunals. Most of them do their best, struggling with different dialects, but they're not perfect. It's not easy work, you know.'

'Are you seriously telling me that none of your staff are professionally qualified?'

'If they were, do you think they would be working here? They would be working for banks, or businesses with financial interests abroad.'

'But surely they must have some sort of qualifications?'

'No. If they have the basics and a good personality, that's OK by me. And it helps if they can bring some clients to my business.'

'Can you at least check on Marina's file and see if she has any sort of qualification?'

She shook her head defiantly. 'I have no files on my interpreters. Anyway, as I said, many of them are immigrants themselves and they don't pay tax. They never tell you the truth about who they are, or where they are from, and I don't ask. The best thing to do is to phone her yourself and ask her straight out what her qualifications are.'

'I have been trying to contact her, but she hasn't answered my calls. Do you know where she is?'

'I know she has exams coming up. She said she wouldn't be available for work because she was studying. That's probably why she has her phone switched off.'

'Have you at least got an address for her?'

'No, she usually collects her cheques here. Actually, I have one waiting for her from that case, so if you manage to contact her, tell her it's here, will you?'

'And if she calls, will you tell her to contact me? It's urgent.'

'I will of course, Mr Molloy.'

Dermot got up to leave, but stopped at the door. 'You have another Russian girl who works here – Elena, I think her name is?'

'Yes. Elena Koratova.'

'Where can I find her?'

'She doesn't work here anymore. She went back to Russia and I heard she left in a hurry.'

'I see. Can you tell me if she ever had any dealings with that murder case?'

Bushba opened a drawer, took out an invoice and glanced at it. 'Let me see ... I have all the claims for prison visits here.' She inspected the invoice closely. 'No, she didn't.'

'Are you sure? She might have gone to the Central Mental Hospital once or twice.'

'No, I have no record of that.'

Dermot thanked her for her help and left. He returned to his car and slumped into the driver's seat. Elena translating for Yuri at a medical consultation indeed. He was right, she killed the old dear and had been in court after all. But why had Yuri covered for her? He rang Tracy. 'There was a tape I left for you from a consultation I had with Mr Armstrong and Yuri before Christmas. Is there any chance you still have it?'

'I don't know, but I will check it out for you.'

'Good girl, drop everything and get on to it straight away, will you?'

'Yes, Mr Molloy, right away.'

Dermot recalled having dropped Marina off at a model agency in Wicklow Street after a prison visit. They might have her home address; it would be worth a try. He didn't like the idea of using her as the sacrificial lamb; but if it turned out she didn't have any qualifications as an interpreter, the Court of Criminal Appeal would probably overturn the conviction. He drove to Wicklow Street and parked his car then walked along the busy street until he came to a door he thought he recognized. A small plaque on the door declared the premises to be that of the Gloss Model Agency. He pushed open the heavy glass door and walked into a modern open-plan reception area. A pretty, red-haired receptionist sat behind a glass-covered reception desk.

'How may I help you?' the receptionist enquired, eyeing Dermot up and down. He didn't look much like a fashion guru, or, for that matter, a fashion follower.

'My name is Dermot Molloy, I'm a solicitor,' he said, handing the receptionist his card. 'I was hoping to talk to your boss.'

The receptionist took the card, looked at it and inspected Dermot again. 'I will just see if she is free. Take a seat.'

Dermot sat on a chrome and black leather sofa. A glass table in front of him was covered with fashion magazines. He looked down at his unpolished brown brogues resting on the white carpet and felt more than a little out of place. Picking up one of the magazines, he opened its glossy pages. He was conscious of the receptionist's gaze as he flicked through page after page of semi-naked young models. Fashion indeed, he thought, tasteful pornography was more like it. He replaced the magazine. He glanced around the reception area and saw that the walls were festooned with photographs of beautiful young girls who were presumably on the agency's books. He felt decidedly uncomfortable no matter where he looked. Taking out his mobile phone he paged through his phonebook.

'Can I say what it is in connection with, Mr Molloy?'

'Yes, I'm running an advertising campaign for our firm and I was hoping to find a suitable face.'

His explanation didn't sound at all convincing. He had thought about telling the truth, but couldn't see the agency giving Marina's address to a stranger coming in off the street. The receptionist grimaced, and muttered something into the phone.

'Mr Molloy, Miss Bannon will see you now, just go on up the stairs.'

'Thank you very much.'

Dermot reached the top of the stairs and found himself in an open-plan office. Seated behind a desk in front of a large window was a fresh-faced woman in her early forties. She was wearing a bright red dress and heavy gold jewellery. She gestured him into a chair. 'Mr Molloy, how can we help you?'

'Well,' he said nervously, 'I am the senior partner in a firm of solicitors and we're running an advertising campaign shortly.'

'So?'

'And I am sure you have just the girl we are looking for on your books,' he said cheerfully.

'Yes, I'm sure we do,' she said coldly. 'But I'm afraid we don't deal directly with customers. What advertising agency are you using?'

'We don't have one at the moment.'

'Then I'm sorry, I can't help you,' she said firmly.

'I don't want to look through your books or anything,' he replied defensively. 'I already know the girl we want: her name is Marina Petrovskaya.'

Ms Bannon cast a suspicious eye over him. 'You must have the wrong agency; we don't have any girl on our books by that name. And even if we did, we would still have to insist that you deal with us through an advertising agency.'

'Look, you don't understand,' Dermot said impatiently. 'This is very important.'

'I am sure it is, love, but I can't help you.'

'I need to know where I can contact her, that's all.'

Ms Bannon stood up and walked around the desk towards him. 'You wouldn't be the first man coming in here looking for details on one of our girls. We don't give out that information, and that's final. Now, I'm sorry, I must ask you to leave.'

'Please, you must understand, this is work,' Dermot protested.

'Leave now,' she replied flatly.

Dermot realized he was getting nowhere. 'Listen, Ms Bannon, I'm sorry for disturbing you and I understand your position. I will be honest with you. This girl worked for us as a translator in a big case and we need to contact her urgently. I'm sorry for lying to you, but it's a matter of great importance.'

'I still can't help you. As I said we have no girl on our books by that name; perhaps she works for some other agency.'

'I know she works here, I dropped her off here one day,' Dermot protested.

'There's a massage parlour next door, perhaps she works there,' she said as she ushered Dermot towards the top of the staircase.

He was making his apologies as he was leaving, but then stopped dead in his tracks. His eyes were drawn to a photo on the wall. 'That's her, that's Marina, only she has blonde hair now.'

'No, Mr Molloy that's not your girl.'

'It is her,' he protested. 'I would know Marina anywhere.'

Below the picture Dermot could make out some small lettering. He reached up and took the picture from the wall.

'Please, Mr Molloy, you must leave now,' Ms Bannon said firmly, but he ignored her.

He took his reading glasses out of his breast pocket and read the name and details: *Uliana Komarova, 19.5.1980, 5ft 11ins, 35.23.34.*

His heart began to pound and he put out his hand for something to support him. Ms Bannon, realizing that he was in shock, took him by the arm and guided him towards a chair. His ashen face was fixed on the picture, which he held in his trembling hand.

'Quick, Rebecca, bring me up some cold water,' she shouted down to the receptionist as the colour left Dermot's face. He loosened his tie and undid the top button of his shirt. He continued staring at the photograph and muttering to himself.

'It can't be! Oh, my God, it can't be.'

'Mr Molloy, are you OK? You look like you've seen a ghost.'

Dermot didn't reply. Rebecca brought a glass of water and handed it to him. Ms Bannon tried to take the photograph from his clutches, but he wouldn't release it.

'Shall I call for an ambulance?' she asked.

Dermot looked up at her. 'Are you sure this is the right name on this photograph?'

He knew the answer to his question.

'Yes, I have a copy of her work permit for the United States on her file. She was supposed to go there earlier this year.'

She went to a filing cabinet, took out a file and handed a photocopy of the girl's passport and work permit to Dermot. He inspected the photograph. It was Marina.

'She didn't go on that trip because of some stupid case she was trans-lating in, that must be the same case you're talking about.'

'Where is she now?' Dermot asked.

'I don't know, we haven't heard from her in weeks.'

There was a long, awkward silence. Eventually Dermot took a deep breath and dragged himself to his feet. He apologized to Ms Bannon, stumbled down the staircase and out onto the street. He took a few deep breaths of fresh air and tried to clear his head. His mobile rang and star-tled him. It was Barry.

'I need to know who contacted Tenko Translations on the morning of Yuri's arrest?' Dermot demanded.

'Why do you want to know that?'

'Just tell me,' Dermot said flatly.

'OK, hang on.'

Dermot could hear voices in the background, but couldn't make out what was said.

'The sergeant here says that nobody from the station officially contacted the agency; the translator arrived shortly after his arrest. But that's not unusual, Dermot, it's a competitive business, and they often get tipped off unofficially by someone involved in the case, or one of the officers at the station.'

'It may not be unusual, but it fits perfectly.'

'What fits?'

'Barry, brace yourself, Marina Petrovskaya is Uliana Komarova.'

There was silence on the other end of the phone.

'Are you there, Barry?'

'I'm here. Fuck, she's been controlling everything from the very beginning.'

'Yes Barry, you, us, the doctors – and, of course, Yuri.'

There was another long pause. Barry continued a little nervously, 'That's why she wanted all the tapes destroyed.'

'What?' Dermot exclaimed.

'Look, I can't go into it on the phone.'

'What do you mean, she wanted all the tapes destroyed? I thought they were destroyed accidentally.'

'I'll tell you later.' Barry hung up the phone abruptly.

Dermot sat in his car and rang Tracy. 'Tracy, any luck with that tape?'

There was a short silence. 'Mr Molloy, I'm really sorry; I never got around to transcribing it. It went straight out of my head.'

'That's what I was counting on, Tracy.'

'I'll stay late tonight and do it.'

'You still have the tape?'

'Yes.'

'I love you, Tracy. Don't touch the tape; I'll be there in thirty minutes.'

'Yes, Mr Molloy.'

'And get on to the Russian Department at Trinity College. I want the best translator they have, regardless of the cost.'

'Yes, I'll do it straight away, Mr Molloy.'

forty-two

Dermot returned to his office where Tracy handed him the tape. He placed it carefully into a brown envelope.

'I have cracked it, Tracy.'

'Cracked what?'

'I know who killed Mrs Komarova, and it wasn't Yuri.'

'Who was it?'

'Marina.'

Tracy started to laugh. 'You're joking, Mr Molloy, she was just the interpreter, why would she have killed her?'

Just then the phone rang and Tracy answered it. 'It's Detective Sergeant Murphy looking for you.'

Dermot grabbed the phone from her hand. 'Yes, Barry.'

'Dermot, I couldn't talk earlier. Some of our lads get backhanders from solicitors and translation agencies for referrals. I have checked with Pat, who was the station orderly on the morning Yuri was brought in, and he has assured me that he didn't contact Tenko Translations on the morning of Yuri's arrest. He has admitted to me that he got backhanders in the past, but he didn't on this occasion, and I believe him.'

'Tell me about the tapes, Barry.'

'I lied when I said they had been accidentally destroyed. During the third interview, there was an ugly scene. Ruth provoked Yuri quite deliberately and she shouldn't have done it. She reconstructed her idea of how he had stabbed his mother, and Yuri fell into the trap and physically attacked her. Yuri's loss of control would have done him no favours at the trial, and Ruth was in a lot of trouble, so I talked to Marina and suggested that she persuade Yuri to agree to the destruction of the tape, and we would forget what happened. I told her that the tapes were often scrutinized by defence lawyers for mistakes in translation. She spoke to Yuri and said he would agree, but only on condition that all the tapes were destroyed. I didn't attach any significance to it at the time, but I can see now she was covering her tracks.'

'I appreciate you telling me this.'

'And I understand that it will all have to come out in the wash if you are to get Yuri released.'

'It mightn't come to that.'

'What do you mean?'

'I have a tape of a consultation we had with Yuri and am getting it looked at. If we are right about all this, I reckon that tape will sink little Ms Petrovskaya, so keep your mouth shut for the moment.'

'Thanks, Dermot, I'll put my letter of resignation on hold.'

'I will ring you as soon as I have any news.'

How was Blair going to take all this? Dermot pondered. He, too, had fallen into Marina's web of deceit and had been used by her. By getting close to him she knew exactly every move the defence team were making, and she was more than happy to see the sleepwalking defence develop. In fact, she had probably fed the experts the material to back it up – just so long as nobody looked at the possibility that someone else might have done it. She even lied about the dark-haired woman in court having been at a consultation in Dundrum. Yuri obviously knew her because she was Uliana's friend.

forty-three

Dermot arrived at Blair's apartment slightly early. Blair answered the intercom and told him to come up. On entering the hall, Dermot saw three large Gucci suitcases bulging at the seams.

'Are you going on a trip, Blair?'

'Yes, I'm off to Barbados first thing in the morning for a well-deserved break.'

They went into the drawing room and Dermot sat down on a large sofa opposite Blair's favourite leather armchair. 'Whiskey, Dermot?' Blair said as he walked across to the drinks cabinet.

'Thanks, Blair, better make it a large one, and for both of us.'

'More earth-shattering theories?' Blair retorted.

'No, just facts; and they are disturbing ones at that.'

Blair poured the drinks into Waterford Crystal tumblers, handed one to Dermot, and sat down.

'Blair, prepare yourself for a shock.'

Blair took a sip of his whiskey and smiled. 'Fire away,' he said wistfully.

Dermot took a deep breath, hesitated, and shuffled nervously in his seat.

'Come on, Dermot, get on with it will you?'

Dermot took a gulp of his drink, and looked Blair squarely in the eye. 'Marina Petrovskaya and Uliana Komarova are one and the same person.'

His words echoed around the walls of the room until they eventually settled on Blair. He didn't say anything at first and showed no reaction. Slowly raising himself from his chair he walked to the drinks cabinet where he topped up his glass to the brim. He then returned to his seat, bringing the bottle with him and placed it on the small table beside his armchair. 'Go on,' he said in a low voice.

'Uliana was working for Tenko Translations under a false name, probably to avoid paying tax. She had been working with the agency for the last year, supplementing the money she made from modelling.'

'Are you sure about this, Dermot, or is it just another one of your theories?'

'Unfortunately, I am absolutely positive. I have all the evidence.'

He took out the photograph he had taken from the model agency and handed it over. Blair studied it for what seemed an eternity. Dermot thought he saw Blair's eyes moisten, and he wished he were somewhere else. Eventually Blair looked at him and, with sadness in his voice, said softly, 'I don't want to hear this, do I, Dermot?'

Dermot shook his head. 'No, and it's hard to tell you. She came here with Yuri and the old lady three years ago. She lived on her own and was working her way through college. There is a suggestion that the Russian Mafia tracked her down and might have been putting some pressure on her to return the icons.'

Blair appeared surprised. 'What have the Mafia got to do with all this?'

'Apparently her uncle had received the icons as a down payment on an arms shipment, but he never completed the deal. One way or another, she was desperate, and demanded that the old lady hand them over to her. They fought continually. On the night of the murder, Yuri went to bed drunk and fell asleep and, as I said before, she arrived late and, after a row, stabbed her aunt. She then planted the knife beside Yuri's bed. She knew he would be arrested because she tipped off the guards. Next, she decided to present herself at the garda station as the translator. She had been there before and the guards knew her, so there were no questions asked. Yuri spoke no English, and she knew she could control everything he was supposed to be saying, in order to deflect any suspicion from her. Yuri had no reason not to trust her and neither had the guards.'

Dermot paused and finished his drink. Blair handed over the bottle, and he poured another large one for himself. Blair appeared deep in thought.

'When the guards asked Yuri about his family, she told them that Yuri was the sole survivor. They had no reason to doubt this, and Yuri had no suspicion that she had mistranslated his answer. They also asked him questions about his mother's financial position, to try and establish a motive for her death. It's quite likely that Yuri told them the truth about the icons, but Marina didn't pass on the information, as she feared the guards might seize them. It's also likely that Yuri was protesting his innocence all along, but she made out that he had got drunk and remembered nothing. All the evidence pointed towards Yuri, and she was happy to keep it that way.'

Blair remained silent, his face stern, as though the full truth was slowly dawning on him. He got up and walked slowly over to the fireplace. He turned to Dermot.

'Don't stop.'

'If it's any consolation to you, Blair, I don't think she planned this from the start. I think it all spiralled out of control.'

Blair raised a dubious eyebrow. Dermot continued, 'She even brought me in on the case because I was a second-rate solicitor who wouldn't do much research. She also knew I was crazy about her and would insist that she be involved in the translation from beginning to end. This was important to her. She could never have another translator involved, as the cat would be out of the bag. She was at all the consultations listening to everything. She was even present when the psychiatrist and other experts were examining Yuri, and she fed them exactly what they wanted to hear. When she heard that sleepwalking was a possible defence, it suited her nicely. Yuri would be blamed, but wouldn't go to prison. Easy on her conscience – if the bitch has one, that is.'

Dermot looked up at Blair who was slouched against the mantelshelf. 'Blair, I don't understand how she knew what was relevant to the sleep-walking defence, but I have my suspicions.'

Blair looked away and returned to his chair. He sat in silence, his head bowed. Eventually he leaned forward placing his elbows on his knees and clasping his hands tightly together. 'Dermot, you realize this is pure conjecture on your part, don't you.'

Dermot stared at Blair in amazement. 'What do you mean, conjecture?'

'You have not a shred of evidence that Marina mistranslated a single word, either in the garda station or, for that matter, to us. You might be right, but you have absolutely no evidence to back up your theory.'

Dermot could see that Blair was in denial and understood why. He decided to press on.

'That's where you're wrong, Blair.'

He pulled a brown envelope out of the breast pocket of his jacket, took out a small tape and placed it on the table. Blair glanced at it. 'What's that?' he enquired.

'I used a dictaphone at the first consultation you attended. I have the whole conversation on tape, and if I'm right it holds the key that will release Yuri from his nightmare.'

'What do you propose to do with it?'

'I hope you don't mind, I asked Professor Urigov, who is head of the Russian Department at Trinity College, to call here tonight to check the translation.'

'That's fine by me. Where is Marina now?'

'She's vanished without a trace, fled the country no doubt.'

Blair poured them both another drink with an unsteady hand. 'It sounds unbelievable, Dermot, almost far-fetched.'

'I know; from the moment she killed the old dear, she has manipulated everybody – the police, the doctors, me, Yuri and, especially you.'

Blair raised an eyebrow. 'And what do you mean by that?'

'Come on, Blair. I know you were seeing her; so did Jenny. She reckoned Marina had a crush on you, but it looks like she was just pumping you for information. Did you give it to her?'

Just then the intercom sounded, it was Professor Urigov. Blair raised his head. 'Let's see what's on the tape first.'

Professor Urigov entered the room. He was a short, stocky man with a grizzled beard, wearing a loose-fitting tweed suit. Dermot greeted him in the hallway and led him into the drawing room. Blair was leaning against the fireplace.

'Thank you very much for coming at such short notice, Professor, this is Blair Armstrong.'

'I know Mr Armstrong well,' the professor replied.

Blair nodded to him, but didn't speak.

'We need you to test the accuracy of some translation; it's a matter of great importance. I have the tape here and will play it for you.'

The professor took out a notebook and pencil and sat down.

'Can we offer you a drink, Professor?' Blair asked.

'Yes, vodka with ice.'

Dermot took a dictaphone machine from his briefcase and placed it on the table. He inserted the tape and pushed the play button. As they listened to the tape Blair watched the professor with interest. The professor's face, within the vivid circle of the lamplight, was unquestionably that of an old man. He listened with a slow and exaggerated precision to the tape and scribbled some notes in his notebook.

'My name is Blair Armstrong, did we keep you waiting?'

The tape continued. The professor gently nodded in obvious approval at the translation. Dermot was perched on the edge of the sofa, his hands steepled as though in prayer, watching the professor's reactions with interest. After a few minutes, the professor abruptly stopped the tape, removed his glasses and looked at his expectant hosts.

'Gentlemen, I am pleased to inform you that your translator is first class. Not a word wrong, she even has the dialect. Usually there are some errors in translation, but she is one of the best I have heard.'

Blair smiled. 'So much for your theories, Dermot,' he said triumphantly.

Dermot looked puzzled. He stood up and walked aimlessly around the room with his head down, his hand furiously rubbing his chin. 'No, I want the professor to listen to the whole tape,' he protested.

'What's the point? You got it wrong, Dermot. Have another whiskey and let the professor go on his way.'

Dermot brushed aside Blair's observation. 'No! Please go on, Professor, it was a short consultation.'

The professor looked from Dermot to Blair wondering who would win the debate. He glanced at his empty glass, which Dermot quickly replenished. 'Very well, if you insist.'

He took a swig of his vodka and resumed making notes as the tape continued to play.

'And family – have you any living here?'

'No, my mother and I moved here three years ago from Rostov.'

Professor Urigov frowned. 'Stop the tape, please, replay that portion.' Dermot replayed it.

'This is very strange, her translation was perfect up to this point. May I translate what was actually said? "And family, besides Uliana, are there any living here?" He answers, "No, we all moved here from Rostov three years ago." He then speaks to the interpreter. "Uliana, have you not told them all this already?" She replies, "Yes, but they want to hear it from you." And then it goes on, "Sorry, did I understand you to say there were no other surviving members of your family besides Uliana?" And he says, "Yes, that's right."

'Then the next question is, "Had your mother money that you hoped to inherit?" and he replies, "My mother had the icons that Uliana has already told you about, and a small amount of money in the bank." The professor stopped the tape. 'Gentlemen, as you can hear, this is not an incompetent translation, but a deliberate misrepresentation of what was said by the interviewers and by the young man.'

'Is there a possibility that she herself may simply have misunderstood the questions?' Blair asked.

The professor removed his glasses and rubbed his eyes. He then slowly shook his head. 'I have no idea why this woman did this, but she has deliberately altered the questions that were asked and also the replies that were given. I am afraid it is a fraud, plain and simple.'

'Professor,' said Dermot, 'I will send you a copy of the entire tape, and I would be obliged if you would do a report on every word of the translation.'

'Certainly.'

The professor took his cue and left, thanking them for the excellent vodka. Blair sat back into his seat and an eerie silence engulfed the room. The crackling fire drew both men's gaze to it. Dermot glanced across at Blair who seemed mesmerized by its riotously dancing flames. Dermot was slow to speak but then hesitantly broke the silence.

'So, where do we go from here?'

Blair didn't answer immediately and continued to stare at the fire. The man, once strong as a statue, was crumpled in his chair. He then spoke slowly, but deliberately. 'You had better notify the DPP and get Jenny to draft an affidavit for the Court of Criminal Appeal. On this evidence they will release your client, pending the hearing of the full appeal.'

'Blair, I'm really sorry.'

Blair turned slowly in his chair and faced him. His sad brown eyes engaged those of his old friend. 'Why should you be sorry?'

'Because I brought you into all this in the first place, me and my stupid sleepwalking theory; it's my fault.'

'You're not to blame for my blindness.'

There was a long silence as Dermot fumbled for words of consolation, but found none.

'It was some deception though; she was a clever bitch, wasn't she?'

Blair seemed distracted and didn't immediately answer. 'Yes, well, you win some, you lose some,' he muttered.

'We haven't lost, Blair; Yuri will be free, and it's still a victory of sorts.'

Blair stood up and walked to the mantelpiece. He studied the photograph of Marina, which was in his hand, then angrily crumpled it into a ball and tossed it into the fire.

Dermot left Blair alone to his thoughts. He got into his Mercedes and let out an enormous sigh of relief. It was all over.

forty-four

Blair settled into his luxurious seat as the Jumbo jet roared into a clear blue sky. An attractive blonde-haired air hostess wearing a well-tailored green uniform served him a glass of champagne with a warm and friendly smile. He put on a pair of earphones and, listening to Dean Martin crooning *Amore*, he reclined his seat and closed his eyes.

His thoughts were of Marina, and how she had simply vanished after the trial. He had phoned her continually for a week, but when she failed to return any of his calls, he gave up. As time passed the memories of their short time together became more vivid. He re-enacted over and over again the evenings spent together and she became lovelier than she ever really was. At first she visited him only in his dreams. Then she was everywhere. He could hear her in the mornings cooking breakfast. In the evenings she sat opposite him on the settee flicking through magazines. He had taken to walking O'Connell Street during the afternoons where he caught a glimpse of her in the faces of other young foreign women. When his phone rang he prayed it was her, but it never was. How he longed to touch her soft skin again. To talk to her about life and watch her earnest young face latch onto his every word.

Then one day he declared to his housekeeper that he was unwell and wouldn't leave the apartment. He drank heavily and often. He knew deep down that this moment was fated, but it had arrived far sooner than he predicted.

After a while Marina left his dreams. She still appeared from time to time around the apartment, but when he heard her voice it had become harsh. Her footsteps were clumsy; her face once beautiful, became twisted and her pale eyes, soulless. He began to doubt everything she had ever said and became convinced she used him from the beginning. His hurt turned to anger and soon he became consumed with a burning hatred.

But he still had some nagging doubts that he clung to. Why had she confided in him her darkest secret? Why had she made love to him so passionately on the eve of the trial? It made no sense as his usefulness by then was surely spent. Was she really just a cold-hearted bitch without any emotions, or did she really care for him? Despite his growing hatred for her, he hoped that the closeness had been real; that the times they spent together had meaning. But at other times he felt he was merely clutching at straws. Day and night, the debate raged in his mind, but he was no nearer a verdict.

Darkness had fallen by the time Blair arrived at the stylish Royal Pavilion Hotel in St James on the east coast of Barbados. His luggage was brought up to his suite. Feeling tired after the long flight, he headed straight to the elegant bar overlooking the Caribbean Sea. The spacious bar, which had a high vaulted ceiling with Moorish columns and exotic plants, had a colonial feel to it. A pianist, sitting at a grand piano tucked away in a corner, was playing soft music that seemed in tune with the sound of the waves gently lapping the white sandy beach only yards away. Blair sauntered over to a glass-topped cane table on the wooden veranda overlooking the beach. A full moon made brief, but spectacular appearances, from behind black thunderous clouds. It was a sultry night, with the smell of rain hanging in the air. A waiter wearing a crisp white uniform approached the table, exchanged pleasantries about the weather and took Blair's order. He returned shortly afterwards with the drink. Blair took a Cuban cigar from the breast pocket of his blue linen jacket and lit it. He turned and looked around the bar. A few elegantly dressed couples were sipping cocktails, waiting to be shown to their tables in the impressive dining room. A pale-faced, bald-headed man in a white three-piece suit was sitting alone a few tables away from Blair, and was staring at him. Blair smiled at the man, who looked back with unfriendly eyes. Blair ignored the rebuff and settled into his wicker chair and looked out at the glistening sea.

Suddenly the shadow of a figure moved across his table. He looked up. Marina, wearing a long cream linen dress and gold flat sandals was looking down at him, her soft blonde hair blowing gently in the warm breeze. She beamed at him as he rose to his feet.

'Hello, stranger,' she said, as she wrapped her arms around him and kissed him on the cheek.

Blair held her softly and slightly at a distance. 'Hello,' he answered coolly.

She sat down opposite him at the table and her eyes, dancing in the light of the lone flickering candle in the centre of the table, engaged his. She looked bronzed and healthy.

'Would you like something to drink?' he asked.

'No I'm OK,' she said, brushing aside the distraction. 'It's great to see you, Blair.'

'And you,' he said, but quickly looked away from her.

'I have missed you.'

'Sure you have.'

She sat upright in her chair, placed her elbows on the table and rested her chin on her hand. 'Why the sarcastic tone? What's the matter with you? I thought you would be happy to see me.'

Blair leant forward, looked deep into her pale-grey eyes and hesitated before answering. Then his eyes narrowed. 'What the hell is all this about, Marina? Why did you ring me out of the blue last week and ask me to meet you here in Barbados?'

'Because I needed to see you.'

He let out a half laugh. 'Just like that?'

'Yes, what's wrong?'

Blair sat back drawing heavily on his cigar. 'Where did you vanish to after the trial?' he asked.

'I had to go back to Russia.'

'Why?'

'Because a friend of mine was in trouble and needed my help.'

'Why didn't you ring me and tell me you were going?'

She smiled. 'Look, Blair, don't be so sensitive. What does it matter? We are here now and that's all that counts.'

Blair looked at her angrily. 'It matters to me. Why didn't you answer my phone calls?'

She sat back in her chair and folded her arms across her breasts.

'I told you, I went to Russia.'

'Without even so much as a goodbye?'

'Look, Blair, you don't own me; I'm not some child who has to account for my actions. I felt like going back to Russia and I went. I didn't need your permission, did I?' she said flatly.

'No, you didn't need my permission, but after all we had been through, you might have had the courtesy to let me know you were leaving.'

'Courtesy!' She threw her head back and laughed. 'You should know by now we Russians have no manners.'

'So why did you want to meet me here, of all places?'

'I was here doing a fashion shoot for an agency in Moscow, and I thought it would be a cool place to meet up, that's all. I wasn't sure you would come.'

'You knew you had me wrapped around your little finger, and I would be on the next flight.'

A sheepish grin crossed her face. 'OK, I was ninety per cent sure you would come.'

'What other reason had you for asking me to come?'

'Just forget it. Let's go up to the room and have some champagne to celebrate.'

Blair let out a raucous laugh. 'Celebrate what?'

'Your great victory in getting Yuri off.'

Blair knocked back his drink and they headed out into the marble-floored lobby. As they strolled towards the lift, Blair noticed the bald man sitting on his own, watching them.

'Mr Armstrong there is an urgent message for you,' the porter called after Blair.

'Yes.'

'A Mr Molloy rang from Dublin and asked that you contact him as a matter of some urgency.'

Blair glanced at his watch. 'Thank you. I will do it first thing in the morning. Good night.'

'Good night, sir.'

The suite was minimally but tastefully furnished, with a taupe-coloured polished stone floor, white furnishings and dark mahogany shuttered doors that led to a large balcony. Blair walked straight into the bedroom, which was similarly furnished, but with a lavish gold canopy over the mahogany framed bed. His three Gucci cases were sitting beside Marina's two canvas bags in the corner of the room. He went into the stone and marble bathroom, undressed and showered. Putting on a white bathrobe, he returned to the living area. Marina was sitting outside at a table sipping a glass of champagne. Blair sat down opposite her, took the bottle of Moët from the silver champagne bucket and poured himself a glass. Marina looked at him and raised her glass.

'Cheers.'

'Cheers,' he replied coolly.

'It's beautiful here, isn't it?'

Blair didn't answer, but regarded her closely. She looked uneasy and shifted nervously in her chair. 'Why are you looking at me like that? You're making me feel uncomfortable.'

There was a long silence.

'I want you to tell me the truth.'

'I told you already; I went to Russia to help out a friend. I don't want to—'

He cut her short. 'No, I want you to tell me the whole truth, no more lies.'

'That is the truth, now let's enjoy ourselves.'

She moved towards him, but he raised his hand and gestured her back.

'No, I need to know the truth.'

'That's the truth,' she snapped.

Blair stood up and looked out towards the sea, with his back to her.

The continual sound of crickets and the odd frog croaking filled the night air as the tension between them grew.

'What's wrong with you, Blair? Why are you acting all paranoid?'

There was a long silence, which Blair eventually broke. 'Where are the icons?'

Marina didn't answer him. He turned around and faced her directly. 'I asked you a question,' he said firmly.

'What the hell are you talking about?' she replied angrily.

Blair sat down opposite her and searched her eyes. 'I know the truth.'

'What are you talking about? You're mad,' she said, turning away from his piercing gaze.

He stood up again and looked down at her menacingly. 'If you don't tell me the whole truth, I'm leaving now.'

'Look, I don't know what you're talking about.'

Blair turned his back to her and looked out at the blackness. 'Dermot went to your model agency looking for you after the trial and found out all about you. I know you are Yuri's cousin, Uliana Komarova.'

A look of horror crossed her face and she buried her head in her hands. She then started to sob, but Blair did nothing to comfort her and seemed unimpressed by her emotional outburst. Eventually after what seemed an eternity she wiped the tears from her eyes and looked up at him. 'OK, do you want the whole truth?' she asked, her voice trembling.

'Yes, I do,' he replied sternly as he sat opposite her. 'And no more lies.'

She took a deep breath. 'OK, I am Yuri's cousin, in fact, he is more like a brother to me. We came to Dublin three years ago with my aunt Anna. My mother and father were killed in the fire in Russia and she and Yuri were all that was left of our family. Yuri's father had broken some deal he made with the Russian Mafia. Those bastards killed my parents.'

She started to cry again, her body shaking with emotion and anger.

'Go on,' Blair said coldly, seemingly impervious to her theatrics.

'From the very beginning I begged my aunt to return those fucking icons to the Mafia, but she refused and locked them away in the bank. I was only twenty-one when we came to Dublin, and got a job working with a translation agency. I knew I would be working with Russians, so I had to use a false name. I was terrified those bastards would eventually track us down. Anyway I lived on my own and went to college. I was doing OK for a while, working nights in a bar, and I met this guy, he was a photographer, and he asked me to go to a model agency for an interview, which I did. They put me on their books, and I had to give my right name, because I needed to travel a lot and had to have a passport. They were the only people who knew who I really was. I never got on with my aunt, but I used to take Yuri out now and again, and one night I stupidly took him to a Russian party. Elena was there, and some other translators from the agency. Anyway, he got drunk and ended up blurting out my real name. I hoped no one noticed, but there were a lot of ears listening. Last September, two Russian guys arrived to my flat. They were animals and threatened if I didn't give them the icons they would break my legs. I went to my aunt and told her what happened. She accused me of making the whole story up just so I could get my greedy hands on them. I begged her for my share so that I could at least buy back my own life, but she wouldn't give in.'

She looked at Blair, tears rolling down her cheeks.

'Blair, I was terrified of those guys – please believe me. They called again two weeks later and this time threatened to kill me.'

Blair looked at her, still seemingly unimpressed. 'Tell me what happened on the night of the killing.'

'The same two guys called around to my flat in Rathmines that evening. They had found out where my aunt and Yuri lived, and threatened me again, but this time they said they would kill them too. When they left I went straight round to my aunt. It was around half past eleven and I let myself in. I went down to Yuri's bedroom, and intended to tell him what had happened and warn him that we were all in danger. But he was out of it on drink or drugs, and I couldn't wake him. I then went to my aunt's room. She was still awake, reading a book. I told her what happened and she called me a lying bitch. I couldn't believe that she wouldn't listen to me and we had a very bad argument. I lost my head and called her names and she called me a slut. I didn't know what to do. We were roaring and shouting at each other. I eventually went into the living room to get a drink and saw Yuri's knife lying on the table. I went back into her bedroom with the knife.'

Marina started to cry again, but after a few minutes composed herself.

'Blair, I promise, I only wanted to frighten her. I went over to her bed and threatened her with the knife. She called me a slut again, and I didn't know what she was talking about. I told her to stop calling me a slut, and then she said it.'

Marina bowed her head and wiped tears from her eyes.

'What did she say?' Blair asked.

Marina lifted her head and, brushing her hair from her face, she looked at Blair through tearful eyes. 'She accused me of seducing my father and nearly destroying her sister's marriage. I couldn't believe it, after everything that happened to me when I was a child; she was telling me it was my fault. She was blaming me for everything. Then all of a sudden I saw my mother's face looking at me and all those horrible memories came flooding back. I lost control of myself and stabbed her. I didn't want to kill her, but I couldn't stop myself. She kept screaming and roaring that I was a slut and I kept stabbing her. All I wanted was to shut her up, to stop her blaming me. Then she fell back on the bed and everything went quiet, she just lay there.'

Marina was sobbing as she continued her story. 'I sat on the floor of the bedroom with the knife in my hand and cried my heart out. I couldn't believe what had happened and didn't know what to do. The whole thing was like a nightmare. Then I went down to Yuri to tell him, but he was still out cold. I sat in the living room for ages just crying and crying, thinking of all those people who had died because of those stupid icons.'

'Why did you decide to frame Yuri?' Blair asked coldly.

She looked at him, tears still streaming down her cheeks. 'You must understand that Yuri is like a child and his mother did everything for him. He could never have survived on his own without her, let alone deal with the Mafia. They would have killed him for sure and I knew that. I came up with the idea of planting the knife in his bedroom and making it look like he'd done it. Then I decided to call the police and get him arrested.'

'But why?'

'It might sound crazy, but I honestly believed prison was the safest place for him right then. At least they would look after him if anything ever happened to me. I was only going to leave him there long enough to return the icons and get those bastards off our backs. So I called the guards and went to the garda station myself. You seem to know what happened after that.'

'I don't understand how you could leave him in prison for so long.'

'I was eventually going to tell the truth, but I kept putting it off,' she protested. 'And then I met you.'

'What have I got to do with it?'

'For some strange reason I trusted you from the moment we first met. I rang you the next day to meet you so I could tell you the whole story.'

Blair raised a dubious eyebrow. 'And why didn't you?'

'I know you won't believe this, but I fell in love with you. When you told me about the sleepwalking defence the next day at lunch, it seemed an easy way out for me. I would get the icons and return them to the Mafia and Yuri would be out of prison.'

'That was a dreadful gamble, what if Yuri lost the case?'

'I knew you would pull it off. And you gave me most of the ammunition for the doctors anyway. If it didn't work, I could have come clean and told the truth.'

'Where are the icons now?'

Marina looked at Blair and then towards the bedroom. 'They are in my bags.'

Blair sighed. 'If you were as terrified as you claim, why didn't you return them to the Mafia?'

'I wasn't thinking straight. After all that had happened, I decided to hold on to them. It was a mistake because those guys will never give up.'

Blair sat back in his chair and looked at her quizzically. 'Is that the real reason you wanted to meet me?' he asked.

She frowned. 'I don't understand, what do you mean?'

'Did you hope I could help you sell them?'

'That's not true,' she replied indignantly.

'And when were you going to tell me the truth?'

She lowered her head and appeared deep in thought. 'I wanted to tell you all along, but I was afraid that you would think I was a bad person. I tried to tell you the night before your closing speech, but you wouldn't listen to me.'

There was a long pause. He recalled how he had indeed cut her short that night, maybe she was telling him the truth, he thought.

'Blair, I have told you the whole truth, do you believe me?'

He shrugged his shoulders. 'What difference does it make whether I believe you or not?'

She started to sob again. 'You're the only person I have in the whole world and I need to know you don't think I planned all this. Please tell me you believe me, I beg you.'

Blair stood up and took her in his arms and drew her close. She broke down completely.

'It's OK, Marina, I believe you,' he said brushing her soft hair from her face.

She looked up at him. 'Do you really mean that?'

'Yes, now sit down and have a drink.'

He poured her champagne. She expected him to sit beside her, but he sat opposite her with what she thought was a grin on his face.

'Why are you looking at me like that?' she asked.

'Like what?'

'Like you don't seem to care.'

'Of course I care.'

She shook her head. 'No, you don't. I can tell from the look on your face that you don't love me any more.'

Blair laughed. 'That's crazy, of course I love you.'

'You think I murdered her in cold blood, don't you?'

'That's nonsense, Marina.'

She stood up and walked nervously around the balcony looking for words and eventually sat back down opposite him, tears in her eyes. 'Blair, things can never be the same between us, can they? The strings are broken.'

He remained silent, with his head bowed, unable to look at her. 'Maybe a few strings are broken but they can be fixed,' he said, in a low voice.

She became agitated, leant across and grabbed his hand with hers. She dug her long nails into his palm and pulled his hand from his face. She looked deep into his eyes.

'Do you hate me, Blair?'

'Why would I hate you?'

'Because I'm a cold, heartless killer.'

He shook his head. 'I don't see it that way.'

'Yes, you do. Ever since you found out from Dermot that I killed her, you have hated me.'

'No, you're completely wrong.'

'And all those special moments we spent together are history and mean nothing to you. I am just a murderer in your eyes.'

'No, I still love you.'

'Fuck you,' she screamed as she turned and stormed towards the bedroom.

'*Ya vso pro tebya znaya s samovo nachala.*' He called out in Russian after her.

His words pierced the evening air and were followed by an eerie silence. Even the crickets and other night creatures seemed to take an intermission from their evening cacophony. She stopped dead in her tracks and stood in silence. Then she turned, and walked slowly back to where he sat. She stood over him with hands on hips, a look of absolute astonishment on her face.

'What did you say to me?' She asked with utter disbelief in her voice.

'*Ya vso pro tebya znaya s samovo nachala,*' he replied.

She slumped down into the chair opposite her. 'You knew about me from the very beginning.'

'That's what I just said, isn't it?'

Her shoulders dropped as she looked at him in amazement. 'You speak Russian.'

'Fluently, I even gave a lecture to the Society of State Prosecutors in Moscow last summer on Ethics and the Criminal Law,' he replied.

Her mind was racing as she buried her head in her hands and rubbed her fingers violently through her hair.

'But I don't understand, why didn't you tell me you spoke Russian before?'

'Because you didn't need to know,' he replied dismissively.

'What do you mean, I didn't need to know?' she roared.

She poured herself a drink and knocked it back in one go. 'So, how long have you known about my secret?'

'From the first consultation with Yuri.'

'I don't believe you.'

'I am telling the truth. Do you not remember at the consultation when

I was asking Yuri about his family history I asked you to make sure that your translation was correct?'

'No, I don't remember that.'

'I knew at that point there was something very strange going on.'

'But why didn't you say anything?'

'Come on, what could I say? Call you a liar in front of Dermot?'

'But if you knew I was deliberately mistranslating what Yuri was saying, you must have known I was involved in the murder.'

'To be honest, all I knew for certain was that your real name was Uliana, that you were really Yuri's cousin and for some strange reason you didn't want us to know that. And, of course, I also knew about the icons, though I had no idea they were so valuable.'

Marina appeared mystified. She got up and walked aimlessly around the balcony. She eventually stopped and looked down at him. Her eyes were burning as she tossed her blonde hair off her face. 'When we met for lunch the next day, why didn't you say anything then?' she demanded.

'I didn't know for certain what you were up to, but the more we talked, the more my suspicions were confirmed. I remember you quickly changed the subject when I touched on how lonely Yuri must be in prison, as though I touched a nerve.'

'And you played along with my little game,' she said in disbelief.

'I suppose I did.'

'And that's why you never asked me about my past.'

'Yes.'

'You deliberately told me what to say to the doctors on Yuri's behalf to back up his case, didn't you?'

Blair thought for a moment. 'Yes, I hoped what I was telling you would filter through to the experts.'

She sat back down opposite him, but remained silent as she looked at him across the table. The man she saw was a stranger to her.

'And all those moments we shared together – it was all lies, just a game for you.'

'No, it wasn't like that,' he protested.

'You were only playing with me.'

Sensing the mounting tension Blair leant forward and grasped both her hands in his.

'You have it all wrong, Marina. I was in love with you and protected you all along.'

She pulled away from him. 'What do you mean, protected me?'

'I knew that you must have been the one who called the guards, and a great deal of the circumstantial evidence pointed to someone else being involved in the killing, but I managed to steer Dermot and Jenny away from it. That's why I concentrated on the sleepwalking defence to the exclusion of everything else. I even went to Mr McNamara in advance of the trial and told him the facts were effectively admitted, so that he wouldn't advise a more thorough investigation into the crime.'

Marina stared at him in astonishment.

'When Dermot rang me with the disastrous news that the guards had unearthed the icons, he wanted me to go to the prison and confront Yuri with his lies.'

'And?'

'I felt that your cover would probably be blown, since the only topic at the consultation would have been why he had lied to us. And even allowing for the skills you had already displayed, I couldn't see how you could dance your way around that.'

She sat back in her chair with her arms folded across her breasts. 'What else did you do?'

'After the trial, when Dermot came to me having discovered that a cousin had appeared and run off with all the money, I tried my best to bat him off. I even created an ethical problem about client confidentiality and told him not to go to the guards with the new information. Unfortunately it was too late as he had already told Detective Sergeant Murphy. Even after he discovered your true identity when he visited the model agency, I still stuck by you. If it hadn't been for that bloody tape of the consultation you would have got away with it.'

'But why, Blair, why did you do all that for me?' she said her tone laden with sarcasm.

'Because I was crazy about you.'

Her body shook with rage. 'And what about your client, what about Yuri?'

Blair pulled back, startled by her aggression. 'I was fairly confident, with your help, I could pull off the sleepwalking defence.'

'And if you didn't, what were you going to do then?'

'I don't honestly know.'

'What do you mean you don't know? He was your client, he trusted you, and you betrayed him.'

Blair laughed.

'What's so funny?' she said, seething with anger.

'Sounds like the pot calling the kettle black.'

'Go to hell! My position was very different. I had the Mafia breathing down my neck. But you deceived everyone because you fancied me and wanted to get into my knickers.'

Her eyes, intense and focused, narrowed and pierced his soul.

'What kind of a man are you?'

His ego, leathered by time, was immune to attacks by faceless critics.

But her arrow, sharp and true, sliced open his armour and peeled away his defences.

'Marina, we're both to blame for this mess.'

'No, you're a selfish bastard and I bet you really only went along with my game so you could win your last big case. It was all about your inflated ego.'

As she said this, she flew into a rage, picking up the bottle of champagne from the table she threw it at him. It narrowly missed and smashed against the wall behind him. She then stormed into the bedroom, slamming the door behind her.

Blair sat on the balcony and lit a cigar. Why had he spoken to her in Russian? That had been a dreadful misjudgement, he thought. He sat alone looking at the stars, wondering how he had arrived at this place. It was a place unfamiliar to him and he was unsure of the road he should now take. He eventually settled onto the sofa, wrapped himself in the bathrobe and fell asleep.

forty-five

A gentle knocking on the door of the suite awakened Blair; it was room service with breakfast. He hauled himself from the couch, adjusted his bathrobe, and opened the door. Two waitresses dressed in pale-pink uniforms greeted him and wheeled a breakfast trolley into the living area.

'Would you like breakfast here, or on the balcony, sir?'

'The balcony would be nice, thank you.'

Blair hovered around in his bathrobe as they spread a starched linen tablecloth on the table and laid out a small feast of croissants, exotic fruit and juices. They wished him a pleasant day as they left.

He gently knocked on the bedroom door.

'Marina, there is some breakfast here for you.'

There was no response.

'Oh, come on, Marina, this is childish, grow up and open the door for heaven's sake,' he persisted.

Receiving no answer, he turned the handle, but the door was locked from inside. He sat on the balcony, looking out at the tall palms dancing in a stiff breeze as he poured a cup of strong coffee and smelt its rich aroma. The sun was dazzling with only the occasional passing wispy white cloud momentarily softening its glare. A perfect day for sailing, he thought.

He returned to the bedroom door and this time knocked harder with his fist. But there was no response.

'Marina, if you don't want to talk to me, so be it, but I need to get a pair of shorts to wear to the beach, so please unlock the door.'

There was still no response. He returned to the balcony and was about to sit down when he heard the sound of the bedroom door opening. He dashed inside only to observe the door being slammed shut and his khaki shorts lying on the floor outside the bedroom door. He put them on and headed off barefoot to the beach.

He hired a catamaran at the beach and sailed out to sea, where he spent the day lost in time and space. The small craft was tossed chaotically around by the howling wind and an angry sea, as were his thoughts. What in God's name had he become? All those years devoted to his profession, lost, along with his reputation and more importantly his self-respect. He had loved the law and almost everything about it, the cut and thrust of the courtroom, and the pure drama. Now all was lost. What in God's name had he done?

Marina's outrage, though ironic, was justified. What sort of a man was he? Her cruel words had resounded in his ears all through the previous long and lonely night. Even today the howling wind hadn't managed to muffle them, as they echoed around his mind.

In the late afternoon a seagull squawked and streaked across the sky. He heard a clap of thunder in the distance and observed the southern sky, streaked and gashed by lightning, was conceiving a storm. The turquoise sea became suddenly grey and angry, like his mood. He revelled in the struggle to bring his small craft to the safety of land, but at times he became tired and wished the sea would take him into its darkest depths. Eventually he reached the shore and hauled the catamaran from the sea as a sheet of torrential rain swept the deserted beach. He scurried into the sanctuary of the hotel.

Darkness was descending as he slowly made his way up to the suite. Within his heart was a determination to exorcise the malignant growth that had gnawed away his soul. Each step became surer than the last, quicker and more purposeful.

forty-six

Dermot nervously paced the corridor outside the Court of Criminal Appeal. His face was grey and he appeared to have slept in his suit. Jenny approached from the far end of the corridor, walking towards him purposefully. As she drew nearer he observed a broad grin on her face. She came to a halt several feet in front of him, cocked her head and looked at him sympathetically. The smile then left her face.

'Well?' Dermot asked nervously.

'Well what?' she replied.

'What do the prosecution say? Is our client going to get bail or not?'

She bowed her head. 'I'm sorry, Dermot, Yuri isn't going to get bail.'

His fingers tightened around the papers he held in his hands so that Jenny saw the whites of his knuckles. As his face became flushed with rage, Jenny intervened, the smile returning to her face.

'Yuri isn't going to get bail because the prosecution are prepared to concede the appeal this morning. The conviction will be quashed as soon as the Court sits.'

Dermot dropped his papers on the floor and buried his head in his hands. Jenny put an arm across his back and ushered him to a bench in the hallway.

'Stay there, Dermot, I have to rush inside and firm all this up in court. But don't go away I'll be straight back.'

Dermot watched Jenny as she breezed into court. He sat alone in the corridor and lazily bent down and gathered the papers he had dropped and stuffed them into his briefcase. He sat back clutching the briefcase against his chest. It was finally over. A sense of peace embraced him. But it was short lived as the strangest thought floated into his mind. What next? What was he going to do next? Was there ever going to be a case so demanding and yet rewarding? He suddenly felt empty as the thought of returning to his mundane practice in the District Court sent a cold shiver down his spine. Better to have loved and lost than never to have loved at all, he smiled to himself. But he had won, and what a victory. And what of his old friend Blair Armstrong? What demons had possessed him? He shut his eyes and banished the disappointment from his mind. Better not to go there he thought. Jenny returned within minutes. The conviction quashed and a miscarriage of justice conceded by the State.

Yuri had spent the previous few months in St Mark's Psychiatric Hospital in Howth. Formally a fine Edwardian mansion it was approached through a gated entrance and a long, tree-lined gravelled avenue. The hospital housed some thirty patients most of whom suffered from fairly minor psychiatric illnesses.

At first they didn't know what to do with Yuri, but kept him locked in his room at night in case he went on walkabout in his sleep. During the day he was given free rein and mingled enthusiastically with the other patients and staff. He volunteered to tend the gardens and even on inclement days he could be observed sweeping the paths and weeding the flowerbeds. The staff liked him and he they.

Dr McCormack, a tall, thin, elderly man with a grey beard, was the resident psychiatrist. He could find nothing wrong with his patient and recommended to his authorities that Yuri be discharged. His advice was ignored. Apparently his patient was to be kept under close observation for at least a year before he could be considered for release. He was unsure exactly what he was to observe but in the meantime had organized a teacher to help Yuri with his English.

Yuri was unsure of his future. He had cried solidly for three days when he heard the news of what Uliana had done. At first despair, then panic, consumed him as he realized he had lost everything. He remained unsure of his status. Was he to be deported back to Russia when eventually released? On reflection it mattered little, as he had nowhere to go in Ireland anyway. At night he prayed that he could stay just where he was.

He was working in the garden when he heard his name being called by one of the orderlies. He dropped his rake and walked into the front hall. The orderly was standing behind a desk where Dr McCormack was seated.

'Well, Yuri, I have good news for you,' said the doctor.

'What is that?' asked Yuri.

'We have just got word that your conviction has been quashed and you are now a free man.'

Yuri looked bemused.

'You are free to go. James here will help you pack your belongings and off you go.'

'But ...'

'But nothing, it's been a pleasure having you with us and I wish you all the best,' the doctor said as he stood up and shook Yuri's hand. Yuri looked at James who immediately glanced away.

Yuri sat on the edge of the bed in his small room. He leant forward and took a framed photograph of his mother, kissed it, and placed it carefully into a rucksack. He gathered his clothes together and bundled them in on top of the photograph. He looked around the room and was reluctant to leave. James who was waiting outside called on him to hurry up and Yuri emerged into the hallway dewy eyed. He could hear the other patients in the day room and wanted to say goodbye, but James seemed in a hurry to escort him from the premises. Back in the front hallway, which was strangely quiet, he signed a form and his travel documents were returned to him. James handed him an envelope with €200 in it. Yuri looked around the hall and then at James.

'Where am I going to go?' he asked.

James patted him on the back. 'Don't worry, you'll find somewhere to stay. There are a few bed and breakfasts down near the harbour.'

'But—'

'Come on, Yuri, I haven't got all day,' James said, as he ushered Yuri out of the front door.

Yuri walked slowly down the gravelled driveway towards the wrought-iron gates at the entrance. On seeing his rake lying where he had dropped it, he stopped. James called to him.

'It's OK, I'll get that; off you go now.'

The electric gates opened smoothly as he approached them. His steps became shorter and his body began to shake. He stopped and turned back towards the house, but James gestured him away. As he passed through the pillars he heard the sound of a car roaring up the road and the sound of screeching tyres as it came to a halt in front of him. He froze on the spot, his body trembling.

The driver's door opened and Yuri saw Dermot's beaming face looking over the roof at him.

'Come on Yuri, get in.'

'But, Mr Molloy, where are we going?'

'We have a spare room in the house and I thought you could come and stay with my family while you arrange your own accommodation. I hope this is OK with you.'

Yuri heaved a sigh of relief and climbed into the passenger seat. He looked at Dermot with tears in his eyes, Dermot smiled back.

'And I have arranged for you to get your old job back too. You start first thing in the morning.'

Yuri rubbed his forehead. Dermot tapped him on the shoulder and pointed to the hospital. Yuri looked around and saw the staff and patients standing on the steps waving and hollering towards him. He opened the window and waved back enthusiastically. He turned to Dermot, tears streaming down his cheeks.

'Mr Molloy, this is the happiest day of my life.'

forty-seven

Blair opened the door and reluctantly returned to an enigma he had been unable to decode.

'Hello, stranger,' Marina called from the balcony.

He walked out to her, looking bedraggled in his shorts, his skin caked in dried salt after a long day at sea. She was sitting at a candlelit table sipping a margarita, looking sensational in a long lime-green evening dress. Her hair was tied up in a ponytail, as it had been when they first met. Her soft, sun-kissed skin was glowing in the candlelight and she looked happy and relaxed. She looked him up and down and frowned in a critical way.

'You look a mess,' she said disapprovingly. 'I have reserved a table for eight o'clock, so you had better clean yourself up and put something decent on.'

His resolve vanished under her spell and he did as she commanded. Shortly afterwards he emerged wearing a royal blue linen suit over a pale blue shirt. She stood up and took him by the hand. The scent of her perfume engulfed him.

'You look much better,' she said as she took him by the hand. 'Come on, we don't want to be late for dinner.'

In the opulent dining room Blair gazed into her eyes and was mesmerized by her beauty. He swallowed hard and fought back the tears as he realized how deeply he loved her, and how little anything else in his life mattered. She leant across and kissed him softly on the lips, as though it were a kiss goodbye. And, as the last strand of her hair brushed against his cheek, he felt she was about to leave him forever. He went to speak, but she placed a finger to his lips and smiled. Then she wiped a tear from her eye, and spoke softly, but firmly.

'Blair, last night I was in shock and said many things I didn't mean. I know that you helped me because you loved me and for no other reason. I also know that whatever we had was special. I never loved a man the way I loved you. All my life men have treated me like a flower, something to admire. But I wanted much more. I needed to be treated like a person. You gave me a gift more precious than diamonds or gold, your respect. I will never forget you and the short time we spent together. I will never forget how you touched me with your mind and body, and how we felt as one. But I have destroyed everything that was dear to me. I took my aunt's life; I betrayed Yuri, and I lied to you. I have to go back to Ireland and give myself up to the police. I need to be punished for what I did, and only then can I start my life again, free of all this guilt and paranoia.'

Blair leant forward and took her hand in his. 'If you go back they will send you to prison for a long time.'

She smiled. 'I know that, but above all else I don't want you hurt by any of this.'

'What do you mean?'

'I know that you covered for me because you loved me and if that love is as deep as the love I feel for you then I can understand how you were driven to do crazy things for me. I don't want anyone ever to find out what you did. It's my turn to protect you, and for once in my life I want to do the right thing.'

'What about the icons?'

'I will hand them over to the police.'

Blair sat back and regarded her closely. 'Marina, are you sure about all this?'

'Yes, but before I do anything I need to know that you don't think I am an evil person.'

Blair leant across and gently kissed away her tears. 'I never believed you were anything but special from the moment I first saw you. I know we have both done bad things, but the truth sets you free, and I am more deeply in love with you now than ever before.'

'Do you really mean that, Blair?'

'Yes I do, and I am going to prove it to you.'

'What do you mean?'

Blair sat upright in his chair and his face came to life. 'I can't live without you. I want you to come to Argentina with me and start a new life.'

'Are you sure, Blair?' she asked, unable to hide the excitement in her voice.

'I have never been so sure of anything in my life.'

Marina began to tremble, and then tears rolled down her cheeks. Blair gently held her hand across the table. 'What's the matter with you now?'

'I never thought you cared for me so much, but you really do.'

'Well, is it prison in Ireland or the beaches of Argentina?'

She lowered her head and appeared deep in thought. Then with a sweep of her hand she brushed her hair from her face as she looked up and gave him a coquettish smile.

'I love you with all my heart, Mr Armstrong, and will follow you wherever you go.'

Blair ordered a bottle of Moët and carried it under his arm as they laughed and giggled their way through the gardens of the hotel, unaware of the pale-faced man who followed behind. A clap of thunder startled them, and they fled through the gardens as the heavens opened and drenched their bodies with warm rain.

They arrived at the suite, staggered into the bedroom and flopped onto the bed. Blair poured more champagne and Marina rolled a joint. She took three drags and then handed it to Blair.

'Try some, its good stuff.'

Blair took the joint from her and drew heavily on it. She removed his saturated shirt and he lay back on the bed. He took her hand and gently pulled her close. He kissed her on the lips, but she slipped from his grasp and slid out of the bed, disappearing into the bathroom. She undressed, and sprayed some perfume on her slender neck. Then she slinked back into the bedroom; only to find Blair lying naked, face down on the bed. He was out cold. She looked at him and smiled.

She lay on her back next to him looking up at the whirling wooden fan above. The sound of torrential rain and water gushing onto the balcony from the canopy overhead was pleasantly mesmerizing. The occasional flash of lightning penetrated the wooden shutters and momentarily flooded the room with white light. She closed her eyes and nestled her head into the soft pillow. For the first time in years she felt at peace and looked forward to the dawn and a new beginning. At last the everlasting voices from her past had been silenced. A strange peace engulfed her, and for the first time in her life she felt loved and secure.

Suddenly she felt a presence in the room and opened her eyes. A flash of lightning momentarily dazzled her. She saw a pale face looking down at her, then a flash of cold steel as the knife penetrated her chest and slid deep into her lungs. There was surprisingly little pain. She gasped for air, but there was none. Her second gasp was shorter and her third was her last. She felt dizzy, closed her eyes and left the chaos of all that had happened behind.

forty-eight

The following morning two waitresses arrived with the breakfast trolley and gently knocked on the door. There was no response from within the suite. They looked at each other and then knocked harder, but there was still no response. Using the master key they eventually let themselves in and called out a greeting to the guests whom they assumed were still in the bedroom sound asleep. They arranged the table for breakfast and looked at each other, wondering how they had failed to disturb the guests. The door to the bedroom was slightly open and one of them knocked gently announcing her presence. Receiving no response she pushed open the door. The wooden shutters were closed and the room was in almost total darkness.

She pulled back one of the shutters and screamed in horror when she saw the bloodstained sheets and two bodies lying on the bed. The other waitress looked into the room and saw Marina's naked body lying face up with a knife stuck in her chest. Mr Armstrong was lying face down beside her and was motionless. She gingerly felt his wrist for a pulse and to her surprise she found one. She then quickly left the room and was met by two hotel security men who had responded to the screams.

They entered the bedroom and looked at each other, unsure of what to do. They closed over the door and stood outside awaiting the arrival of the police.

Detective Sergeant Samuel Jones and three uniformed policemen arrived after fifteen minutes. They drew their guns and burst into the room. Blair was still lying motionless on the bed. The detective sergeant yelled at him to get up slowly with his hands in the air. There was no response. He gestured to one of the policemen to cuff him, which he did as the others stood pointing their guns at Blair. They dragged him violently to his feet. Slowly he began to come around, at first not knowing who these strange figures were or what they were doing in his room. His bleary eyes began to focus and he saw the blurred image of Marina's naked body lying in a pool of blood on the bed. Seconds passed and when the image became sharper he let out a loud roar and violently pulled away from the policemen in an effort to get to her. They struggled with him, but such was the ferocity of his resistance three of them were unable to restrain him. He broke free and fell face down on the bed beside her. The detective sergeant put the cold barrel of his gun against the back of Blair's head.

'Don't move or I'll shoot.'

Despite the warning, Blair moved his head towards Marina's and gently kissed her on her forehead. The policemen grabbed him and pulled him away. Blair stopped resisting and was led from the room. He glanced to his left and saw that Marina's canvas bags were missing. He was marched downstairs and through the lobby past a group of shocked guests who had gathered out of morbid curiosity. When they arrived at the police car the sergeant placed his hand on Blair's shoulder.

'You are under arrest for murder, do you wish to say anything?'

Blair looked at him with tears in his eyes, and shook his head.

The sergeant stared at him in bewilderment and then took his suspect away.

Leabharlanna Poiblí Chathair Bhaile Átha Cliath

Dublin City Public Libraries